Praise for *Any Other*

Michael Croley's *Any Other Place* is a stor........................
power. Croley masterfully gathers disparate ....ough his sym-
pathy and generous grasp. As the characters approach their truths of
home, family, and duty, we witness the gorgeous possibility of what
ordinary men and women seek—love, acceptance, and forgiveness.

—Min Jin Lee, *Free Food for Millionaires* and *Pachinko*,
finalist for the National Book Award

Like the best writers, Michael Croley takes us into the lives of ordinary people who have been thrust into the extraordinary circumstances of everyday life. There is not a wasted word in these thirteen
taut and thrilling stories of grief, exile, and devotion. We leave *Any
Other Place* feeling as if we know each of these sharply drawn
characters and traveled to their places in the world, all of which
Croley presents with startling clarity and complexity. This is one of
the most exciting and beautiful story collections to come down the
literary pike in a long time and announces a major new talent who
infuses every story with emotion that leaves us feeling gut-punched
in the best of ways. *Any Other Place* is a stunner.

—Silas House, *Southernmost*

In these thirteen stunning stories, Michael Croley delves deep into
the lives of characters undone by grief and betrayal with crystalline
compassion and deft surprise. How do we reckon with the troubled
legacies we inherit? How do we square our own stark limitations
with our desire to create love? *Any Other Place* is beautifully unafraid
of such vast and thorny questions. This magnificent collection is the
kind of fiction that will expand your comprehension of the world, a
debut that reads with the precision and punch of a writer already in
full command of his powers.

—Laura van den Berg, *The Third Hotel*

Michael Croley shows us the lives most of us inhabit—simple on the surface, with a rich and complicated inner life. His people yearn, fight, and love, make mistakes and gain success, and remain optimistic despite tough circumstances. This book will teach you about humanity and about yourself.

—Chris Offutt, *Country Dark*

Writing with assurance born of bone-deep knowledge and insight, Michael Croley brings us these taut, brilliant, understated stories from the new "global South"—each one occurring in a charged, liminal space, its characters caught at the crossroads of their lives, between countries, between past and present, between conflicting loyalties or desires. Each perfect ending is a surprise, yet perfectly realized, reverberating in the mind long afterward. *Any Other Place* is a revelation.

—Lee Smith, *Dimestore: A Writer's Life* and *The Last Girls*

Any Other Place is a beautiful and moving collection. Michael Croley is a master at locating those quiet moments that reveal a character's truest emotions; his balance between their inner lives and the surrounding complexities of daily life is extraordinary.

—Jill McCorkle, *Life After Life*

Unlike some writers, Michael Croley isn't afraid to lay it all out there. These are some of the most emotionally honest and beautifully moving stories I've read. What does it mean to say that Croley's stories help me feel a little better about the human race in these times? They are not soft, not prettified, they don't pull punches, but they're comforting in their deep empathy for humanity itself.

—Brad Watson, *Miss Jane*

ANY
OTHER
PLACE

Michael Croley

BLAIR

Printed in Canada
Cover design by Laura Williams

Blair is an imprint of Carolina Wren Press.

The mission of Blair/Carolina Wren Press is to seek out, nurture,
and promote literary work by new and underrepresented writers.

We gratefully acknowledge the ongoing support of general operations
by the Durham Arts Council's United Arts Fund.

Library of Congress Cataloging-in-Publication Data
Names: Croley, Michael, author.
Title: Any other place : stories / by Michael Croley.
Description: Durham : Blair, 2019.
Identifiers: LCCN 2018057564 (print) | LCCN 2019003373 (ebook) |
ISBN 9781949467017 (eBook) | ISBN 9781949467000 (pbk.)
Classification: LCC PS3603.R6365 (ebook) |
LCC PS3603.R6365 A59 2019 (print) | DDC 813/.6—dc23
LC record available at https://lccn.loc.gov/2018057564

For Olive and Arlo
There's no place I want to be without you two.

CONTENTS

SLOPE

WREN ASHER IS nearing thirty, and over the summer, like his father before him, he's fallen in love with a woman who lives in another country. But that's where all similarities end. For one, Hannah is an American who grew up outside Boston and now lives in Paris. And second, she lives with a boyfriend, a man for whom she moved to France. Wren knew from the beginning getting mixed up with her was a bad idea, and when they parted in August he thought whatever he felt for her would fade. But since her return to Paris she calls him every night at two in the morning because of the six-hour time difference. She waits until the boyfriend is gone for work—and before she goes to the high school where she teaches English—then she dials Wren. He likes to be wakened by her voice and sleeps with the cell phone beside the bed so that before he answers he sees the picture he snapped of her in the Metro in DC.

"It wasn't strange?" she asks one night.

"What?" he says.

"Growing up there."

"Of course it is now, but not then. It was just my childhood, and it was as happy as most, I think. Happier, probably."

Her boyfriend is Algerian. She hasn't told Wren much about him, and Wren hasn't asked. One night she told him, "I'm drawn to people with backgrounds different from mine."

Now she says, "But you have so many stories about how backward it is there."

"It is and it isn't," he says, feeling the need to defend his hometown against the stereotypes about Kentucky. "My best friends' parents were doctors and lawyers. Insurance salesmen. I don't know anybody whose father worked in a coal mine, but plenty of them worked at the railroad. It was suburban more than anything else, I guess. I just got a cool accent in the breakdown," he tells her, but there's more to it than that because he knows that while Fordyce is a town and not the country, it's not by any stretch cosmopolitan or refined.

Hannah sighs through whatever wires or towers make calls possible anymore, frustrated, it seems, by his answer. He knows she's in bed too, and he tries to imagine the room she's in, her black skirt and silk blouse across the back of a chair, the indention of her boyfriend's head on the pillow beside her.

"Sometimes," she says, "I think you and I are more different, culturally, than I am with him." She never says his name, though Wren knows it's Henri. On Facebook Wren has seen the pictures of them in and around Paris and vacationing at St. Tropez. The two of them look happy with the city lights or the blue of the Mediterranean at their backs, and when he thinks about the possibility of a future with Hannah, he thinks he'll never compare with the images on the computer screen. In a race between his love and France, France will win.

"What do you mean?" he asks.

"I don't know," she says.

"Yes, you do. You said it. You've been thinking of it." His room is completely dark except for the red glow of numbers from the alarm clock he's turned against the wall so he can't count the minutes until she calls.

"It's nothing," she says. "Forget I said it."

"How am I supposed to forget it?"

"It was just something stupid I said. I don't even really know what I meant." She has dropped the subject, and the only way for them to come back to it is if she brings it back up.

For a month, they've been going this way. They met at the beginning of Wren's internship in DC last summer. Hannah was teaching in a summer college program and was the friend of a girl in the senator's office where Wren worked. They met in a big group at a bar, and by the end of the night they were alone, everyone else having begged off for early mornings at their offices. Hannah turned on the barstool, her crossed leg revealing itself under her summer dress. She edged closer to him, and he ran his fingers along her calf. "Is this okay?" he asked. She smiled, giving a quiet nod. "And this boyfriend you mentioned earlier?"

The smile disappeared, and she narrowed her eyes. "He's not here now."

It was only a matter of time, and a week later when they found themselves in the same bar, cashing out, ready to head home, he felt her behind him. She reached up and laid her hands across his chest, putting her weight against his back, and she felt soft, like a thousand feathers pressed next to him. He finished signing the credit card slip and held it up to the bartender. "Thanks," he called out and then turned, held her gaze, and took her hand to walk out. Hannah let him lead her through the crowd spilling out of the Adams Morgan bars, and when they were finally on a quiet part of Connecticut Avenue, before a block of row houses, he stopped and stood before her. His heart was beating fast, and sweat ran down his back. Light from a street lamp fell through the leaves of an oak tree, and shadows danced on her face. "It'll be a mistake," he said, but she was up on her toes and kissing him before the words were out of his mouth. They caught a cab back to his place, and later, while she slept and he was still awake, sobering up and holding her, he was already giving himself over.

HE REMEMBERS BEING eight years old at Kmart and in the checkout line with his mother. It was a bright day, and the sun came through the big panes of glass at the front of the store and bounced off the cars in starburst reflections. He'd asked for a Snickers, but his mother ignored him. She was distracted, looking toward the automatic doors at some man. She was so lost in her thoughts that the cashier had to call to her. "Ma'am," she said, "the candy bar?"

"No," she said and took it from Wren and put it back. She paid quickly and moved toward the man, walking right up to him. "Did you lose something in my face?" she said.

The man looked confused, as if he wasn't sure she was talking to him. Then his mother started in again. "You were looking awfully hard for somebody that hasn't lost something. Do I know you?"

"N-n-no," the man stammered but then straightened up, regaining his confidence. But before he could say anything Wren's mother was done with him.

"I didn't think so," she said and took her son's hand.

People in Fordyce had always watched her when she came into a store. They'd see her olive skin, soft almond eyes, the long dark hair, and they'd wonder where she was from, who she was. She'd told him stories about managers following her up and down the aisles of the Dollar General Store while she shopped and grocers at the Pic-Pac who spoke to her in slow, overenunciated ways when she paid.

Frightened, Wren asked what the man did.

"He wouldn't stop staring at me," she said. "Nobody can look at me that way." Her hands were shaking, and she needed a moment before starting the car.

It is Wren's first memory of fear. In the car, his own pulse quickened, worried if the man had struck his mother what he, being a boy, could have done to defend her. He hadn't told his parents about the taunts at school. He was constantly being called Japanese or Chinese. Nobody ever guessed Korean. And later, in middle school and high school, he was called *gook* and *chink*. One boy called him *ching-chong* over and over, singing a song about it, but no one ever called him a *slope*, something Wren learned in graduate school was the correct slur for Koreans, but he had no idea why one slur was more logical or appropriate than another. In Fordyce they were all the same.

Out in the world, away from his hometown, his slanted eyes and dark hair haven't seemed out of place. In New York or DC, he's marked more by his Kentucky accent and the country sayings he picked up around his cousins and uncles. People sometimes ask him to repeat what he says, as if he's a form of entertainment and his speech has the quaint air of someone who is simple.

THE LAST NIGHT Wren and Hannah spent together he booked a hotel room in Georgetown. He didn't love her then, but that was coming. He had a sense that once they were away from each other it would be easy for her to forget him, but he pushed that from his mind. They spent the day walking in and out of the shops along M Street, and despite the stickiness of the day, she held his hand, and every so often, when waiting for the light to change to cross the street, she leaned her head on his shoulder and sometimes kissed his cheek. They followed the towpath along the Potomac, hoping to catch a breeze, but the air was still. Overheated, they started back for the hotel, and then Hannah stopped at a fountain, hiked up her green dress, and stepped over the lip and into the cool water. Wren watched her. She piled all that dark hair of hers on top of her head, giving the fair skin of her neck to the light, and she laughed and smiled at him, splashing him once.

"Are you ready?" he asked, but he wanted her to stay in the water just a little longer so he could watch her playfulness. She had the hem of her dress balled into one hand and traces of light shimmered from the water and onto her legs.

Back in the room they passed the afternoon in each other's arms, making love with the curtains wide open and then watching bad television and movies, including one set in Paris.

"What're the odds?" Wren said. Outside the sky began to purple, and the sounds of the students out on the quad died out. Hannah was laughing at the movie, telling him how they had spliced the film so all the famous landmarks appeared to be near one another. A little Peugeot zipped past the Louvre and crossed under the Arc de Triomphe, and the Eiffel Tower was almost always in the background. He imagined her in the city, walking its streets, and he thought about his lone visit there, that old European architecture, walls the color of sand turned dingy with soot and grime and centuries of history lying in their cracks. In a week's time they'd be half a world apart, and he wouldn't know her the way he did now, lying next to her, listening to her laugh. The images of Paris reflected off her eyes. The sun had completely disappeared from the sky, and when she saw he wasn't paying attention, she turned to him and smiled, crinkling her nose. They switched off the TV, and the room was filled with early beams of moonlight.

"WHAT HAPPENED?" HIS mother says.

"Nothing. I got in a fight."

They're at the airport in Lexington, and other travelers are looking at him with his bulging black eye and the bruise on his right
cheek.

"With who?" his mother asks, examining the swollen skin and
small cut along his nose.

"Nobody. Some punk at the gym."

"You're too old to get in fights."

"Well, I guess not."

She reaches up to his face, and he pushes her hand down. "It's
fine, Mom."

"It doesn't look fine," she says. "You need to watch your temper.
I worry about you all the time and how angry you get."

"You're one to talk," he says, but it comes out nastier than
intended.

"Hey," she says, stopping their walk to baggage claim.

"I'm sorry," he says. "Let's get my bag and get out of here."

On the ride home his head pulses with pain. He knows he's too
old to get in fights. And if Hannah hadn't called him that day, he
probably would have been able to let the kid's comment at the gym
pass. The pickup game was already too physical, and when the kid
said to Wren on the foul, "You got me with that samurai chop,"
Wren went after him. He put his hands on the kid's throat, got him
down on the ground, choking him, and watched the kid's eyes bug
out. He thought he could kill the kid right then—that he was capable. Then it was Wren who had fear running through him, and he
opened his fingers wide, releasing his grip as if he had grabbed hold
of a fire that was searing his palms.

Two guys on his team pulled him up by the arms, and the kid un-
loaded two quick shots with his left and opened up Wren's eye and
bloodied his nose before anybody wrapped the kid up. It was Wren's
only real fight since high school, when he had come up from the

lunchroom to grab his books for chemistry and found that someone had written *Gook, Go home* on his locker.

His size—six feet, two hundred pounds—had prevented a lot of fights back then. He played three sports, and people admired his ability to catch touchdown passes, hit jump shots, and throw strikes. His friends were other athletes, the cheerleaders and girls on the dance team, but he never felt part of the clique they formed, and those words on his locker confirmed his feeling of being an outsider.

The writing on his locker continued for a week, and none of his friends told him who was doing it, but Wren figured it out and confronted a boy from the football team. Wren had never taken a punch and wasn't sure if he could. He'd always been afraid of being suspended or of ruining his reputation as a good kid, but he understood that if he ate shit then he'd be eating it for the rest of his life. The first punch came easy, right at the boy's chin. His red hair was in bangs that hung down over his eyes, and it flew back with the impact of Wren's fist. The boy threw Wren into the lockers and a metal lock dug into his back. Then a teacher came running. "What's going on here?" he asked. He had been a colonel in the army, but to Wren he didn't look like an army man. He was soft in the middle and taught Romance languages. He kept the two boys apart with a firmer grip than Wren expected.

Wren told his side of the story, above the other boy's denials, and then the colonel sent them off to class instead of the principal's office. After that, Wren never doubted he could stand up for himself, and the next year, when Alvin Harrison called him a *Japanese motherfucker* as they were headed out for the layup line, Wren cornered him against a wall and put a hand to his throat, and it was the look in Wren's eyes more than anything else that forced an apology.

On the interstate, headed home, Wren thinks about his mother's confrontations in Fordyce, her own slights, and how it has always been a bigoted place. He's not lived there in more than ten years, but when he thinks about being growing up there, he finds it harder and harder to remember what was good and easy for them in that place.

"One of these days you could really get hurt," his mother says.

"Maybe," Wren says, thinking about Hannah's call. Her crying. "He knows everything," she said. Over the phone, he heard French police sirens wailing.

"Where are you?" he asked.

"At a pay phone down the street," she said. "He got the phone bill yesterday and saw all my calls to you, and then he hacked my email account and found our messages."

Wren was sitting up in bed by then, his heart beating fast. "You weren't paying for the phone bill? He hacked your account?"

"I know," she said.

"You wanted to get caught," he said. "Look at how you've handled this. What are you going to do?"

"I don't know," she said.

"What about our plans for you to come home this fall?"

"I don't know about that either."

"We can make this work," he said. "I know you're scared, but if you get back here and we see each other again, it will be all right."

"You're always so sure about that," she said.

"*You're* the one who said you wanted to come back home to me," he told her.

She was breathing heavily into the phone. "My phone card is running out of time. I need to go to the store and get a new one. I can call you back."

"What did he say?"

"He said he wants to talk tonight when he gets home from work."

Wren knew her boyfriend was going to ask her to work it out, and when he did, she would stay. "Call me tomorrow," he said.

"Okay," she said, barely audible.

"I want you to come home," he said. "You know that, right?"

"I do know it."

He closed the phone and stood up in the dark of his apartment. He went to the window and looked out over the barren street below him. He tapped a fingernail to the glass and listened to the hollow clink, thinking that in eight hours *they* were going to have a conversation that would decide *his* future. He went to his desk and opened his laptop, and there was an email from Henri to Hannah, blind copied to Wren. *Do you love me?* Henri asked her. He wrote in English for Wren's benefit. *Or do you think about Wren when you are fucking me?* Wren closed his laptop and leaned back in his desk chair. They'd both been so caught up, and once they had started down this path, they couldn't stop themselves, even though they saw the danger ahead. Now his and Hannah's long exchanges, their secrets and desires, had been pored over by someone else.

"What's wrong?" his mother asks. "What are you thinking about?"

"Nothing," he says. The hills of Kentucky roll past at seventy miles per hour. Hills that are imprinted on him along with each bend and curve of I-75.

"You've barely said anything. Aren't you happy to see your mother?" she teases.

"I'm okay. Tired, is all."

"You can't lie to me, son. Are you depressed? Did something happen? You haven't called us as much as you usually do."

He relents, wanting to tell somebody what's happened, how he feels. "Things went bad with this girl I was seeing."

"I didn't even know you were seeing anyone."

"Well, I'm not really. I met her over the summer at my internship. She lives in Paris."

Her head snaps back. "Kentucky?"

"No, Mom. The real Paris. It didn't work out." He doesn't tell her more, though. She worries about him too much already.

"Why?"

"Because she lives across the ocean for one."

"It worked for your dad and me," she says.

He never asked his parents how they met or fell in love. He knows his father asked her to wait for him when he went to Germany to finish out his army service. Six months they spent apart, held together only by his letters to her.

"I guess that's right," he says, and he smiles at her, feeling the pain in his cheek.

ON WREN AND Hannah's last night together they left the hotel room and went back to the bar where they met. It was late, and the kitchen was going to close in ten minutes. Their bodies were spent, and they sat across from each other with weak legs and glossy eyes.

"Would it matter if I told you I don't want you to get on that plane?"

"No," she said, "but it's nice to hear."

"I want you to stay," he said, and knowing it wouldn't come true made it easier to say.

"And what would we do if I stayed?"

"We'd figure this out," he said.

"And what would we find?"

"That you're trouble," he said.

"And you're not?"

"I didn't say that."

He ran the backs of his fingers over her hand. "We needed more time," he said. "But that wouldn't change anything would it?"

"It might have," she said.

They made small talk then, avoiding what they were feeling and, Wren believed, trying to convince themselves the entire summer hadn't been some big mistake and that when he got on the train tomorrow they would leave each other and not think about what could have been. And later, back in the room, with daylight drawing close, tangled in the sheets, he said to her, "Do you love him?"

"Yes," she said.

"Then why are you here?"

They had almost had this conversation once before, but they had both been drunk and she started to cry, saying he must never ask about him, that he could never question her about her relationship.

"I wanted to be," she said.

He was holding her from behind, and he kissed her shoulder, then her neck. "If you love him then I want you to go over there and give it your best shot," he said. Fear rose in him and dried his mouth, and it was hard for him to keep speaking, but he went on anyway. "If you really love him, you owe him that much. Don't tell him about us. Go over there and give your heart to him."

She pushed herself up from the bed, out of his embrace, almost frantic, he thought later, and said, "How can you say that?"

He turned from her, onto his back, and looked at the ceiling. His stomach was completely hollow. He licked his lips and tried to measure his words, steady his voice. Her visa expired in May, and either way she was coming back to the States. "What else can I say? I want you to go over there, and when spring comes and you're back home, I'll still be here. I'll be waiting without waiting."

He knew she was angry with him. She propped herself up on an elbow and looked down on him.

"You know how I feel about you," he said. "Don't act like you don't."

"You really want me to go back to him?"

"No, but there's nothing I can say that's going to change your mind about leaving. You've said as much. If there is something, tell me."

"No," she said quietly, retreating.

"Then don't get angry with me for telling you that."

They lay apart for a long time, and when she was finally asleep, he listened to her breathing and the soft talking noises of her dreams and remembered that within their first week together he had woken up one morning to find their foreheads were pressed right next to each other, their breath passing back and forth like two slow-moving trains. He wasn't sure how long they had slept like that, but he closed his eyes and soon he was asleep with her again. That was the moment when it stopped being a fling for him, and he began to feel closer to her than he ever had to anyone else. The room was ripening with sunlight, and he finally understood what it meant to fall for someone. His feelings for Hannah, for what was going to happen to them, were the same as if he had stepped off a cliff and, tumbling through the air, grasped at the firm ground above him that grew more distant with increasing speed. Beside him Hannah let out a sigh and he rolled to her, running a finger along the curve of her hip, and then he put his arm around her and she took his hand and clutched it, bringing it near her heart.

"YOUR DAD'S MAD at me."

"Why?" Wren asks. They've just pulled into Fordyce. New fast-food joints along the roadside stand out against the sheared gray mountainsides.

"One of his cousins died a few weeks ago and was so poor his wife didn't have enough money to pay for a funeral. So Dad called your Aunt Janice and said we wanted to help pay for it, but she told him that his cousin didn't want anybody's money."

"Why not?"

"Your dad thinks she didn't want to feel like she owed anybody."

"So what'd they do?"

"The funeral was last week, and Janice and Tom went out there and helped her dig the grave at the cemetery."

"They dug the grave themselves?"

"I reckon," she says. Wren smiles at this, marveling at just how long she's lived in Fordyce, how she talks like a country woman. "That's what Janice said. She called to see if we wanted to go help, but your dad said to let them do it by themselves."

"It's the twenty-first century and they dug a grave using shovels?"

"I think so," she says.

"The county didn't take a Bobcat out there or anything?"

"I don't know," she says. "That's what your aunt told me."

"Damn," he says. "So why is Dad mad at you?" They make the turn by the post office, where the high school football field is—the centerpiece of town—and cut through the underpass and make their way to Main Street.

"Well, he said we needed to start thinking about where we were going to be buried and what kind of funeral we wanted, and I told him I didn't care. I said, 'I don't have a country anymore. You can just spread my ashes in the ocean.' And he got real mad at me. He started cussing and saying, 'This is your country. What makes you say things like that?' I tell you, he gets sensitive about those kinds of things. He doesn't understand."

"No, I don't guess he does."

They pass the ball fields where he used to practice Little League football, and for a moment he imagines the figures and shapes of his past, the coaches that were so young then standing in shorts with baseball caps on backward, getting down in three-point stances and yelling instructions. He sees the ill-fitting shoulder pads and the helmets on him and his friends and remembers the sting of the first blow he ever took, the sensation of it running from the top of his neck, through his spine, and into his toes. Not all his memories of home are bad, he thinks. "Where *do* you want to be buried?" he says. "In Masan?"

"I want to be cremated," she says. "Masan isn't my home anymore, but neither is here."

He aches with sadness for her. She gave up everything for his father, for this place where they raised him.

"Are you going to see this girl again?"

"I don't know," he says. "I doubt it. I wasn't very smart about things."

She's not one to pry, but they've always talked. They're friends as much as they're mother and son. As he's grown older, he's become aware how important his happiness is to her. He tries to shield her from his disappointments and pains.

"It'd be nice for you to have somebody," she says.

He thinks about the early years of his parents' marriage, of how much trouble his mother had adjusting to Kentucky. Wren doesn't understand how she dealt with her misery, but his parents made a life together—a life for him—and the only explanation is that they loved each other.

"Sometimes I think you like being lonely," she says, pulling into the driveway.

"Why is that?"

"The things you get yourself into," she says. Then, feeling bad, she corrects herself. "I shouldn't say that. You'll find someone."

"I'm not worried about it, Mom. You shouldn't be either."

"You're not?"

"No."

He gets out of the car and grabs his bag and walks his mother around the house to the back deck. Cold air rocks through the trees, and the wind chimes hanging from the eaves go sideways and clang.

"Are you coming in?" his mother asks.

"In a minute," he tells her.

But she comes beside him. He feels her looking up at his eye. "You should put some ice on that," she says.

"I will," he says, still staring ahead.

"You know," she says, and he turns toward her, but then she shakes her head. "Never mind."

"What? What was it?" he asks. He feels guilty for not telling her more about Hannah. All she's ever done or wanted to do is help him. She wants to take his pain and make it her own.

"It's nothing," she says. "I'll go make you a cold pack." And she turns to go in before Wren can stop her.

One night, after he and Hannah made love, he rested his cheek on her stomach, and she asked to tell him a story in French. It was so dark in the room he barely saw her face, and when she began speaking he didn't hear her but felt the vibrations of her talk through her skin. He had no idea what the story was about, but it was filled with feeling, with pauses and contemplation. He listened to the emotion of her voice, and at times she was so moved she had a hard time continuing, but she'd gather herself, and when she was finished, when the beautiful rhythm of the language and sentences was complete, they lay in the dark for a long time, not wanting to ruin the silence.

"I don't know why I did that," she said, at last.

"It was nice." He pushed himself up so that his face was beside hers.

"Did you understand any of it?"

"No, but that wasn't important," he said, sure, somehow, that might be the most of herself she would ever give him, the most she would ever let him in.

He puts his hands in his pockets, bracing himself against the weather. He looks up at the thin poplar trees swaying in the stiff breeze and the autumn leaves swirling and twisting as they fall. The mountains surround them, and he wonders if he'll one day look at any other place the same way again, with the same feelings of comfort rising in his chest, when his parents are gone and there is no reason for him to return here.

LARGER THAN THE SEA

WANTED TO FIGHT. I told Seo-Yun that the Japanese were only men, but she didn't want to hear that. She wanted me to run away, like so many others, into the mountains and wait until the soldiers passed through our village.

The Japanese needed men for the war. They were traveling from village to village, kicking in doors and marching men out at gunpoint. Since Sook-Cha was born, I had lived in greater fear that they would come for me. We heard they were only three days from Masan and I was afraid, but I didn't tell Seo-Yun that. I only said when they came I would be right beside her and our daughter.

It was evening and the child was already asleep in her corner of the house, as near to the fire as we dared put her. "Look," Seo-Yun said, and went to the girl. "This is why you must run." She squatted beside the child's pallet and pushed back a small curl of hair on the girl's forehead.

I went below the house to stoke the fire of the ondol that warmed the floor where we slept. I crawled on my stomach, feeling the earth's coolness against my body. I heard Seo-Yun's feet padding above me in the tiny kitchen. Then she stopped and there was a tapping, and I knew she was waiting by the door for my return. I took my time lighting the fire, stacking small limbs on top of the burning coal and blowing on them to fan the flames. The fire bloomed brighter, and I shut the stove door and rolled to my back, looking at the dark underside of the floor. *They are all I have,* I thought, *and they are all I want.* And in the next moment I said aloud, "And yet."

"And yet what?" Seo-Yun said when I stepped up to the small ledge of our porch.

"Nothing," I said, and I dusted myself off and stepped past her, onto the warming floor. A small set of bowls and cooking utensils sat in the corner and a strip of moonlight landed on the crock of water, sending silvery dances of light onto the soot-covered clay wall. Seo-Yun had not moved.

"We need to talk," she said.

I knew where it would go. I saw every angle of her argument laid out like stones in a path—neat and in line. "I'm tired," I said.

"Promise me you'll go," she said. "Promise you won't stay and fight."

"I can't promise that."

"Even for her?"

"If I stay it will be because of her. That's why I must fight. They can't have everything. Why can't you understand that?"

"Why can't you see that I need you?"

We both had our eyes on the child, unable to look at each other. I saw her side, but it didn't stop me from feeling my own arguments, of remembering when my father was taken from me at ten and always wondering what had happened to him and how he had died.

"There is no honor in dying," Seo-Yun said. She touched my arm, turning me to her. Her eyes were nothing but anger despite the tenderness with which she held me. She wasn't a woman who cried. "You have to go," she said. "I won't argue about it anymore."

"And what I feel doesn't matter then?" I said.

She met me with silence.

I walked to the beach and sat on the rocks jutting out in the water and let mist spray me. The ocean was so loud, and the foam lapped and lingered at my feet. I was filled with anger and guilt for leaving, but I couldn't be in the house anymore. I had no energy to go through the pushing and pulling of my will with Seo-Yun. I knew I should do what she asked and leave. I had no gun. I had no training, but now that Sook-Cha was here with us, I also didn't see how I could walk away from the two of them. None of that would make sense to Seo-Yun when all she was thinking about was survival, but I was thinking about independence, dreaming of the day when we would no longer be under colonial rule. I wanted to feel I had fought, in some way, for that freedom. Sook-Cha's life colored these thoughts. The world—all of its joys and sorrows—seemed so much heavier now. Neither of us had ever loved someone or something so much, and the child bore the weight of our hopes and our worries.

Last year, the Japanese had taken Seo-Yun's brothers from her parents' home and shoved them out into the street, pushing them to their knees and pissing on them. They forced them to say it tasted like sugar water before they pulled them back up and paraded them out of the village. Weeks later we learned both were dead. Since the beginning of the war, the Japanese had taken Koreans and dressed them in their uniforms and put them on the front lines of their Emperor's army as human shields to absorb the gunfire and mortar shells of the Americans in Okinawa. My wife had suffered so much, but I still couldn't make myself bend. I had my own principles and my own sense of what she and Sook-Cha needed.

"And yet," I said again.

I came home much later than I intended and opened the door to see Sook-Cha, her little body aglow by the fire's light. She slept peacefully on blankets Seo-Yun had arranged next to our sleeping pads on the floor. Seo-Yun was beside the child, sitting up.

"You've been waiting for me?" I asked.

"They won't be in our country forever," she said. "They're going to lose this war. The Americans will come to help us."

"They've never helped us," I said. "Why should we believe in them now?"

The fire lit the three of us in flickers. Seo-Yun leveled her eyes to mine. "The Americans will win this war," she said. "And then she can run free. I want you to be here to see it. Please," she said.

She had never pleaded with me like this before or spoken so softly to prove her point. It was my turn to reply with silence, but I wanted to say, *I am tired of watching my brothers and fathers die.* I couldn't begin to think about a day when I would never see her or Sook-Cha again, but I couldn't live another day in which the lives of everyone I knew seemed to disappear into the roar of the ocean. I turned my head from her because her eyes were so sharp and intense, and I listened for the ocean I'd walked away from, which was too distant to hear, my imagination filled with its crashing waves and tidal waters.

"Hyo," she said, "look at her again."

"Don't say anything else. I've heard it all," I said. "I can't lose you, either. But I can't lose myself."

My voice had risen and the baby let out a wail. We both froze and waited to see if she would wake in full. When she resettled, I whispered, "What will happen to you and her if I'm not here? Did you think about that?"

"We will be fine," she said.

"Unless they take you."

"They won't. They need men."

"They have taken women."

A silence filled up between us once more. Sook-Cha's life, despite the joy of her existence, had somehow caused so much silence between us. It had only been five months since she was born, and

I felt Seo-Yun slipping away from me, both of us moving into a current of constant worry for our daughter. I missed my wife's hair on my face in the mornings when she woke me for breakfast. I missed the way we talked after I came home from the boat, my hands cut and scarred from nets and hooks, and I soaked my hands in a balm she made and waited while she brought out the rice and soup and kimchi for our dinner. Even as the world unfurled into madness and war changed our country once more, we had each other, we believed. Always that. I wondered how much this new war, newly dying Koreans, had affected my feelings and pushed us away from each other.

We went to sleep without another word, though that night I slept between the front door and my family.

AT SEA, MY eye wandered to the horizon. I tried to picture the war, the men, the landscape of another country. Mr. Gong's little boat rocked in the waves, and I held firm to a bloodstained gunwale. It did not happen often, but I could still find myself sick if I did not keep my focus on our fishing and a fixed point on the shore. Mr. Gong chided me and smacked the back of my head. He had known my father when they were young men. He knew where my mind was. "Do what she asks," he said.

"She can't tell me what to do," I said.

"That's where you're wrong. What do you think will happen if you stay? Do you think the Japanese will be afraid of you?"

"I'm not a coward."

"Yes, yes," he said, shaking his head. "I know. Everyone knows that Paek Hyo is no coward. You're tough and strong."

"You think I am young and foolish."

"I think you are fooled. Your wife loves you. She's worried she'll never see you again and she'll have to raise Sook-Cha on her own."

"Didn't you and my father want to fight them?"

"Of course we did. But what could we do? You act as if we have choices in life."

He bent over his gunwale and reached down for the net. I did the same, and our hands ran through the water, seaweed brushing the backs of my fingers until we snagged the net. We pulled and heaved with our backs, carefully picking through the net to throw the crabs back and keeping seabass and cod. We worked quickly to contain their flailing bodies in the net and pack them in the bow on a bed of ice.

Mr. Gong picked up his oar and began rowing toward our next buoy, and I did the same. I watched his back, still strong and defined, although on land he walked with a bend, as if his spine had been turned into a worn-out spring from a lifetime of sitting in the boat and then extending to grab the nets. We stopped at the buoy, and the boat swayed with the water. Mr. Gong put his oar down.

"When those men come, go to the mountains," he said over his shoulder.

I put my eyes on the peak of Muhaksan. I tried to think of my friends already hiding there. I imagined them passing canteens and bowls of rice back and forth. The tree canopy was thick enough to hide the women who walked up the trails to deliver supplies to them.

"Hyo," Mr. Gong said. "I'm not your father, and I can't tell you what to do." He paused a moment and turned from me. He looked to the mountain as well. "You are my son," he said. "Do you understand? Hide. Bravery can be doing something you don't want to do."

I knew it had been hard for him to say this, and I did know what he meant. After my father was taken, I had become his charge. He showed me how to work the nets and to sell in the market and work with brokers. He gave me the home we lived in because he had no sons of his own.

"It doesn't bother you?" I said.

"I was a boy when they came," he said. "It bothers me more than it could ever bother you, because I remember our country before they arrived. I remember a Korea that is only alive in my dreams."

I tried to see the Korea he spoke of in the beach and mountains, but I could not see anything except my own life.

That night I came home with a seabass wrapped in newsprint and gave it to Seo-Yun to filet. I took Sook-Cha in my arms and lifted her to the sky. Her little legs stuck straight out, as straight as the oars in my boat, and I flew her around the room and watched her face come to life.

"Be careful," Seo-Yun said.

"We're playing," I said. I pushed her higher into the air and felt her tender rib cage resting on my fingers. "Abeoji would never drop you," I said to her.

Seo-Yun allowed herself a smile, and I played with Sook-Cha until she became sleepy. Then I put her down for a nap. The house smelled of searing fish, and I went to Seo-Yun and kissed her on the back of her neck and brushed a strand of hair from her temple and tucked it behind her ear.

"I will go," I said. "I'll hide."

Her shoulders stiffened. "You promise?" she said. She kept her eyes down.

"I do."

She turned her face to me, and I saw she was trying not to cry. "What changed your mind?" she asked.

"Mr. Gong."

"Of course," she said. "You listen to him but not me."

"I'm leaving," I said. "Isn't that what you wanted? What's the problem?"

She concentrated on the fish, turning it in the pan and then pouring hot water over tea leaves. I was exasperated. "I'll leave tonight," I said. "After we've eaten."

"I'll pack some squid jerky and sweet rice for you to take."

She still had not turned to me, though.

"I thought you would be happy," I said.

"There's nothing to be happy about. It's dangerous either way."

We ate without talking, and Sook-Cha still napped. I thought of those tiny hands being the size of her heart and lungs, and I did not know how something human could be so small and full of life.

Then we heard the rifle shots.

I scrambled outside. A pair of soldiers headed toward us. They were entering the village with their rifles pointed skyward. The dusty road that wound through the village's small homes was lifeless and empty. The dusk light seemed to vanish faster than it ever had, a curtain falling, and the rifles' muzzles sparked like lighters with each shot. I could not be sure from so far off but the men appeared to wobble in their walk.

I ducked back into the house. I scanned the two rooms for something to defend us with, but there was nothing except a hot poker for the fire and my fishing knife.

"You have to hide," Seo-Yun said.

"Where?"

"Under the house," she said. "Behind the ondol."

Sook-Cha stirred and wailed. I tried to put my palm to her head, but Seo-Yun pushed me out the door. I jumped down to the ground. There was very little space between the stove and the house's pillars, and a jagged edge of stone sliced my back as I pushed myself through the opening. The gunfire was louder, out in front of our house. I tried to keep my breathing even. Sook-Cha was screaming so loudly I wished I could reach through the floor and pull both my wife and daughter down there with me. I heard Seo-Yun walking her back and forth, trying to calm her, but the baby kept screaming so long and loud she lost her breath, and I thought she would choke to death on her tears.

Heavier steps pounded on the floor. Seo-Yun shouted. The soldiers ordered her to quiet the baby, but Sook-Cha kept screaming. I placed my hands against the floor, as if I could push against the clay and calm the child and will those men to leave. There were more shouts from the soldiers.

"Leave!" Seo-Yun screamed. "There is no one here. There are no men. Only a coward enters the home of a mother and child and fires his rifle into the air. You are nothing but drunks."

I did not hear the slap. I heard the bump against the floor and a piercing cry from our child, and I knew Seo-Yun had been hit so hard she dropped the girl. Then came the louder tumbling of Seo-Yun falling to her knees to scoop up the baby. She yelled at the men in a voice so loud and indecipherable I thought they would kill her just to shut her up. I gripped the warm brick of the ondol. I saw the dim light at the edge of our house, and I knew if I went forward and pulled myself out from under the house it might mean death for all of us. The vision of Sook-Cha's face, wet with tears, kept me in place.

I heard three hard stomps and knew they were from Seo-Yun, telling me to stay put. Then silence. I did not know what was happening. The worst of my imaginings sprung forth, and I had to close my eyes. I had never felt so scared and so strong in all my life, filled with anger and vengeance, and I understood what Mr. Gong and my father had known and what those men in the mountains might never know, which is that such anger is another kind of empowerment, driving you to the unspeakable with righteousness on your side.

Another stomp came. Seo-Yun said, "It's okay," much too loudly to be telling the baby. "You're safe. You're safe."

She had given us away. The clear voice of a soldier called to her. "Where is he?" he asked.

I moved in position to wrench myself up from under the house.

"Who?" Seo-Yun said.

He did a *tsk-tsk* sound. "The husband you stomp for," he said. "It will be easier for you both if you tell us."

"He has gone to hide with the others," she said. "He's in the mountains. All the men are gone."

"What kind of man leaves his family behind?"

"The kind that wants to live to see his daughter grow up."

The soldier let out a loud laugh. He asked the other soldier if he could believe this woman. His Korean was very good, though with the clipped accent from the north like people from Seoul. He was clearly educated. "Maybe we should look around?" he said.

"I told you he's gone," she said.

"We will find him."

I came out from under the house, and the night air felt like my first breath, cold and filling. My body shook with fear, but I took one step, then another, and came up the porch and into my house.

"I am here," I said.

"My dog sleeps under the house when he is scared," the soldier said to me. The other soldier had his rifle pointed at Seo-Yun and Sook-Cha.

"We don't want trouble," I said.

"And we don't want to be in this dog-infested country. But we have our orders.

"You're a fisherman?"

"Yes," I said.

"I can smell it on you."

"Leave," I said, more calmly than I thought I could.

"This fisherman is brave."

"I just want my family to be safe. I'm not brave."

"That's true," he said. "A brave man wouldn't have hid and left his wife and child alone."

Then there was a crashing into my temple, a burst of lightning in my vision, and I was on the ground. The other soldier stood over me. The butt end of his rifle hovered in the air. He brought it up with two hands, as if it were a fencepost he was readying to drive into the ground, but the first soldier, the one who had done all the talking, stopped him. I knew blood was on my face, but I refused to touch it. I let it run it run into my eyes. The cut was large enough that the air burned my split skin.

"My friend doesn't like all your talking," one of them said.

"I don't like yours, either," I said.

"Yobo," Seo-Yun hissed.

"Listen to your wife, fisherman."

Blood trickled into my mouth. I tasted its salty metal, and then I spit it into my hand. I tried to stand but fell. The soldiers laughed. I stood up quickly, fighting to keep my balance.

"Clean yourself up," one of them said, and spit into my cut.

I didn't move. I turned to my family. I did what I had done every night since our daughter was born. I searched for her breathing in the rise and fall of her belly, and when I saw it, a sense of relief came over me about whatever would happen next. Seo-Yun's fingers squeezed the child's waist, and I allowed myself one glance to her eyes.

Had there only been one man I would have lashed out, but with both of them there I thought there was only one thing to do, which was to surrender.

"Take me," I said. "I'm ready."

"No!" Seo-Yun cried.

"Leave my family and I will go quietly," I said. "Let my daughter live."

Sook-Cha was close to Seo-Yun, and she was remarkably quiet. My face had gone numb with pain. There was nothing but a throb in my head.

"Why should any of you live?" the soldier asked.

"She's a child. Our only child," I said. "Spare her and her mother."

There was a burst of light as before, then another. In between the bursts I saw Sook-Cha's face, heard her begin to cry. I tried to remember her smile, that first smile when she started to become a child and not just a baby. Seo-Yun pleaded, but the bursts came faster until I no longer heard my wife or daughter or anything at all.

I AWOKE TO Mr. Gong sitting beside me. My vision was milky. I rose quickly, pain shooting through my body and my ribs seeming to crack in two. "Where's Seo-Yun? Sook-Cha?" I asked.

"They're fine. They're here," he said. "Resting. Asleep."

We were in his home. He told me the soldiers had left me to die. Seo-Yun ran to his house with Sook-Cha, and then he had come back for me, carrying me on his back. Seo-Yun had not wanted to stay in the house alone.

"You've been asleep almost two full days," he said.

My mouth was dry. He put a wet cloth to my lips.

"What did Seo-Yun say?" I asked.

"She said you were lucky. That all of you were lucky."

"What would you have done?"

"I wasn't there," he said. "You need to rest. You're talking too much."

"Tell me."

"A broken man is nearly as useless as a dead man," he said. "I told you to go."

"I was going to. I wanted to have one more meal with Seo-Yun. They came more quickly than we thought."

"Babo," he said. He rose. He paced. His voice was low and his words pointed. "You never listen to anyone. You only do what you want, when you want. You should have been gone days ago, when you first heard they were coming."

"That's my family," I said.

"That nearly died because you couldn't stay hidden."

He left the room. Minutes later Seo-Yun came in with Sook-Cha. Her cheek was bruised, and I saw that her face was scratched. The child appeared unharmed. Seo-Yun sat down next to me, and I put my finger in Sook-Cha's little fist. She squeezed it.

Seo-Yun was distant. She couldn't look at me.

"Are you mad at me?"

She didn't answer, and not wanting to fight, I sent her away. I told her we would leave when I could walk.

She got up without saying anything else, and I knew she had turned away from me.

Hours passed. I woke in the dark and my whole body throbbed in pain. Sook-Cha gave a cry, and then it was quiet again. I fell back and pulled the blanket under my chin. I was cold and every little movement hurt.

I thought of all the homes where men now slept again. Why had those soldiers left us? Why had they only beaten me? The fire was nearly out, only a faint crackle every few minutes. I only remembered the world disappearing, nothing after. Seo-Yun was so angry that I felt I could not ask her to come back to the room, to build up the fire and let me see the baby. I closed my eyes and then opened them very quickly.

I rose with a start, ignoring the sharp slices of heat that tore at my ribs and back, the dizziness of my aching head. "Yobo," I shouted. "Yobo!"

The child cried out, and I heard footsteps coming toward me.

"What is it?" Seo-Yun said. She was out of breath.

"What did you do?"

"What are you talking about?"

"What did you do? What did they make you do?"

"Nothing."

"You lie," I said. "Why am I still alive? Tell me, I must know."

"You already do," she said.

I braced myself against the wall and fought not to retch. Seo-Yun guided me down to the floor, back to my pallet and covers, and then she went to the fire and stoked it. I closed my eyes. I could not bear to look at her and think about what I had caused.

"I'm sorry," I said. "I'm sorry."

"Our daughter is safe. That's all that matters."

"You saved us," I said, the words between a whisper and cry.

She put her hand to my forehead. The familiarity of her touch was gone, though. I leaned toward her. "Rest, Yobo," she said.

I tried not to think about the crashing of their boots into my head, the world gone dark, the cries of pain I did not hear while I was unconscious. "Will you ever forgive me?" I said, my eyes on the fire.

"There is nothing to forgive."

I believed she meant it, but she was wrong. There was much about what had occurred that was unforgivable. There was no way to forget what she had had to do, what we might have avoided.

TWO DAYS LATER, we were back in our own house. The baby was happy, making smiles and soft giggles when we nuzzled into her neck. It was morning, and I was preparing to leave for the boat, though Mr. Gong had told me to rest. The air was cold outside, and I hobbled to the fire.

Seo-Yun had pushed our blankets to the corner of the room, close to the wall. She almost seemed to be cowering as I grabbed my fishing knife. She nursed Sook-Cha, and I thought of how she was giving the girl life from her body, how she had been the one to shield us.

"I must go," I said.

"Stay," she said. "You're too hurt."

"I'll manage," I said, but I wasn't sure if I could. I thought I might just be in the way both on the boat and at home. She walked with me to the door and held the baby on her hip.

"Do you think they'll come back?" I said.

"I don't know."

I pointed to Sook-Cha. "Is she okay?"

"I think so."

"And you?" I asked.

The bruise on her cheek had begun to lighten. She could only nod, turning the question back to me. "You?"

I told her what felt true for both of us. "I don't think so," I said. "I never will be."

I stepped away from the door, readying to leave, though I did not want to. "Yobo," Seo-Yun said, stopping me. "Can we walk with you?"

The three of us went to the beach in the dawn light. Small step by small step, and each one was like a knife in my side, another kick in my head. Mr. Gong waved to us from the pier and came toward us, taking Sook-Cha into his arms, lifting the girl up in the air where she spread her arms like a bird as if to fly away. She smiled as the sea breeze blew and waves crashed into the rocks.

"I'm sorry." I said it because I didn't think it was possible to say it enough, because I didn't want her to slip away from me.

"No more apologies," she said. She took my hand. Her knuckles were red.

Mr. Gong flew the girl back into Seo-Yun's outstretched arms, and my wife pushed the child up into the sky once more.

Out in the ocean, pulling in the first net, my eyes on the shore, I saw the pair of them—my wife and child. I saw them there all day. Mr. Gong and I did not talk about the events, what those soldiers had done to my wife, what she had given herself over to in order to spare our lives, and why they had agreed to spare us. At day's end, he gave me two sea bass, and that night I walked home with my family. I stoked the fire and carried Sook-Cha outside while Seo-Yun cooked.

All that had happened could have occurred anyway, which is why I had wanted to stay and try to prevent it. But now we both believed it could have been avoided if I had not been there. I saw that in Seo-Yun's eyes, and I knew I would always see it.

I watched smoke from the chimney trail up toward the mountain. I thought of the men who had walked up there and then back, safe, eager to see their families and hold them close again. They had avoided everything we hadn't.

I held our child close to me, pressed her soft cheek into my rough beard, careful to avoid the bruises and cuts. "We love you so much," I whispered. "Your mother's love is larger than the sea."

Seo-Yun appeared in the doorway. She said it was nearly time to eat. Above her the smoke thinned to wisps, the moon rose, and past the mountains, over the treetops, a dappling of stars began to burn in the fast-approaching night.

TWO STRANGERS

THE LAST THING I wanted—or expected or needed—was to be standing in the doorway of Carly Ray's room, watching her clutch a picture of Burl up to her face. She's so tiny, but at the same time there is something very adult about her appearance. Maybe it's the light spreading over her shoulders from the nightstand lamp, her slick-straight, brown hair lying limply behind her. Something about her seems too mature for ten years old.

"Carly Ray," I say, hesitant, fearful. "It's time to go to bed. You've got school tomorrow." I expect her to turn with cold eyes and resentment toward me, but she doesn't. She puts the picture away, under her mattress, and rolls to her back.

We both know she's used to Burl being here, maybe telling her a story or just sitting on the edge of the bed until she falls asleep. I'm not sure of what. She's only ever known me as her father's friend, who comes in every so often, bringing her a present from some far-off city she's never visited. She doesn't see me in any sort of fatherly way. I'm not even like an uncle.

"Goodnight, J.D.," she says.

I turn off the lamp and she closes her eyes, feigning sleep, and my mouth becomes dry. I close my own eyes with the hope that when I open them I will be in my own apartment, a thousand miles away, the sounds of the city rising up from the street and through windows, crashing against my bookshelves and furniture, echoing

down the hallways. But when I open them, I am in her room, a
strip of light slashing across a Gillian Welch show poster that was
Burl's doing for sure.

I pull the covers up to her chin, something I've seen people do
on television, and whisper a goodnight to her.

MOM WAITS FOR me in the living room, flipping through a *Time*
magazine. She puts it beside her on the sofa when I walk in.

"How is she?" she asks.

"Good, I think. I can't tell."

"What do you mean you can't tell?"

"I mean, I don't know. I've never been around her enough to
know. I'm not sure about all this."

"Well, you're going to have to be, aren't you?"

"I guess," I say. I think about the phone calls I have to make this
week. The one to St. Vincent's to tell them I'm not coming back.
The one to Julie to tell her what I've avoided the last few days. "It
doesn't seem real," I say, but not really to Mom.

She rises from her seat, ready to comfort me.

"I never thought I'd be back," I tell her. "When I was in college
I thought I might still come back, but after that, once I was in my
residency, I knew I never would. I didn't plan on this."

"Plans change sometimes, honey. Burl was your oldest friend
and he asked you to do this for him. You can't take her from here,"
she says.

"Why not? Why can't I raise her someplace else?"

"Because this is her home," she says.

"People move all the time, Mom. Think about the life she could
have in the city. I could take her to see plays and museums. She
could go to better schools."

"You grew up here and turned out just fine," she says.

"For every person like me how many are there that stuck around when they could have left?"

"That's not the point, son."

"Well, what is the point? My whole life is going to change."

"And hers hasn't?"

LATER, AFTER MOM has left and I'm on the porch, phone in hand, the frenzy of the last two weeks hits me. The phone call about Burl's death, my frantic flight home, that first night with Carly Ray. When I went to see Chris Molloy about Burl's papers, I found out he left me everything. Not just custody of Carly Ray, but his house, his pickup truck, half of his insurance policy, and a letter telling me what he wanted for Carly Ray if it ever came to this point and I had to take care of her.

The paperwork was tough to sift through. Molloy coached us both in Little League, and he got choked up as went over the documents with me, lifting his glasses off his face so I could see the impressions they'd made on the bridge of his nose as he wiped away a few tears. "Just doesn't seem right," he kept saying to me every few seconds. "You two were good boys. Still are," he'd say and then go back to the will and explain what it all meant.

He said normally the term *godparent* is just a title, but in this case Kentucky law says with Tracy having run off and not keeping contact for ten years and Burl naming me custodian, unless something crazy happens, I'm in the clear. She's my responsibility as long as the court declares me capable. "There's no reason they won't," he said, and with that I left his office with a folder full of documents.

I thumb the numbers on the phone, trying to summon up the courage to call Julie, but I can't. I keep thinking of Burl. I want to remember the things he and I did as kids in this town. The nights we drove to Swafford's, the bootlegger out past Woodbine, and sipped on lukewarm beers, setting our empty cans on the railroad tracks and waiting for the trains to run them over. I try to think of all the high school football games we attended on my visits home from college and med school, how we spotted the kids wearing our old numbers, but all I can see is the picture I have of him in my mind falling from that roof. One minute he's hammering away at shingles, the frame of the house drawing yellow lines against the forest behind him. He's bare-chested, skin turned brown as a biscuit, sweating under the July sun. Then it happens. He stands to stretch, loses his balance on the pitch, and he's tumbling. Nails splay from the canvas 84 Lumber pouch he has tied around his waist. They sprinkle, like jacks, the spot of earth where he will land. I hear the snap of his neck as it bends past ninety degrees and the thud of his heavy, muscled body hitting the ground. He folds on himself like a sheet kicked off the foot of a bed. Nails prick his skin and his hammer lies beside him, the shiny silver glinting in the sun.

I see my friend, the only one I had remaining here, lying in the grass, the life escaping his eyes, and I shudder at the sight, at all the distance that came between us when I left Kentucky and went to New York. And now that I'm back in our hometown, here to raise his daughter, I think how I've always thought our lives were moving in opposite directions and that home was our only connection to each other. But *home* doesn't even sound like the word to describe Fordyce anymore, it's been so long since I've lived here. I don't know what I can claim of it.

I look at the big oak and maple trees lining the street. Their branches hang over the pavement, shading the ground from the moonlight in jigsaw-patterned shapes. The quiet here compared to the city unsettles me, and this lets me know how far I've gone. *My life's only beginning*, I think. I finished my internship a year and a half ago, and St. Vincent's is a nice hospital, close to where I live. After my shift today I would have gotten Tone, the x-ray tech on the third floor, and we would have walked ten blocks down to the Carmine Street Rec to play hoops, and then after we'd have gone to Two Boots Pizza across from the hospital. Then there's Julie.

We've been dating four months. Long enough that I want her around, but not long enough that I'm sure it's okay to ask her to come to Kentucky and live with me. And even if I did, there really isn't much for her in the way of work. She's in public relations, and the closest thing we have to that around here is the local newspaper, maybe something in a state congressman's office.

These are selfish thoughts; there's no way getting around that. But when I think about what has come to pass, this promise I've made that I never thought in a million years would be called in, I can't help but be resentful. I've had to give up everything for a girl I don't really know and a friend I became separated from. ·

I'm ready to dial Julie's number when I hear Carly Ray open the front door. She has on baby blue pajamas with daisy chains around the ankles and chest.

"J.D.," she says.

"Yeah," I say, turning on my hip and setting the phone down. "Can't you sleep?"

"Not tonight," she says. "It's not an especially good night for sleep."

I smile at her child's way of speaking like an adult.

"What would Dad do if he were here?" I ask, too quick to realize this may be the wrong thing to say.

"Nothing. He'd probably just sit here with me and talk till I got bored."

I ask her if she wants me to read a story, but she says no. She says she just wants to sit outside for a bit.

"That's what we'll do then. It'll be hard to get up in the morning for school, though. You'll be tired. Fifth grade can wear a girl out."

IN THE MORNING we're running late, and I hustle Carly Ray out to the truck, handing her some money for lunch.

"Dad always made my lunch," she says.

"Today you'll have to buy your lunch," I tell her. "I forgot." I want to tell her that after she fell asleep on the porch and I carried her up to bed, I came back outside and called Julie, and she kept me on the phone until nearly three. I want to tell Carly Ray that Julie is probably the first woman I've ever even felt close to loving, to saying, "I love you," to and not having it feel hollow and out of some form of obligation.

Carly Ray doesn't know any of this. She is looking at me, hateful and upset. "I hate the school lunch," she says.

"I'm sorry, Carly Ray, I really am. I won't forget again."

She gets in the truck and holds her backpack in her lap. I flip the collar down on my sport coat and slide in, smelling sawdust in the floorboards. I've not driven a car, much less a stick, in four years. I pop the clutch three times before we ever make it out of the driveway and onto the road.

Carly Ray is sullen. She pouts, refusing to look at me or to even look straight ahead in the truck. She only looks out her own window.

"I really am sorry," I say to her, hoping to make peace.

She says nothing and stares ahead. In two weeks it seems I can't do anything right. When I tried to clean up the house, getting rid of some of Burl's old magazines she asked me why I was throwing them out. And when I started to pack his shirts and put them in boxes, she came into the room, looked at me, and then turned around without saying a word.

I have no idea how to handle her. I'm lost in how to get her to open up, in even knowing what she needs from me at this time in her life. The muffler has a hole in it, and the truck rumbles when I downshift and give it gas. It sounds like a sputtering lawn mower on turns.

On Adams, I pass the house where I grew up and see the new homeowners have taken down the basketball goal where Burl and I used to have our games. I see him and me, our younger selves dribbling and blocking each other's shots, Burl streaking past me as I stand lead-footed, my neck craning, to watch him lay the ball in.

Carly Ray is looking out her window, gripping and then regripping her bag, like she's kneading dough. I think to tell her this, to give the images I have of her father, but I keep quiet until we get to her school and I ask her if she'd like for me to come in with her.

"What for?" she says.

"I don't know. Do parents go in with their kids at the beginning of fifth grade?"

"You're not my parent."

She doesn't say this with malice. She says it like it's a statement about the weather, the way a person says, "Looks like rain today."

I grip the steering wheel harder. "I know that," I say. I want to remain calm. I want to say the right words. "I just meant do you need me to go with you?"

"It's okay," she says. "I can do it by myself."

"I'll wait here until you get inside then." She gets down from the truck, and I hand her the backpack.

"Bye, J.D."

"I'll see you at two-thirty." I wave to her, but she has already shut the door and is walking up the small set of steps. She is greeted by a young woman standing at the door in khaki pants and a bright red blouse. The woman waves to me and ushers Carly Ray inside, and I pull away, almost popping the clutch again.

ON THE PHONE the previous night, I told Julie I couldn't do this, which led to an obvious question from her.

"Why don't you bring her back here?" she said.

"Mom doesn't think it's a good idea."

"Your mother isn't in charge, J.D. You are. Your whole life is here. Your job, your friends. What about us?"

"I know, I know." There was a long pause on the phone until I finally said, "I think she has to grow up here. You don't understand that, I know, but it has to be *here*."

"I don't even know what that means. People don't have to grow up in small towns."

"What am I supposed to do, Julie? I gave him my word. You think I want to be here?"

"So, what? It's settled? Is that what you're saying? We can't even talk about this? You just said you couldn't do this. We talked about doing this together. At least trying it. You were going to bring her up here after Labor Day and then we'd enroll her at a good school, let her get adjusted to the city. What happened to that? Didn't you tell me he was always telling you how proud he was of you? How much he wished he could have gone off and done the things you did? Don't you think he'd want you to still live your life too?"

"It's not that simple. Maybe if she were older. It's too soon to move her." I looked up at the sky, the field of stars, and I felt my throat closing, fighting back the urge to let go of my emotion and tell Julie just how afraid I was and how much I was beginning to love her just as I had to leave.

Then the phone went silent again, and I heard Julie tapping her fingers against the window in her apartment, looking out over the traffic on Houston. "I thought we were in this together," she said and what she meant by "this" wasn't Carly Ray but life. I didn't have to tell her how I felt, she already knew.

"Things are hard. She's just a little girl. I don't know if the timing is right and—"

"Of course the timing isn't right, J.D. Her father died. But you sound like you're giving up on everything. You don't have to make every decision right now, do you?"

"I promised him," I said, but even that seemed so hollow to me. I thought about Julie's face, the soft point of her chin that rested on the windowsill, her light reflection in the glass as she leaned her forehead against the window.

"You're unbelievable," she said. "Listen to yourself. Have you even thought this all the way through? What if I came there for a few weeks? I have the vacation time. I could use a break."

"There's no need for that," I said.

"Why won't you let me help you? I love you, J.D. It's not just a tough time for Carly Ray. You have to think about yourself too."

I SPEND MOST of the day cleaning up the house. I'm reorganizing the living room and Burl's—now my—bedroom but leaving as much as possible the way it was for Carly Ray's benefit. I cut the grass and pull weeds from the flower bed and then make a list for the grocery store, leaving enough blank spaces for Carly Ray to fill in what she wants.

The sun comes through the trees in specks, and the heat feels like it has a hum to it. I wheel the lawn mower back in the shed and feel welcomed by the cold air resting inside. Everything is so neat and organized, hanging off of screws driven into boards. In the corner is a mini-fridge where Burl kept his stash of beer, afraid to let Carly Ray know he liked to drink one from time to time.

I open up the door and pull out one of the silver cans and pop the top. I hear my throat rising and falling as I gulp down nearly half of it in one long pull. I sift through the drawers of a small filing cabinet that has all the invoices for customers built up over the years. I see Burl made a good living framing and roofing houses. I think in all those years I've been away he must have grown closer to other people, that when he died there's no way he could still consider me his best friend.

I finish the beer and grab another. And then another. I sit in the shed all day and drink Burl's beer. I forget about our childhood races up and down Roosevelt Street on our bikes. I forget about the night we stayed up until dawn at my father's cabin after graduation, matching each other shot for shot from the Maker's Mark bottle, standing on the railing of the balcony, seeing which one would fall first while our friends cheered us on. I try to forget about his phone call to me when we were in our junior years of college, me at UK and Burl at Eastern, telling me Tracy was pregnant.

I sat up still groggy with sleep. "I thought you were smarter than that," I said. "Didn't you wear a rubber?"

"It was just the one time, J.D. I swear."

"Well, that's all it takes, right?"

"What am I going to do?" he said. "I ain't ready for no kid."

"You don't have to do anything about it tonight. You've got a little bit of time, man."

"What's that mean?"

"You know exactly what it means."

"Shit. That ain't no kind of advice. I can't ask her to do that."

"Why not? You think she's found some religion all of a sudden?"

"No. It just don't seem right to me, that's all."

"Well, what then? Marriage?"

"Shit," Burl said. "That ain't no kind of advice, either. She's crazier than a shithouse mouse. You know that yourself."

"She's always been crazy for you," I said, allowing a slight smile.

Burl huffed into the phone and let out a sigh. "I'm in a fix this time. I'm going to have to quit school. Get a job."

"Don't do that," I said to him.

"That kid's going to need a father. There ain't nobody but me and her to take care of it."

But it turned out he was the only one. Tracy took off after the birth. Never told anybody where she was headed. Just gone. Her parents moved off to Florida a year after Carly Ray was born, Jacksonville, I think, and like Tracy, they never kept contact. Burl was it. He was all Carly Ray had, and as I take the last beer out of the fridge I realize I'm now all she has.

Cans are scattered at my feet. I stand up and start stepping on them in hard strokes, flattening them out. My skin is hot from the alcohol; a patch of sweat on my back feels cold. I keep stomping the cans until they are all discs. I kick at them, pushing them like hockey pucks into the yard.

I go to kick another and miss, losing my balance. I fall backward and try to catch myself on the workbench, but my fingers slip and I fall. My coccyx cracks, shooting pain up my spine, and my left hand slams beside me, the last three fingers jam against the ground, bending the top knuckles backward. I hold my hand out in front of me and clench my teeth as I push them back into place.

I walk out of the shed and into the house, straight to Carly Ray's room. I shove my hand, my bad hand, under the mattress and ignore the thousand spikes of pain tingling under my skin and pull the picture of Burl out. I look into it.

Burl's in between two other men with his arms draped over their shoulders and grinning that easy, warm smile of his. His sandy blond hair is lighter than normal because of the sun, and his tool belt hangs around his waist, sloped down over one hip. A farmer's tan at the sleeves of his tee shirt and the lines of an older man already around the edges of his eyes. I never saw him this way. My visits were too short, too sporadic to ever know what became of his life in the way a friend should know these things.

I expected this picture to be of Carly Ray and him, but I see the appeal is how fully he fills the space, how engaging and bright he looks. I cuss him. I yell at him for dying and making me come back here to this place.

My voice screeches in my throat and my temples pulse when I shout. I pound the wall with my good hand, feel the sheetrock crack. I grab at the poster on the wall as I fall to floor. My hand throbs with pain and I crumple his picture, believing I can press all the pain concentrated there into his image. I open my hand and look at the creased lines on his face. Tears run down my cheeks and I look up, to the doorway, where I see Carly Ray standing with Mom holding onto her shoulders.

"J.D.," Mom says. "What in the hell are you doing?" She looks around the room, sees the poster ripped and lying on the floor, the imprint of my fist in the wall.

Carly Ray jerks away from her and runs down the hallway and out of the house. I go to the window and watch her run away, her little legs pounding into the sidewalk, her arms swaying side to side, trying to cut the air. I hear my mother's voice on the porch calling for her, asking her to stop.

Mom walks back in the room.

"What the hell's wrong with you?" She grabs my cheek and pulls down on my skin. I jerk away from her and the picture flies out of my hand, falling on the carpet.

"You're drunk," she says.

"I am not."

"You were supposed to pick her up from school an hour ago,"

she says. "Her teacher had to call me because she couldn't get an answer here at the house."

"I forgot," I say and try to walk past her, into the living room and then outside, but she grabs my arm. "What?" I shout.

She slaps me in the face as hard as she can and one of her nails nicks me. She can't control the contortions in her face. She looks at me more disappointed then than at any other time I can remember. "We've got to go get her," she says.

The beer is bouncing in my head. My steps are wobbly even though my mind is starting to clear. I realize what it is I've done and why I've done it and how it must look to Carly Ray who doesn't know anything about life and decisions, sacrifices people make for others.

"How could you?" my mom says to me in the car. "She's just a little girl and she has to come home to see you there, destroying her room, ruining the one thing she has left."

I stay quiet because there is no explanation, not one that would matter to her or me, really. I press my forehead against the window and look at the rows of houses that haven't changed since I was a boy, everything so unflinchingly the same.

"You're a grown man, for God's sake," she says. "Getting drunk in the middle of the day. And then. The gall you have to do something like that."

She goes on. Keeps repeating herself, keeps saying the same thing to me over and over, and I feel like a child. I feel like I'm ten years old and have broken a window by accident and she's yelling at me for something I couldn't control. And I want to say something to this effect back to her, to stand up for myself, but what I did is indefensible, inexcusable.

"I get the point," I say.

"Do you? Well, congratulations. That's great. You get the point.

There's a little girl you're supposed to take care of running around town because she's just seen you destroy her room and her father's picture but you get the point. Thank God for clarity."

"I didn't ask to take care of her." I say it so softly that even I'm surprised I've said it.

Mom slams the brakes and, having forgotten to put my seatbelt on, my head flies into the windshield before I can catch myself.

"You didn't ask to take care of her? You didn't ask to take care of her? She didn't ask for her father to die, J.D. That little girl hasn't asked for shit and that's exactly what she's gotten her whole life."

I keep touching my forehead.

"Get out," she says. "She can't be far. Start calling her name."

JUST AFTER DUSK, when the mosquitoes start to get thick and I can hear the frying of bugs in blue lights on back porches, I find Carly Ray sitting out behind the shed at the house. It's been almost two hours, and I've been crossing through the same yards Burl and I crossed twenty years ago when we were about her age. My head aches from the beer and the knot on my head. Some lightning bugs pop and katydids are whining, but there is still enough light that I can make out her face and see she's not been crying.

"Hey," I say as soft as possible. I'm not sure if it's to comfort her or to make sure I don't scare her.

She looks up to me, but she's quiet. Just like her father.

She goes back to staring in front of her, ignoring me. I feel the pull of a thousand mistakes in my life compounded into this one chance I have at redemption.

"Why me?" I asked Burl. We were twenty-five and he'd come back from putting his father in the nursing home.

"You're all the family I got, man. Tracy's never coming back. Her parents don't care about Carly Ray. I know if anything happens you'll take care of her." We were on the back deck, and instead of this shed being here, there was a dead maple tree, its trunk almost rotted out.

I didn't know what to say to him then except that I was honored and that, of course, I'd be Carly Ray's godfather. Burl and I never talked about it again, but as I look at Carly Ray and consider all the years in the past and the ones she has coming, it's on my mind how often I've not thought about it. The nobility and conviction of my word to Burl doesn't have the strength it did seven years ago. I've let myself forget what it meant to Burl to ask me, for me to be the one, and in doing this I feel like I'm unworthy of taking care of his daughter.

"Are you hungry?" I say, knowing I'm stalling. "My mom will be back any minute now and she'll cook you some supper."

I squat down in front of her, like a catcher, and look into her eyes. They are Burl's, round with small irises that give her the appearance of always being focused.

"I messed up today," I say. "I really messed up." I think how awful this sounds, how unapologetic it is.

Carly Ray blinks past me to the back of the shed, the chipped white paint on the boards and the dandelions that have grown up at the base.

"Did your Daddy ever tell you about me, Carly Ray? Do you remember when I used to come visit you and him?"

This breaks her stare, but she still won't hold my eyes with hers. She is thinking.

"When your daddy asked me to be your godfather I was proud to tell him I would do it and take care of you. And now all I can think about is what I did today, and how he would feel about it, what he would do to me if he was here."

"He'd kick your ass," she says, and this time there is venom in her voice, the anger of her father's death I've not seen until now.

It's what keeps me from laughing and forces the sting deeper.

"You're right. He'd beat me black and blue. He was a way better fighter than me," I tell her. "I—" but I stop short of finishing.

Carly Ray looks right into me, so hard I blink and almost fall back. "Why'd you do what you did today? Why did you rip my poster and punch my wall?"

"I was angry at him for leaving. I was angry that I'm the one who is supposed to take care of you."

"You don't want to take care of me." She says it as a statement, not a question, and this hurts the most. This little girl who has nothing anymore, who is the daughter of my oldest friend.

Mom's car pulls into the driveway and illuminates the yard in a sweeping motion. I get up and walk out from behind the shed and wave to her. "She's right here." I point.

Mom comes running up and bends down to hug Carly Ray. "Lord, you scared us to death. We looked all over town for you. I was fixing to call the police. Don't ever do that again," she whispers into her ear and turns up to me when she says this. "Don't ever run off again."

They walk past me into the house, and I'm left standing in the dark, my hands in my pockets and dew collecting on the tops of my shoes. I pick up the cans from earlier and throw them in the trash. I lock up the shed and go sit on the porch steps and smell hamburgers frying inside.

Mom puts Carly Ray to bed and says she's going to stay the night. I'm still outside, slapping at gnats and mosquitoes, and I tell her I'll sleep on the couch. She's too angry with me to say much more than this, and I don't blame her. I watch the red light of a radio tower flashing off by the railroad.

After the house is quiet I walk inside and grab a burger from the fridge and walk outside again. I can't even stand to be in the house. I'm on the steps, and I lay my head back and feel the wood, cool and grainy, against my neck.

Carly Ray comes outside, and I open up my eyes. She stands over top of me and then sits down beside me. I raise up and offer her a bite of my half-eaten burger, but she shakes her head.

"Can't sleep?" I ask.

"No," she says.

"You'll be tired tomorrow."

"Yeah," she says. "I was tired today too."

"You need to get your rest. School's going to be tougher this year than last year, right?"

"I guess."

"Sure it will be. That's how it works," I say, but then I stop myself. There's no use trying to talk to her like this. She's too smart to not see what I'm trying to do. We are quiet on the porch, listening to the trains being connected in the distance and the rumble of their movements echoing above us. I'm ready to pitch my burger into the bushes when Carly Ray speaks up.

"I miss him, J.D."

"You always will," I tell her. "You can talk to me about those things when you want. When you're ready to."

She nods her head and folds her arms over her knees and lays her chin down on them. "Do you miss him?"

I think about this for longer than I should. I hadn't seen him since last Christmas and only then for a few beers. Our conversation felt strained and our emails became reduced to nothing but forwarded jokes. I do miss him, but not in the way I think I should.

"Yes," I tell her. "I miss him."

She stays quiet and I look out at the road with her, neither of us moving or talking until I say, "You know when we were kids and I'd make a mistake, your father would never say anything to me. Just go quiet for a few days and give me these awful looks. He wouldn't sit by me at lunch and wouldn't call me at home. Back then I had a car and he didn't, so I'd usually pick him up, and when he was mad,

I'd wait for him on the curb every morning. When he wasn't mad anymore he'd come out and get in the car and we'd go to school and act like nothing had ever happened.

"He made me think by doing that. And if I tried to mention what had happened or tell him I was sorry, he wouldn't let me. Just say, 'I already forgot it.' Even then as a kid that's what he did. That's funny, ain't it? A person acting that way?"

Carly Ray is sleeping, though, and she leans into me. I put my arm around her and expect her to knock it away, but she nudges closer. Her breathing is soft and blows lightly against my skin. I pick her up and she rouses a little but falls back asleep, and I carry her into her room. The poster is taped up and hanging in its place on the wall. I think about the way my own father used to carry me to bed and how warm it felt next to him and how strong his arms were wrapped around me.

I pull back her covers and lay her down and then pull them back up. She rolls to her side and then onto her back. The streetlamp outside goes off and the room is suddenly dark. I lean down and whisper, "I'm sorry, Burl," in her ear.

She opens her eyes to me but doesn't say anything, and we stay like that for more than a moment. Two strangers staring at each other.

SINCE THE ACCIDENT

THEY NEVER CALL it what it was. They never discuss what happened. Emma thinks she can get past it, that it's just a phase, and when she does, her life with Richard, their marriage, will return to normal. But in quiet moments—as in the shower this morning—she can't remember what normal was like, how everything felt months ago, before the misshapen hoods and the hissing steam and rising smoke. She sometimes feels like a child who has let go of a balloon in the wind and run through a field after it, only to watch it fly farther and farther away.

"What are you doing here?" Emma is at her desk. The last class before winter break has just let out, and she hears her seniors in the halls, loud and boisterous, feeling the rush of freedom.

"I wanted to take my wife to lunch," Richard says.

"You don't work until tonight," she says, pointing at his police uniform. She still likes the sight of him in it, the shield shining against his chest and the patent leather holster shining in the fluorescent light.

"We had to go over to the rec center today to meet the kids the Optimist Club is sponsoring for the Christmas Angel project." He thumbs the bulletin board where she has put up a display of Adam Smith's Invisible Hand theory. "They like it when you look official. Looks better in the paper," he says and turns to face her.

She comes out from behind the desk to give him a kiss and sees the sky is threatening snow. Across the street the telephone poles are decorated with garland-covered candy canes and snowmen with lights around their edges. "Let me grab my papers," she says and turns back to the desk to stuff them in her shoulder bag. He reaches for it when she is finished, but she stops him. "I can get it," she says and shoos him off.

They walk out into the hallway where they fell in love as teenagers. Back then all Emma felt inside the walls of the school was that she was stifled. Everything seemed small and plain, too normal and too easy. Inside her group of friends there were no odd characters, no crazy free spirits. They went to the football games wearing their boyfriends' jerseys and class rings wrapped with thread around the band to make them fit their small fingers. They did not pick on anyone, and they were not picked on. When she pulls into the parking lot some mornings, she thinks back to her days as a girl and how she never could have imagined that as an adult she would find her way back into this place. But teaching suits her, and she enjoys the back and forth with her students, the mothering she can offer them on their small problems that seem so large and defining. The only thing that seems to be missing in her life—that everyone has been asking about for years—is a child of her own. *When are you two going to have children?* Always the plural. She and Richard smile politely at these inquiries, wanting to believe they are well-meaning but knowing this is the way it is in their hometown. A family is a sign of success, and they are failures.

They stop by the main office so she can turn in her grades and tell everyone Merry Christmas.

"He's taking you to lunch," Margaret, the secretary, says when they walk in.

"He is," Emma says.

"Such a good husband," Margaret says back. "I couldn't tell you the last time Larry took me to lunch." Emma and Richard look at each other then back to Margaret. "He's the sorriest old thing ever was a husband," she continues. "But I love him. What else are we going to do but love our men? They need our love."

"That's right," Emma says.

"They're helpless without us," Margaret says. "You two have a good Christmas."

"You too," Richard replies. Then he gives Emma a knowing squeeze and says, "I hope Larry gets everything he wants."

Outside the school they laugh at his remark. "She didn't know what you meant," Emma says.

"Oh, she knows. All she can do is love that man."

They laugh again and the wind picks up. Flurries are starting to fall. Emma grabs hold of Richard's arm as he walks them toward his cruiser and opens the door for her. She hates the smell of his police car. A mix between stale, rotting wood, body odor, and coffee that Richard has spilt too many times in the floorboards.

"Maybe I should take my car," she says.

"Why?"

She can feel what's left of the warm air inside escaping past her into winter. "It smells bad," she says.

"I put a new air freshener in there this morning. Take a whiff."

"I have errands to run," she lies. He looks at her confused and maybe hurt. She goes on, "That way we won't have to come back here after we're done."

"OK," he says, but she knows he is upset by this small thing.

"I just don't see the need for two trips," she says and then kisses his cheek to try and soften everything.

They go to the Chinese restaurant in the shopping center. The parking lots outside Belk-Simpson and J.C. Penny are full, and the restaurant is busy too. Six years ago this restaurant opened up and Emma never believed she'd see hillbillies lined up to eat Chinese food, but here they all are at the buffet like it's a Sunday dinner at the church. Some of her students are in a corner. They wave to her, and she waves back as Richard gets them a table.

"How're you feeling?" Richard asks when they are sitting across from each other.

"About what?"

"In general," he says. He is tiptoeing again, something he has done more and more of late.

"I'm glad the semester is over. We need to go Christmas shopping. I still haven't gotten your mother anything." She picks at her food, waiting for what's next, knowing he will ask about her health.

"I was thinking we could go to Lexington next week," he says and puts his fork down.

She looks up at him and decides to play dumb. "The malls will be so crowded," she says. "I'm sure I can get everything I need here at Belk's and Penny's and online."

"Not to shop," he says. "I mean, we can, if you want, but I was thinking maybe we should see a specialist."

"You heard what the physical therapist said. As long as I follow—"

"I'm not talking about your neck," he says. He lowers his voice. "I meant, a fertility doctor."

The teenagers in the corner hoot and holler with laughter, and for a brief moment Emma believes they've heard their conversation and are laughing at her and she flushes. "Can we talk about this later?"

"Only if you promise to actually talk about it."

"What's that mean?"

"You don't want to talk about it. Ever. We've been trying for months and nothing's happened. Maybe there's something wrong with me."

The implication that it is him who is at fault makes her distance from him these months seem all the worse. She turns to her plate of food again, pushing the rice to one side, and feels her neck seize up in the simple movement of looking down. She makes a face and reaches a hand back to rub the spot.

"Are you all right?" He reaches across the table and puts his hand on top of hers.

"It's nothing," she says, feeling the sting lessen. "I just need to ice it."

"Maybe we should find a specialist for that too," he says.

"It'll go away."

"It hasn't yet."

They stare at each other. "I don't need to see a doctor about anything," she says at last. "My neck will be fine and we'll have a baby when it's time. I don't want to go to some clinic and have them run a bunch of tests on us only to find out we're normal."

"But what if we're not?"

"We're fine," she says. She gets up from the table and goes to the restroom, taking her purse. At the sink she wets a paper towel and presses it to her forehead and then the back of her neck, taking in the coolness on her skin. She turns her head left and right and wants to feel her neck pop, but it hurts to turn it too much. Then she opens up her purse and pulls out the birth control pills. She keeps telling herself she will stop taking them, that she should have stayed off of them, but when the accident occurred, she lost her hold on the world and feels she still hasn't gotten it back. She cups a mouthful of water into her palm and takes the pill.

"Are you ready?" she asks back at the table.

"We just sat down. You haven't eaten," he says.

"I guess I'm not hungry."

She sits across from him and places her napkin on top of the uneaten food. Through the window snow is starting to fall in big, full flakes. She is unsure of what to say and knows she is losing him. They sit in silence, listening to the scrapes of forks and the loud foreign talk that sounds like screaming to them from the kitchen. Emma wants to push through this wall they've formed. Their love for each other is not what has been called into question, but as she watches him move the food around on his plate, not even lifting the fork to his mouth, she isn't so sure she is right anymore.

In the mornings, when she wakes, she feels the strain. Something akin to a pulse and a tightening of the tendons and muscles where the shoulder meets the neck. This is her only physical reminder of what took place. The others don't seem as subtle, though. And now when Richard leaves for his shift, after the ten o'clock news, she has a fear about being alone. Once she's in bed, the house shifts and settles, bringing creaks and groans that no longer seem familiar and warming, and she imagines all the terrible things that could befall him. Scenes from television dramas and stories she's read in the paper pop into her head, and she sees Richard's chest caved in by a bullet, his cruiser run off the road by a Ford pickup truck and careening down a mountain. Him pulling a car over on the Falls Highway, standing beside the driver's door awash in swirling blue lights and then his head struck by a crowbar from behind, and he is left on the oil-covered road. Yet these seem implausible because she has lived in Fordyce her whole life and knows it is a small town, has always seemed a safe place. But bad things can find you anywhere. She also knows this. And, when Richard returns at dawn and lays his holster over the back of her chair at the sewing table and undresses and comes to bed smelling of the cold wind, she is filled with relief but not comfort.

He pushes back from the table, throwing his napkin down.

"You're done?"

"Might as well leave. Neither of us is eating," he says.

"I don't want you to go in tonight," she says and is surprised to hear herself say it.

He looks at her and frowns. "Why? What's wrong?"

"Nothing," she says. "I just don't want you to go in tonight. It's a feeling I have—that I've been having."

"What do you mean?"

She feels childish, foolish. "Nothing," she says. "Forget it. I shouldn't have said anything."

"Don't do that. Please."

"What?"

"Shut down on me. I want to talk about this."

"I don't know what to say or what it is—" but she can't finish the thought and bring herself to tell him what's on her mind, what she's kept from him since that day. It doesn't even make sense to her, these fears, this feeling that has come on her.

Frustrated, Richard gets up from the table, pausing for a moment, then goes to the counter to pay.

Outside the snow has already covered the windshields of the cars. "I'll see you in the morning," Richard says and leans down to kiss her goodbye, but she backs away.

"You're not coming home before your shift? You've got almost six hours before you have to go in."

"I have errands to run too."

"You're mad. You're pouting."

"I'm not."

She waits for something else from him, but there is nothing. Snow lands in his hair and melts into drops. Now, it is him who is kissing her to soften their talk before he gets in his car. He drives away and enters the bustle of holiday shoppers, weaving through and past their cars. She has always liked the pace of Christmas, the cold weather and early nightfall and lights on houses and lawns, but this year she is empty. She watches his cruiser mix into the snaked line of taillights on the hill that leads out of the shopping center, inching toward the top until he is at the red light by McDonald's. Then he turns left and disappears below the horizon while snow blankets her shoulders.

RICHARD'S INCREASING DISTANCE is her own doing. He loves her more than she feels she deserves at times. To her he still looks like the boy at the top of the steps freshmen year, cutting up with his friends and his laughter echoing all the way down the hall to her locker. That he is a police officer now seems like a strange twist of fate when she considers how unserious he once was. He is still playful, but that has lessened over the years with what he has seen.

So many of their friends—not to mention their parents—think it strange they have waited so long to start a family, but unlike the girls she grew up with, and who still live in Fordyce, Emma was in no rush to be a mother. She has resisted Richard's longing for a child because she wanted to travel and have a full life before having a family. She still has never been on a plane, but she and Richard have driven everywhere, even to the Grand Canyon where they had a Japanese tourist snap a picture of the two of them that sits on the mantle next to a picture another Japanese tourist took of them with their original photographer. It was Richard's idea, and in the picture the three of them are laughing, their eyes closed in delight at the lens before them.

She has seen so many places but only ever been a part of this town. She thinks of all the miles they've logged in the car across the highways that tether the country together like cables and doesn't know how a simple run to the Food Fair to get a watermelon for the church picnic is where everything changed. She doesn't know how many times she's driven at night during summer vacations, in the flat prairies or the Blue Ridge Mountains, and wondered what it would feel like to lose control and tumble through time and space.

When the woman crossed into her lane there was no way Emma could have avoided her. Her teeth rattled together and the airbag exploded in her face and burned her skin. Nothing was how she imagined it. She only heard the loud thunder of the cars ramming into each other, not the sounds of metal twisting or glass crunching. Her car spun sideways and that was like a freefall, but when it came to a rest, all she had was a ringing in her ears and a headache.

In the aftermath, among the shattered glass, Emma saw the woman. Her head hung at a sickening, unnatural angle and appeared to be held in its place by the thread of a single tendon. Her glasses swung back and forth, like the pendulum of a grandfather clock, from a small gold chain around her neck and her eyes were open but they saw nothing. Dust from the airbags filled Emma's car, and she closed her eyes tightly then and said a prayer. But later, when she sat in the back of the ambulance with Richard, giving her statement and watching the cars being loaded on the flatbeds, she could not remember what she had prayed to God for.

At the hospital they sat on the examination table together in one of the small rooms in the ER, and Richard said to her, "Don't think about it too much." She knew he was trying to comfort her. He'd seen a lot of car wrecks, heard the wails of those who did and didn't make it, and because of that, like any emergency worker, he'd become numb to the most fatal tragedies. But Richard didn't make jokes. He was never flip about what happened or what he saw. He just seemed to push it some place inside him that even Emma didn't have access to. She sometimes thought she could fill up the halls of the high school with all that he kept from her.

The doctor who looked in on her was a young woman, young as they are, and she had been curt. She didn't even put Emma's x-rays up to the light box when she examined them and then said they weren't "remarkable." She told her to monitor her pain, gave her some samples of naproxen, and was on her way when Richard stopped her.

"Yes," she said from the hallway, a hand on the doorframe.

"It's just she's—we're—trying to get pregnant."

The doctor gave a slight smile. "Everything should be fine."

Then she moved off and they were alone in the room again, and Richard said to Emma, "She must have places to be."

"Must," Emma said, getting down from the table. "Let's go home."

That night they both lay in bed together, Richard having called in even though Emma told him not to. His lips puttered while he slept, and she looked out the window, wanting to see the stars, but they were drowned out by the yellow glow of the streetlights. She had not been shaken by the woman's death, at least not the way she thought she might. She felt sad and she thought of the woman's family and what they must be going through, but she didn't feel guilt and this surprised her. She was told the woman had a heart attack and lost control of her car, that at impact she was killed instantly, but Emma still doesn't know what that means. Everything takes time even if it seems like it doesn't.

She had just gone off the pill two weeks before this. They were going to start their family, and she had been excited about it, planning the baby's room, its colors and toys. But the night fears started shortly after the accident, and in the shower one morning the pain in her neck was strong, so sharp and biting that she fell to her knees in the water and gritted her teeth and took deep breaths. Then it went away. She got dressed for school, kissed Richard goodbye, and drove to the Dairy Mart at the corner and called in sick. She made an appointment with their family physician and had every intention of telling him about her neck, but when he came in the room and asked how she was, she told him she'd quit taking her birth control and wanted to go back on it. "I'm not ready to be a mother," she said.

"You're just nervous," he said.

"No. No, I'm not." *Unwilling, yes. But not nervous.* She had handled plenty of babies. Had cared for her nieces and nephews. She knew they could both care for a child and love it and that they would be good parents.

"You'll be a fine mother," the doctor said.

"I know," she said. "When I'm ready." That stopped the conversation.

He told her she needed to get a morning-after pill and then start taking her pills again as she had before. On her way out she had her prescription filled and then drove to the state park in London and stared into the woods. She held the morning-after pill in her palm then set it in the cup holder. She had gone to the doctor for her pain but had come away making a huge decision she didn't even bother to tell Richard about. She thought about the look on his face, the concern, when he'd asked that young ER doctor about her health, about how the accident might affect her chances of getting pregnant. She'd never seen him scared before. And she thought about the raids he was going on, cracking down on the surge of meth labs in and around the county. His job was more dangerous than it ever had been. The wind blew against the car, rocking it, and the trees bowed under its force. When she got home that afternoon, she took the morning-after pill in the bathroom while Richard was in the kitchen making them dinner.

She's never hidden anything from him before. They have grown up together, and he knows her better than anyone. She doesn't know how she's kept her secret so long without him finding out, without him sensing what she has kept from him. But when you love someone you find a way, she tells herself, to make things right and make them believe whatever they have to in order to spare them pain.

AT HOME, AFTER going Christmas shopping for Richard's mother and buying her a scarf and some lotions, then to the supermarket, Emma puts away groceries. She checks her cell phone again, afraid she has missed a call from Richard, but there is nothing. They have not spoken since lunch, and she wonders what he has been doing all day and why he hasn't called. Her mother told her when they married that her only job was to do her part. "If you just do what you're supposed to, then you can make a marriage work. You can get through your problems." She thought that meant only being there and being ready, like showing up for work, in a sense. Each one of them had their own roles to play, and hers was to be dependable and faithful and, later, to push him outside of Fordyce on those long journeys to faraway places. It made them both happy. But when she goes to the window at night, not able to sleep from too much thinking, and imagines Richard patrolling their hometown, no matter how hard she tries to convince herself that everything will be okay, she can't. She paces the house and watches television by flipping through channels too fast to pay attention to any one thing. A stack of books lies by the bed, in each of them a bookmark placed just a few pages in, where she has stopped reading. She can't get used to the sound of her own breathing it seems, and only rational thought keeps her from panic on some nights. She doesn't know how many times she has wanted to call him, to ask if he's all right, to ask him to come back home.

She's never needed him like this.

A cup of tea in one hand and a liquid gel pack from the freezer in the other, Emma stands at the picture window looking out on the neighborhood. Christmas lights sparkle on the thick, fast-falling snow. There is so much on the ground that even though it is well into the evening, it still appears to be dusk with the reflected light from the lawns. She shifts her neck into the gel pack, pressing the cold farther into her flesh. She is waiting for something, she feels. Perhaps Richard's car, hoping he has changed his mind and will come home before his shift begins, but all she can see up and down the street is the snow covering everything, one layer being laid over the other. The world changing, she thinks.

THE LIGHTS ARE crashing off the walls, and they fill the living room. Emma has fallen asleep on the couch, and when she hears the doorbell ring, at first she believes it is all a part of a dream, but it rings again followed with a loud knock on the storm door. She kicks off the afghan, and when she rises, she feels her knees go weak with the sight of the cruiser at the curb. She stands, looking outside. The snow has stopped falling, and if not for the lights that color her living room and the pluming exhaust from the car, everything would look calm and peaceful.

"Will," she says, opening the door, and hugs herself against the cold. "What is it?"

"Richard's in the hospital," he says.

"Oh, God," she says and bends at the waist, grabbing his outstretched arms. Before she can ask what happened he is pulling her up.

"He's okay," he says. "He's going to be anyway. But something happened."

She stands tall and still holds his forearm, squeezing it harder. "Tell me," she says.

"He was out on 25, in front of Walmart and a car ahead of him had smoke coming out of the trunk. He pulled it over. Didn't suspect anything other than something was on fire. He'd just gotten off his break. He wasn't thinking." Will is a big man, bigger than Richard, with a deep country accent and kind, soft eyes. His body blocks the cold wind coming through the door. He tells the story calmly, and this calms her some. "The car pulled over and the driver didn't want him to look in the trunk. He ordered him out of the car and made him pop the trunk. He wasn't thinking," Will said again.

"As soon as the lid is open he sees meth cooking in the back of it. It's a bomb on four wheels. The driver panics and tackles him into the ditch, gets on top of him, and hits him in the head with a rock and runs for it."

"He didn't hit back?" she asks.

"Too stunned, I guess. It's not like him. Like I said, he wasn't thinking. He's got a pretty big bump on his head and is a little out of it, but other than that he's all right. He'd already called the fire department when he had the guy pulled over, otherwise he'd probably still be lying by the side of the road."

"He's okay, though?"

"He's fine. His pride is hurt a little is all."

"Can I see him?"

"I'm here to take you to the hospital."

She rushes to put on shoes and grab a coat. She doesn't realize how much snow is on the ground until she steps onto the walkway and her ankle is submerged and snow falls over the lip of her boots. She then thinks of Richard in the ditch, the snow coming up past his ears and his body lying prone and still while cars roll past him on the highway. She thinks of him looking up at the sky with blood trickling onto the white snow and an empty can near his head and the long grass poking through the snow's surface. She is in the car and it is warm and the police radio crackles, and she hears Marlon's voice. There's a crash on the other side of town, near the old Clancy's hamburger joint at the foot of the hill. Two cars. No injuries.

Will picks up the radio and says he'll be there in fifteen minutes, after he drops Emma off at the hospital.

The roads have been scraped, but it's only packed down the snow, making it hard and slick. "Nobody should be out in this," he says, putting the radio back in its cradle. "You ought to pull over anybody that's out on a night like this."

Emma pulls her coat tight at the collar and looks at the houses with their lights off. It is late, well past midnight, and the sky is clear. Each star is like a bright shining pinprick in a dark fabric that blocks the light. She knows she will have to tell Richard about going back on the birth control and about her fears when she gets to the hospital. And he will forgive her and say he understands what she's been going through, how an accident like hers can do that to people. She will have to correct him then and say, "It wasn't an accident. It was a crash. It was two cars colliding, and I'm the only one that lived to tell it. You can't know what it was like." That's when it strikes her that she has been part of a death, of an ending. She grabs at the coat collar, tighter now, and bites down on her knuckles.

Richard will love her anyway, though. Her deception will change nothing in his feelings for her, but he can't know how it felt, how it now feels. He must understand that. He can know how it would feel for him, but he can't have her feelings too. He can't know that when she went to the park that day in London after visiting the doctor, in her mind she saw the car coming at her. She felt the impact again and the way it ran through her body and into her life. It has been rippling through her skin ever since without her knowing what it meant or how it changed her.

She gets out of the car, and the snow has melted into her socks and her ankles chill in the night air. Will only drops her at the curb and tells her he will be back later. She waves goodbye. The hospital sits on a leveled mountain, and she looks down on her hometown and remembers when the building behind her was being built. Nothing has changed so much since then, at least not from so far away. The town lights still look the same to her, and roads wind and cross in their familiar directions. But a thought occurs to her that she had once in New York City. They had been walking through SoHo, and Richard had hated it. He didn't like the way the people dressed and the little black glasses that everyone seemed to wear. "I bet they don't even have prescriptions," he said. "They're just frames with glass." "Hush," she told him. She was looking at all those buildings jammed next to each other, thinking of the thousands of lives in them, stacked on top of each other, separated only by drywall and carpet, plumbing and electrical wires. She wanted to know then what those lives were like. How much different were they from her own? How much different could they be? Standing on the mountain in the winter, bracing herself against the wind, she looks at her hometown and realizes she knows nothing of the lives that sleep below her, the secrets each of them keeps.

She turns and enters the hospital, gives her name to the receptionist. When she comes to Richard's room, he smiles and sits up in bed. She rushes over to tell him to relax, to lie down, but he refuses. He scoots over, giving her part of the bed, and she sits. She puts her hands to his face, asks if he is okay. Even after he tells her that everything is fine, that they can go home in a few hours and he will make her pancakes and they will sleep in, she doesn't get up from the bed. She lies down beside him and pushes as close to him as she can. She has until tomorrow, she thinks, to keep her own secret. One more day and she will tell him everything, and then her fears—all of them—will go away. She feigns sleep when he asks if she is still awake. And before long he is asleep and her breathing finds rhythm with his, and she holds onto his arm all through what's left of the night.

SMOLDERS

THE FIRE BURNED bright. The flames climbed to the height of a small pine and sent smoke to settle in everyone's hair and clothes. This was the last party of the year. The last time Wren Asher figured he might ever see any of the other bright pink faces standing around the bonfire. They all drank from large cups filled from the Dairy Mart soda fountain down the road and spiked with vodka, bourbon, Mad Dog 20/20, and whatever else they'd been able to score the night before graduation from Swafford's Auto Body Shop—the front for the local bootlegger. Some still wore red mortarboards with the gold tassels brushing their cheeks as they laughed and talked. Wren held no drink in his hand. He wore a pair of cutoff khaki shorts and a Che Guevara tee shirt he got from a street vendor on a school trip to New York in the fall. In his car was a mason jar full of moonshine his uncle had given him as a graduation present. When Wren had reached for it his uncle had not immediately let go and looked the boy in the eye. "That stuff there will knock your dick in the dirt," he told him. "I don't doubt it," Wren said, but he had never had a drop of alcohol in his eighteen years.

In a week he was leaving, and he had come to the party more out of obligation than excitement. A rite of passage, really. He wanted to be here because he had known these people all his life but he had never truly felt part of them because he was half-Korean, different from everyone else, the lone minority. But Lucinda was here and that was always enough reason to attend. To call her his crush seemed too immature and to call her more than that was false.

Someone walked to a pickup and grabbed a wood pallet out of its bed. Skids they called them at the shipping warehouse where Wren had worked the summer before. Presumably, he thought, for the way the forklift just slid right underneath them and lifted the cans of shrink-wrapped soup, cereal, or whatever else they distributed. The boy lifting the skid over his head was Danny Jackson. A big, strong kid slated to head to Georgia next year on a football scholarship. Wren hoped his friend wouldn't be back home by Christmas. The town had seen it all too often. Once Danny got down there with all those preps and blacks and got his ass whacked a few times on the field, it wouldn't matter how damn strong he was or how fast he ran. He'd cry homesick and miss being the big shot he was right here in the middle of the same group of friends he'd had since kindergarten. He'd come home, enroll in the local Baptist college, and become an attorney or pharmacist. Fordyce, Kentucky, was littered with men who had been just like him, and like those men, Danny would probably die where he was born. So few people ever really left, Wren thought. He had never thought of Fordyce as a place to escape, and it wasn't hard for him to imagine staying there forever himself, but his parents had never encouraged him to stay.

He took in the group around the fire—remembered nearly all their faces from kindergarten—foreheads reddened with sweat from their proximity to the blazing fire. Many of them, though certainly not all, had treated today's ceremony like an ending. Despite the loud music and booze, a funereal air had been looming over the festivities for the better part of the night. More than once a teammate from the football or basketball team had come up to Wren and hung his arm around the boy's lean, broad shoulders and said,

"This is it, brother. We're out of here. The best days of our lives are over." Their coaches had drilled this sentiment into them as a means to tell them that not only was their youth fleeting, but so were their opportunities at glory and that the two were inextricably tied. There was no glory in old age. Not in Fordyce. Not for them. To each one of his friends, Wren wanted to reply, "If these were the best days of our lives, our lives are really going to suck." But he only nodded and shook his head. There was no point in ruining their buzzes.

She appeared beside him, her lips turned red from Hawaiian Punch. "Still won't drink with me?" Her long hair hung to the middle of her back, and she pulled it away from her face, revealing the crisp green eyes he had first seen in third grade and the soft white nape of her neck. He had kissed her there once, not knowing skin could be so soft. They were on that long ride home from New York, and Lucinda had curled beside him on the chartered bus, saying, "You're the only boy here with any kind of manners, Asher." Somewhere around Pittsburgh she nuzzled close to him, performed that exact same move with her hair, and in the darkened bus with everyone sleeping around them, Wren leaned in for the kiss. She had not even flinched, as if she knew he'd waited his whole life for such a moment. She pulled him closer, causing an erection to press against his jeans.

"There'll be none of that tonight, Asher. Just sleep," she said without ever opening her eyes.

The fire threw embers into the sky that seemed to melt with the night. Wren thought about how much he would like the chance to lean in once more. "I've got some moonshine in the car," he said. "Gift from my uncle." He stepped closer to the fire.

Lucinda broke into a smile. "Does he know what a pussy you are?" she said.

"No, ma'am," he said. "He's mistaken me for someone who is tough."

"Never touched a drop in your life and you've come here with a full jar of corn mash. That's what Daddy calls it. I like how that sounds, don't you?"

"It's got a ring to it," he said. Her tee shirt was low-cut, and the fire's yellow light danced on the tops of her breasts. If she had said to him in that moment she wanted him to marry her, he would have. He would forgo everything in his own future for the chance to put his lips to that neck once more, to feel the curves of her body under his trembling fingertips and hear a cry of pleasure from that sweet, sugarcoated mouth.

"What am I going to do without you next year?" she said.

"What are you going to do without me for the rest of your life?" he shot back. They had always been friends and nothing more, and the impossibility they could ever be together emboldened Wren.

"You don't think we'll keep up? Stay friends."

"We might," he said. "Hard to tell."

"I'm hurt by that, Asher." She never called him by his first name.

"Cindy, you're going to have so many boys calling you in the first three weeks of school that if you even remember me by Thanksgiving I'll be surprised."

"I could never forget you," she said. "You'll be famous someday."

"At what?" he said.

"Probably whatever you want."

She was not drunk, he thought, but on her way. This was his best chance to make a move, to make some lasting memory with a girl he'd always loved. Another skid was thrown onto the fire. Somebody turned up "Sweet Home Alabama" on a car stereo. Even though this was Kentucky, everybody let up a whoop and screamed, "Turn it up!" along with the song. Wren joined in too. He took

Lucinda's hand. He squeezed it tight, interlocking their fingers, and noted she did not let go.

"I'm not going to sleep with you," she said.

"I know it," he said but imagined what that might be like. He was still a virgin. "But you will drink with me, won't you?"

"I will," she said.

"And you'll watch out for me?"

"I can."

Another skid was placed on the fire, and red sparks lifted above the flames, twisting and winding up into nothing.

"Eighty degrees out and we've built a fire," Wren said.

"You can't have a party in a field without a fire."

"We're like cavemen," he said.

"What do you mean?"

"Gotta have a fire. Gotta have light."

"I don't get it," she said. She sipped from her drink.

He didn't bother explaining. "You look empty," he said. "Let's get you a refill. A small one."

They walked to his car, a beat-up Buick sedan that had been his mother's for ten years before it had been his. He popped the trunk and pulled out the jar from the wheel well of the spare. When he turned she was right in front of him. She stood so close the fabric of her tee shirt brushed the backs of his fingers with each rising breath. She said nothing, and he felt the electric pulse of sex between them.

"Let me see what you have," she said. She took the jar in her hands, the red nail polish fresh and glossy, and swirled it around. "Watch," she said and came beside him, holding the jar up to the light. "When there is only one bubble left that's called the bead, and the longer the bead lasts before it bursts, the stronger the liquor."

"How do you know this?"

"There's a whole world of things I know, Asher."

"Will you share them with me?"

"Maybe," she said. "But not tonight. That's all you get." She twisted open the mason jar and handed the ring to Wren, then pried off the sealed cap. The whiff of grain alcohol burned his sinuses and nearly made his eyes water.

"I'll go first," he said.

"The hell you will," she said. "Ladies first. And not too much for you, either. Take a small sip now and then another later."

The jar seemed to tip itself to her lips. Her eyes were closed and she didn't even make a face when she swallowed, but she did immediately take a sip from her own cup to cut the burn. "Your turn," she said. "I can't believe you're going to take a drink."

"First time for everything," he said.

The liquid was clean and clear at first but seemed to sear his esophagus as it made its way toward his stomach, where it formed a small stone of heat. "One more," he said and quickly took another shot.

"Well, I'll see you in the morning," she said.

"Are you leaving?"

"No, but you are." She laughed. "Let's head back." She grabbed his hand and led him toward the fire. Sweat was already on his temples, and the music was loud. No one spoke. They all stared into the fire, watching its moves, its hues. This is what he had been trying to explain to her minutes before. The fire was the big show that over the course of a hundred high school parties, in fields just like this one, there had always been a moment when everyone shut up and simply watched a fire burn itself up, the movement of flames, the melding of orange and red and blue. He would tell her later, when they were alone, he thought. The night sky was filled with more stars than he could ever remember, more than he thought were even possible, and he had spent many nights like this outside his house looking up to them, dreaming of the worlds beyond earth and the towns and lives past Fordyce. Lucinda leaned against him and pitched what was left of her drink against a burning skid, and he watched the Styrofoam melt in seconds and the watered-down alcohol expel a few puffs of fury.

"I'm not sleeping with you," she said.

"I'm not sleeping with you, either," he said. He put his arm around her shoulders. Her body felt as if it was a thousand degrees, and the small blonde hairs on the backs of her arms were bronzed from the fire's glow. From across the way he saw someone give him a thumbs-up, but he ignored it and concentrated on the smell of Lucinda's hair, the rhythm of her breathing beside him.

"You should have another drink, Asher," she said.

"Why is that?"

"You'll be able to keep it up longer." She laughed and he did too.

"We're not sleeping together," he said.

"But you will with somebody someday," she said. "I won't always be here to teach you everything."

"Why does it have to be that way?"

"We both know it will be," she said.

"Do we?"

"I do." She hooked her arm through his. "I feel warm."

"Me too."

"Let's go sit in your car with the AC on."

They walked back through the field, leaving the party behind. He opened the door and helped her inside the car, and she clutched his arm for balance. She seemed to have gotten very drunk very fast.

"I had a few shots before I came over to you," she said. "I'm almost faded."

"That explains it," he said.

"Will you drive us away from the noise?"

"You want to leave?"

"No. I just want to be away from the noise."

He moved the car closer to the road they had come in on. This was someone's hunting camp. Two hundred acres out in the county somewhere. The translucence of the fire was visible from where they sat, just over a small hill. The air conditioner cooled the car down quickly, and Lucinda put her head in his lap and let her sandaled feet hang out the window.

"What do you think those girls will be like at Harvard?"

"Smart, I guess. Boring," he said.

"Am I fun to be around?"

"Yes. Always."

"Then I must be stupid." She smiled up to him, eyes closed.

He pushed the hair from her eyes and feathered her cheeks. "There won't be anybody like you up there."

"That's a nice thing to say. You watch too many movies."

"You don't watch enough."

The music roared again, and the party was gathering its second wind. "Should we go back?" he asked.

"No. I like it here. I don't want to be anywhere else."

He took in the muscled contours of her legs and the clasped hands on her stomach. He'd not known what he should do with his own hands, so he found himself gripping the steering wheel and feeling like an imbecile. She opened her eyes. "Here," she said and reached up for his hand and placed it on her stomach, under the waistband of her jeans shorts. "That's better," she said.

"For who?"

"Both of us."

She'd always had boyfriends, mostly boys from the nearby college, but he had never even been on a date. He was always too afraid to ask. She scooted herself up so that his hand went lower into her pants. She unbuttoned her shorts, and then she took his hand and showed him how to stroke her. The music from the party seemed to move away from them, and the car grew darker as a cloud passed over the moon.

She sat up and pulled her shirt off and unsnapped her bra, and then she unzipped Wren's shorts and took him in her hands. "Push the seat back," she told him, and he did. Then she straddled him and guided him into her. "Breathe," she said. "Try not to think about it too much." She smiled. "Feels good, doesn't it?"

He could only nod. Her movements told him she knew he'd never done anything like this before, and he felt embarrassed and excited at the same time. "It's okay," she said. "Go ahead. I'm on the pill." He had a hold of her waist. He was looking up to her face, to the hair cascading down and covering her breasts. He thought he might not ever see or feel something this magnificent ever again. She raised herself just slightly and then came back to him in a soft, barely perceptible stroke, and he felt the surge inside of himself. She pressed herself closer then. "That's it," she said. She rocked herself forward, once, twice, and then he couldn't hold on any longer.

He felt his whole body spasm, and his toes curl inside his tennis shoes. Nothing had ever felt so warm and so tingly. That was the word that came to his mind, and this made him feel even more inexperienced than the act that had just occurred. She slipped off of him and back into her seat. She opened the glove box, where she knew he kept extra napkins, and handed a couple to him and took some for herself.

"I couldn't let you go up north without doing the deed," she said.

Her face was flushed, and she pulled her hair back into a ponytail. "Now you won't fall in love with the first girl you take back to your room," she said.

"I already know that won't happen—"

"Don't start on saying you love me. We're friends. Nothing more."

"Because you won't let it be anything else." This was not the first time he'd tried to tell her.

"I don't like you that way."

"What way is that? The fuck-me-and-then-tell-me-you-don't-like-me way?"

"Something like that." She grinned. He only stared hard into her face. "I'm kidding," she said. "It's a joke."

"Not this time," he said. "It's not a joke to me." He wanted to be happier. He'd just lost his virginity to a girl he'd pined after so long and so hard his friends had shook their heads in pity at him. He'd thought things were turning.

"For all I know, I'm never going to see you again," she said. "In fact, I know I won't."

"How do you know so goddamn much?"

"You know it too," she said. "You're just trying to act like you don't. You've been wanting to get out of here ever since we were kids and you're the only one that is."

"That's not true," he said.

She huffed. "Asher, you're arrogant. You think you're better than everybody else."

"I do not," he said.

"You do," she said. "All you ever talk about is life away from here. When we were in New York you acted like you knew everything about the city, but you grew up right here like the rest of us in this shitty little ass-backward town."

"I don't think of it that way," he said. He had once only thought of living here, of going off to college and coming back to coach the football team. He had told his father of these plans, and his father, with nearly the same anger Lucinda displayed now, had snapped his fingers at the boy. "You're not going to do that." Wren asked why not, and his father replied, "You've got a brain. Go use it." His father had never said anything like that to him before, and when he told his mother about it, she had agreed. They raised him to leave.

Lucinda came at him again. "Except for the ones going off to the army, you're the only one in our class who won't be living in Kentucky next year. Think about that." Her voice was softer on the last sentence. Then she said, "I wish I could go with you."

"You can. You could." He thought of her with him in Harvard Yard and the small restaurant where he and his mother had pizza after his visit. But those were the only places he could envision her. The thoughts of him alone there, of Boston winters and no one sounding a thing like him, were private fears he harbored, that he would never share with anyone for years to come. The music from the party still reached them and he heard a loud shout, a teammate from the football team, a wild child through and through who would probably take over his father's car lot one day. She was right about him. He was arrogant. He had already mapped out most of his friends' lives, but he also envied how easy the future seemed to be for them.

"I'm gonna go to UK," she said. "Get my accounting degree, and that's all my imagination can conjure."

How could he tell her she could be more than this? That her life, like so many others, didn't have to feel like it was closing down on this night? In four years they'd be into a new century, the Twenty-First, the century of science fiction. His mind was focused on the future, always it seemed on that and not much more, but now Lucinda was beside him, buttoning her shorts back up and brushing out her hair with her fingers, and he wanted to stay in the present longer, wanted to imagine this night catapulting the two of them into more nights just like it.

"I could stay," he said. "I could go to UK and then we'd have the summer."

Her head snapped straight. "Are you out of your mind?"

"No," he said. "I don't want to . . ." but he did not finish the sentence and say he didn't want to leave her.

"You're not going to give up Harvard for me. I don't want that kind of pressure."

"It's not about you," he said. He lied. Of course it was. Of course everything was. Nearly every decision he made as a teenager had been about her, and she had to know it or, at least, sense it.

"I've never wanted you that way. I never will."

"But we just—"

"Had sex and that was it," she finished. "I wanted that. I don't want this."

He was crushed, and yet he couldn't show this to her. He didn't want to be vulnerable in front of her. He steadied his hands on the wheel to keep them from shaking. He did what he had always done as an athlete and channeled his pain into anger, gripping the wheel tight, flexing his forearms so that the veins rose and marked his forearms like small streams. He said nothing else.

"Don't be mad," she said. "Don't—"

"I'm not," he said, taking his turn to cut her off. He parked the car back in its original spot.

"Wren—"

"Asher," he said.

"What?"

"You always call me Asher. It sounds weird when you call me by my first name."

"Asher," she said, softly. "I'm sorry. Let's go have a good time. We graduated today."

"We did." Everything had changed. He knew he couldn't really consider attending UK, but he wanted it to be a real consideration. He wanted her, for once, to look at him for who he was and what she meant to him. He was young, but he knew what he felt and what he wanted. He also knew her mind was made up. He had to reconcile that.

He pulled the mason jar out from under the seat. "One more for posterity?" he asked, holding the jar up to her.

"Not for me," she said, "and only a small one for you."

"You don't get to tell me what to do," he said, but he did listen to her and took only a quick sip and closed up the jar.

"I am going to miss you, Wren," she said. "I'll miss you more than anyone else."

Why had she wasted these last four years with other boys when they were so clearly good together? He wanted to remain angry with her, but he could not bring the heat of anger when it came to her. He forgave her as he always had, writing it off as an unknowable trait of the heart. He did not reply to her remark but instead gave her a nod and opened the car door.

They stepped out and rejoined the party, noticeably thinner now with folks having paired off and moved to their own cars. The fire was dimmer but still burning. The music had been turned lower, and Wren thought if he looked hard enough to the east he might see light on the horizon. They sat on a couple of wood stumps, and Lucinda curled next to him again.

"Are you scared to go away?" she said.

"Some," he said. "But when I told my mom I was scared she

looked at me crosswise and said, 'Boy, I moved five thousand miles away from my family and to a different country. I think you can move to Cambridge for four years.'"

They laughed. "Your mother is awesome. So tough."

"She's the toughest," he said, and he tried to imagine her at his age leaving Korea and heading off into some great unknown. As he got older he would wonder more and more how she had done it, how she had worked up the courage and fought through her loneliness and isolation, but right then he only marveled in it with Lucinda. He took up a stick and poked at the fire, watching its tip blacken.

"I don't want this to be the last night I ever see you," she said with a suddenness that surprised him.

"It doesn't have to be," he said. "I can come back to visit. You can fly to Boston."

She didn't respond. She took up her own stick and poked at his. "You are arrogant but that doesn't mean I don't admire that from time to time. I won't ever leave this place," she said. "I know I'll end up right back here."

"I don't understand," he said. "How can you know that about your future? You sound so defeated by it too."

"I know it the same way you know you won't ever come back. The same way you knew you could get into Harvard."

"But I didn't know that, and I don't know the future."

She turned to him. "You tried. You had the guts to try. Think about that. Look around us," she said. "No one else here lets themselves dream past a year. You've got a whole life planned down to the final detail, don't you?"

He didn't. But ever since his father talked to him, when he imagined life, he had not thought of Friday night football in Fordyce or taking his children to Cable Hill for sledding in the winter anymore. He had some ideas about a city—any city—tall buildings, cabs, public transportation. But in every version of the dream there was a woman like Lucinda, tall and athletic, hair that shimmered under the light, hands that reached for him in the night as hers did now and held him close. She had been both the only clear and murky thing in his life until now.

Within minutes she was asleep, and he was left watching the fire alone. The people were gone. The radios had silenced. It was only Wren and the yellow light and its dying heat suffocated by dew. He picked Lucinda up, cradled in his arms, and carried her back to his car and set her in the passenger seat. He grabbed his graduation gown from the backseat and placed it gently over her and then kissed the top of her head. He went to the back of his car and sat on the trunk and turned east. The stars began to fade, the sky lightened, birds began to call, then the earth was filled with light, and behind him the fire was in smolders.

DIAMOND DUST

WHEN EDDIE JACKSON struck out—looking at a fastball right down the heart of the plate—we felt like *we* had let *him* down. Every single one of us. Across the field the sun was setting, casting warm yellow light on all that beautiful, sharp-tipped grass. He came toward the dugout, his Dr. Pepper jersey streaked with dirt and grass stains at the knees, and before any of us could move away from the chain-link fence to console him, his father, Tripp, was out on the field waiting for the boy's return. He didn't say anything immediately. He gave his son a cold look as Eddie passed by. In the stands our mothers and fathers were milling around, gathering up their trash, pressing half-eaten bags of popcorn into red, white, and blue Pepsi cups. For a moment, we turned from Eddie to see Gatliff Coal jumping up and down, celebrating the Little League championship.

We were twelve that year, but what happened that day, what happened for the next six years, has never left us. Not because it was purely awful, though it was by any stretch of any imagination, but because many years later, as grown men, there is the knowledge that none of us tried to save Eddie. Perhaps we were too young to know how to save someone we called a friend.

Tripp followed Eddie down the dugout steps. Tobacco juice was seeping out of the corner of his mouth, and he spit to the side of Eddie's cleats. Through a clenched jaw he said, "God bless America."

His teeth were brown with flecks of tobacco, and his neck was red from the day's heat. "What the hell was that?"

A small spray of juice landed on the boy's cheek, which made him flinch, and when he did, Tripp grabbed his chin, straightening him out, and looked him dead in the eye. By then we were watching with our bodies backed against the fence. The stands were clear, and our fathers' heads could be seen over the dugout's roof as they talked to one another about jobs and school, the chances of us, their sons, making the season-ending all-star team.

"You took strike three right down the damn middle," Tripp said.

Eddie tried to shrug and turn his shoulder, but Tripp grabbed his arm and pushed him into the cinder block wall of the dugout. His small bones and muscles met it with a hollow knock.

"Where the hell do you think you're going?" he said. "I want you to stand up and apologize to your teammates." Tripp turned to acknowledge us as a group for the first time since his pre-game speech. "Stand up and tell your teammates you're sorry for letting them down," Tripp said, pulling off his hat and readjusting it on his scalp. He had a thin strip of white flesh from his tan line across the top of his forehead, and he spit again at his feet.

The last place any of us wanted to be right then was watching Eddie get up, the tears and pain visible only behind his eyes, and tell us he was sorry. That afternoon he had walked only one batter and given up only one hit, but it was a homer to dead center that Sam Miller had swung at with his eyes closed while pulling out of the box. We lost the game 2–1, but before that we owed our only run to Eddie and the long fly ball he had placed in the middle of a gray Ford's windshield. All season long it had been the same story. Eddie was our best hitter, our best fielder, our best pitcher. He popped homers the way the rest of us did Flintstones vitamins. He threw the ball seventy-five miles an hour as a twelve-year-old.

He was featured in *Sports Illustrated*. He was everything we weren't. Athletic, graceful, broad-shouldered, a man.

Tripp's chest was heaving up and down. If breath had any sort of color we could have seen it leaving his nose in two long beams all the way to his toes and spreading the spare dust on the dugout floor.

"I'm sorry," Eddie said and the only comfort we found then, that any of us could find in his unnecessary apology, was that for one moment Eddie Jackson was like us. He was a kid again. Human. Vulnerable. Capable of doing wrong.

Tripp turned from Eddie to the rest of us still lining the fence. Baseballs and bats were scattered at our feet. On the field a couple of men were carrying a table full of little gold trophies and setting it behind the pitcher's mound. Eddie sat on the bench, his batting gloves still on his hands, and caught our eyes. What could we have looked like to him? What did he see in our faces? He shrugged his shoulders then, staring past each of us.

Later, when we were out on the field to accept our second-place trophies, somebody told Eddie he played a good game. Eddie, his head hung, looked up toward the empty bleachers behind home plate and said, "We lost. Doesn't matter what you do if you lose."

WE KNEW NOTHING of Tripp Jackson back then except that the summer before he coached our Dr. Pepper Little League team he had divorced his wife, who immediately left and went back to Michigan, where she was from. She had given Tripp full custody of Eddie, and as far as we knew had not spoken to either one since the day she left town. Before this we had only seen Tripp when he came to pick up Eddie from school in a rusty, brown and yellow Toyota Corolla. Tripp Jackson was a rough-looking sort, a constant stubble on his thick cheeks, a little paunch to his belly that seemed to be a hard kind of fat, stout and taut. He often wore shorts, even in winter, revealing his hairless, smooth-muscled calves. He wasn't from Fordyce like most of our parents, and because of that he didn't carry judgments about him from his youth. Eddie once said he had played single A ball in Jackson, Tennessee, and his father did have the bowlegged walk of a former athlete, but he was, for the most part, a mystery. We didn't understand how he could be so cruel to Eddie and so kind to the rest of us on the team.

He was a good coach, and at practice he kidded around. He showed us how to field grounders and open our hips on an inside fastball. We were one of the few teams in the league that turned double plays on a regular basis. When we faltered in our execution, he was always right there to tell us we would do better the next time. He would put his arm around boys like Ben Jenkins, whose spastic, high-kneed running style often led him to fall when he came charging in from right field for a line drive, and tell him it was okay. And when Alvin Blanton's limp-wristed throws soared high in the air, only traveling twenty yards, he'd swat him on the backside with his worn leather glove and say, "Hustle and heart are the most important things." He was patient and kind with everyone except his own son. He simply couldn't stand to watch Eddie make mistakes. One day after Eddie hit a triple into right field, going with the pitch, he snapped him up by the collar for not sliding into the bag, even though he beat the throw in easily.

"How many times do I have to tell you to get your tail down? Get dirty. I don't care if your legs are covered in strawberries from your ass to your ankles." Almost always after something like this he'd turn back to one of us and tell us "Good job" on the play. Eddie would stand there, hands on his hips, and we'd see him looking at his father, but he never showed disgust or anger. He took what his father dished out.

We were powerless in these displays, and more than once we didn't give our best in the hopes we might spare Eddie from his father's wrath. But no matter what the boy did, no matter how well he played or distanced himself from the rest of us, no matter how much more talented he was, none of it was good enough for Tripp.

While we went home to separate (and mostly happy) lives, Eddie was at home undergoing further instruction. Push-ups and sit-ups, sprints up the steep hill that led to their house. Early in the evenings, just before the lightning bugs claimed the night, we would see Eddie and Tripp outside, behind their house, as Tripp knelt off to the side and tossed tennis balls to Eddie that he smashed into a makeshift net strung between two maple trees. They both glowed in the soft light, and from that distance we saw what could pass for love between the two, but when we were in those moments with them at practice, we weren't sure how anything Tripp said could ever feel like affection to Eddie.

As we got older, middle school then high school, Eddie continued to outshine us all. Our sophomore year he was clocked at ninety-four on the gun, and he had more home runs than the rest of the team put together. Scouts from big-league clubs started to show up at our games. Some came more frequently than our own parents, but Eddie was never so lucky. No matter where we played, Tripp found a spot, usually along the first-base line, away from the rest of the crowd, and stood with his arms hanging over the fence.

Mostly, he yelled encouragement to us, pounding his thick hands together in loud claps when we came off the field, but he still had his outbursts. His voiced carried through whatever park we were in, and each of us felt embarrassed when he blistered an umpire for a missed call or kicked at the fence, walking up and down in the grass, shouting as loud as he could. It was hard to imagine what Eddie must have felt like when Tripp's voice singled him out for either good or bad, to know that his father was the owner of the voice so many people couldn't stand to hear. But because Tripp wasn't our coach anymore, in some ways, everything he said felt different and carried a lighter weight than it had when we were children, and because of this, nothing he did then ever seemed as nasty as the day he made Eddie stand up and face each of us. We wanted to believe the old man had calmed down and mellowed out. Maybe, we hoped, he finally saw what everyone else did. That on a baseball field his boy was beautiful.

But that wasn't the truth.

Near the end of that year, when we were playing in the region finals, the old Tripp Jackson revealed himself to us again. For five innings against the Middlesboro Yellow Jackets, the second-best team in the state, Eddie was untouchable. His fastball darted left and right, his curve looped toward hitters' heads then dove into the strike zone. Our bats were hot, the constant ping of metal was like a church chorus on the field. Then, in the top of the sixth, Eddie hit a batter. Right in between the numbers on the kid's back. The kid fell to the ground, wheezing and heaving his body, trying to reclaim the function of his lungs. His coach came out from the dugout, yelling at Eddie, saying he hit him on purpose. "Nobody with your control throws a wild pitch," he said. Eddie stared back at the man, holding his glove up to his chest, as if ready to deliver another pitch, but he never said anything or changed his disposition. The boy eventually got up off the ground, rolled his shoulders, and walked to first base, taking in shallow breaths.

What we wouldn't know until later was the shock Eddie felt. It is the only explanation for what then happened. He walked the next batter. The next hit a double in the gap. They closed the score to 4-1, and Eddie finally looked shook. Our coach went out to calm him down. There was a lot of nodding between the two, a pat on the back. Eddie threw the ball in his glove and refocused. But the next hitter sent his first pitch sailing over the right field fence, and the score was tied. We went on to lose the game in extra innings by two runs.

Afterward, as our coach gathered us together in the outfield, standing in the middle of the circle we formed around him, he told us we had a good year and to be proud of ourselves. He said we were losing some good seniors, but we had a lot to look forward to next year. When he said that last part he was looking right at Eddie. But Eddie was toeing the grass with his cleats, and for the first time in our lives we saw tears in Eddie Jackson's eyes. He didn't sniffle or change his breathing. They simply mixed with the eye-black he'd put on and now ran down his face in smudged, ghoulish streaks.

None of us had known what to say to him in the dugout. While we gathered our equipment, Eddie sat on the bench staring ahead of him at the lit field where the chalk lines were now smeared and broken. A few of us put a hand to his shoulder, but nobody said a word. No "Good game" or "You did all you could." We let him sit on the bench in silence until we had loaded up the bus and were waiting for him. Coach Phipps went back to the dugout where Eddie still sat, and when the two of them were coming toward us we heard the yelling, muffled at first, but then clear as we rushed to the side of the bus and pulled the windows down.

"What the hell was that?" Tripp said. "You just quit out there. In all my life I've never seen someone quit like that." He took hold of Eddie and threw him into the side of the bus.

Coach Phipps tried to get between Tripp and Eddie, but Tripp pushed him out of the way. "He's not your boy, Darrell," he said, looking at Coach Phipps. "Stay out of this." He turned back to Eddie. "Look at me," he screamed. Eddie's chin had been down, but he looked Tripp in the eye. A look of failure was on his face, but he said nothing.

"Goddamnit," Tripp said and slammed his hand into the bus right beside Eddie's head.

Coach Phipps moved toward him and called out Tripp's name. Tripp turned to face him full-on. "Damnit, Darrell. I ain't going to tell you again. You raise yours the way you want and I'll raise mine the way I want. This ain't got nothing to do with you."

"The hell it doesn't," Coach Phipps said.

Tripp came forward, and that's when Eddie moved away from the bus and stepped in front of his father. "Get on the bus, Coach." Coach Phipps didn't move. "Go on," he said. "Dad's right. This ain't your business." He turned back to Tripp. "I'll see you at home," he said, and then he turned to see us, the entire team, hanging out the windows of the bus, looking down on the three of them.

We scrambled back to our seats when Coach and Eddie came on board. The bus rocked side to side from our movements, and Coach Phipps stood at the front and said, "Not one word. Keep your mouths shut until we get back to school."

Eddie took a seat in the front, and we did ride back in silence, each of us wondering if what we had just witnessed was the end of his night or only the beginning.

SHORTLY AFTER ALL this was when Eddie began showing up to school with bruises. We only saw them when we were changing for practice, usually along his chest and shoulder blades. And though we knew where they came from, none of us said anything.

That night after the game in Middlesboro, word spread that some saw Eddie Jackson walking home. His father had not come for him, and long after many of us had already left, they said you could see him walking through the streets of downtown still in his baseball uniform with his cleats tied together and slung over his shoulder. He walked as the dark night descended upon everything and the little stores lining Main Street, closed and vacant, glowed with just a few bulbs still burning inside them. He had refused the offers of those that had cars to drive him home and begged off the parents that pulled up beside him that night as he made his way across town to the small house by Lynn Camp Creek. His walk was a shuffle and his hands were firmly tucked inside his baseball jacket. His figure slumped along the sidewalk, and what we found out later was that when he got home what was awaiting him was a fist to his gut. We imagined his shoulder cracking the drywall and Tripp not punching but making sure to slap the boy's face. Eddie took it "like a man," and when his father was done, he showered and let the warm water running over his body sting the bruises deeper into his flesh.

The effect of Tripp's beating, and the subsequent ones, was that his son played more ferociously than any of us had ever seen. We watched in utter amazement at the way he dove for fly balls in the gap. We came out of our seats when he, somehow, stretched singles into doubles, doubles into triples with his choppy, grinding gait. It was almost as if we didn't know how he did it. His talent alone couldn't explain it. But, of course, we did know. We knew that after one particular game, when Eddie had only gone two for five, Tripp had put him through a sliding glass door. Eddie's face and arms were nicked and cut, his cheek green and black from the blow, but he still suited up the next day and ran full speed into the fence trying to chase down a foul ball in the corner.

Coach Phipps ran from the dugout as soon as he saw it, but before he got there, Eddie was up and waving him back.

"You don't have to keep playing this way, son," Coach told him.

Even from the dugout we saw the answer to this in Eddie's eyes.

There was both a pleading and incredulity in the boy's look. There was no other way to play. There was only giving everything he had.

They stood looking at each other, and then Coach Phipps smacked Eddie on the tail and ran back to the dugout.

Undressing after the game we saw the red and raw marks along Eddie's ribs, but if he was in pain we never would have known it. He answered questions from a local reporter and smiled the whole way through it. We were seniors then, accustomed to the exploits of our best athlete and aware of the hell he lived with at home, because when he wasn't present we traded what we knew about him, the separate pieces of his story he offered to us individually. More than once we said we should do something, and more than once one of us would say, "But remember that day Eddie told Coach Phipps it wasn't any of his business?" And that seemed to close up the conversation and we went about *our* business. It wasn't as if we ever stopped wondering how Tripp could be so hard on him or how the man could constantly bring his fists to the hardest playing kid on the team. But we also wanted to be carefree teenagers and have fun. What concerned us most were our girlfriends and college decisions, our lives away from the ballpark and what might be awaiting us in a future that did or did not include Fordyce and its smallness.

So it was easier than it should have been to forget Eddie. He was a boy who, because of his talent, was always popular among us and everyone else in the school, but his popularity was derived only from his feats on the fields of play and had very little to do with anything in his personality. In fact, in the moments when we circled the Trademart Shopping Center in the cars our parents gave us or parked behind the Belk-Simpson after it was closed, our memories of Eddie and what he said were never clear. We never remembered laughing at his telling of a story nor did we ever go to him with our own private confessions. He was friendly and he had friends he ran with, but no one was close to Eddie.

Maybe these are the selfish and shameless reasons we turned away from Eddie. Maybe we believed that even though his arm had gone dead the year before and the scouts had stopped coming around to our games that Eddie would somehow will his way toward something bigger than where we were. We believed he would do what he had always done, that he would always be better than us.

The cumulative effect of all those beatings, though, had left Eddie believing he was only the one thing. A future that didn't include baseball had become, in his mind, not a future at all. In those last waning days of our senior year, when the world had seemed alive with nothing but possibility for so many of us, Eddie Jackson's future was extinguished somehow. And though we knew how important the game was to Eddie, how hard he tried to prevent our losses, it wasn't until our final game when we came to know how much he had always needed us.

What had begun in the sixth grade continued through the last game of our lives when we were beat out in the finals of the region for the third straight year. Eddie is still the only person, as far as anyone knows, to be named the regional tournament MVP from a losing team. He hit over six hundred in three games with five homers and twenty RBIs. He threw a two-hitter in the final. The only run of that game was when our catcher let a sinker ball slip through his legs and roll to the backstop. The runner on third came home and didn't even slide. But unlike that Little League game six years before, when we were separated by different teams, the entire town felt the despair when Eddie scorched a double down the line and one after another of us came up and could not advance him home. While the Harlan Green Dragons ran out to the pitcher's mound,

Eddie Jackson stayed on second base, squatting with his hands on his head. His forearms were rippled with veins and his long, boyish black hair snuck out from under the flaps of his batting helmet. School was already over for the year. Our graduation had been the week before, and with the final out of that game, nothing was left to tie us to Fordyce High School anymore. Eddie's uniform showed traces of the crushed red brick that made up the ballpark's dirt. In front of him the boys from Harlan tossed their hats and gloves in the air, they piled onto their pitcher, and our coaches exchanged quick handshakes at home plate. But Eddie refused to move, as if doing so meant the final out of his life.

Tripp Jackson moved away from his spot on the fence. The stands emptied. The litter of stray peanut shells and aluminum foil that once held hot dogs was lifted by the breeze. In the parking lot, boys much younger than us, boys we had once been, played a game with wadded up paper cups serving as a ball and their hands as bats. In their own makeshift diamond they ran circles, left ghost men behind to run their bases and dreamed of the day when they too would be on the big field with the green grass, the chalked lines, and their own dirty uniforms.

They did not know disappointment in the way we did, but that would come. They too would learn to accept it or live with it, and like us they would go on to lead lives that were predictable and, in many ways, ordinary and full. There was not an Eddie Jackson among them that we knew of, but there almost always is, we came to find out, just as there is almost certainly a Tripp Jackson too, who was pulling away from the park at the moment his son finally stepped off second base, relegating himself to defeat.

Across that field I still see Eddie's eighteen-year-old figure in the way our minds sometimes refuse to let a person be more than what they once were. When I see him around town I don't see the man he is now with two little boys of his own, to whom he's never so much as raised his voice in public when angry with them. I see the kid who I grew up with on second rising from his squatted position. Eddie was our star, our bright boy. It may seem strange, but I know what we all felt in those six years we were teenagers and even now that we are adults. But because we did so little to ease the weight he carried, how can I believe that any of us who really look at him can't see the boy he was, walking alone, past a celebration that he—that we—had always dreamed would involve him? Later that night, after the trophies were handed out and the lights from the ballpark were off, we were not surprised to see Eddie walking through downtown in his jeans and tee shirt, his ball cap pulled low on the front of his forehead. He wasn't headed home, though, like the rest of us. He was going in a different direction that we could not follow or ask about, which did not carry the burden of unmet expectations, and where we could never fail him again.

THE WORLD'S FAIR

THEY'D TRAVELLED TOO far to turn around. That's all Maggie could tell herself as she saw the cars ahead of her pulling into the median for U-turns and heading back north. She looked to the backseat, where her children slept, the slightest bit of sweat on their foreheads. They were only thirty minutes from Knoxville but had been stopped on I-75 for more than two hours because of a crash, and she had been reluctant to give up on the day, especially after everything that had happened in the last month with Jake's leaving and the uncertainty about their future.

Her patience was waning when, almost by wishing it were so, the cluster of cars she'd been stuck behind began to creep forward around the bend. Then the lead car burst forth, the wreck having been cleared, and the anticipation of being able to move all-out on the freeway after being still for so long made her feel hopeful. She looked in the rearview mirror, just in time to see the children waking from the movement of the car.

"Sleepyheads," she said.

The boy and the girl were twelve and seven. Bobby was a miniature version of Jake with the same sandy blond hair and green eyes. He was the oldest and had been asking so many questions about what was going on between his parents in the last week that Maggie, out of desperation—out of her own fears and loneliness—had given him Jake's number at the little motel across town and told him to call his father and ask him. She had immediately regretted it, but she didn't know how many more lies she could tell the boy.

"Where are we?" Bobby asked.

"Almost there," Maggie said. "How was your nap?"

Both kids yawned and stretched. Remained silent to her question. She'd had no one to talk to about anything that was going on, her family lost to her. Her existence now seemed confined only to her mind and her actions, to these children she was sure she was losing.

They came around a big curve, and the tall buildings of downtown Knoxville rose up around them.

"There it is," Maggie said and pointed ahead. In the distance, the Sunsphere shone against the blue sky. Its gold-colored glass reflected and shimmered in the light, resembling an oversized disco ball resting on a radio tower. The children craned their necks to get a better look but were only momentarily impressed.

"That's all it is?" Pam said.

"I guess so," Maggie said and bit her lip. "C'mon, though. That's something."

"It was bigger on television," Bobby said. "Do you think the president is still here?"

"No, he was only here on opening day," Maggie said.

"I have to pee," Pam said.

"We'll be there soon," Maggie said. "You two wait and see. This is going to be a good day."

THE 1982 WORLD'S Fair, inexplicably to Maggie, had ended up in east Tennessee. Two weeks before the fair opened on May first, she had turned thirty, which was followed by Jake's departure into the cold spring night. He hadn't gone far, just to the Cardinal Motel by the drive-in theater, but she felt his leaving in the night, after they had celebrated her birthday with the children, meant he might never return. They had been restless with each other for some time, ever since Jake had been hired on at the railroad and was working second shift in addition to constantly being on call. "It's how they break you in," he told her those first few weeks. "You have to work your way up."

"You never see the kids anymore. Anytime they call you have to leave us and go there. It's too much."

"We can't walk away from this kind of money. You know that. A year from now I'll be a yardmaster and get a normal schedule."

Lately, there had just been one fight after another conducted in the darkness of their bedroom. They weren't so much fights as constant flare-ups over the smallest things. Cracker crumbs on the floor, a curling iron left on in the bathroom, forgetting to change the oil in the car at precisely three thousand miles. They were these maddeningly little tics in the behavior of each that spoke only to the surface of what troubled them.

The night of Maggie's birthday he had come home late from work and was eating supper when the fight broke out about the kitchen sink and its slow drain.

"Call the plumber," he had instructed.

"I have," she told him. "He doesn't want to listen to a woman."

"He gets paid either way. You're just imagining things."

"It's not my imagination when I've called him every day this week and he still won't come out."

"Then call another one," he said.

"You told me to call Mills. You said he's the best." They were alone in the kitchen, and Maggie was covering her birthday cake with plastic wrap. Jake raised his head from his plate. A single candle that Bobby insisted on putting in before he was shuffled back to bed stuck up from the slice.

Calm and deliberate, Jake put his fork down and got up from the table. He walked to the shed behind the house, grabbed his toolbox, and came inside and started pulling everything out from under the sink, setting bottles of detergent and S.O.S. pads against the cabinets.

Maggie stood over him, not believing how he was behaving. He moved under the sink, holding a small flashlight in his mouth. She stared at his torso and legs. "Why do you act this way?"

"'Cause I get tired of listening to your mouth," he said. The wrench he was using slipped, and he cracked a knuckle against the pipe. He cussed and pulled himself out from under the sink. He rubbed his hand and looked to her.

"I just want it fixed," she said. "I don't see why that's such a big deal."

"You never let up. You never cut anybody any slack."

She had left and gone to the bedroom at that, and when he came in the room, hours later, they lay still in the dark, not saying a word. Jake turned on his side to face her, and before he could speak, she cut him off. "What?" she said.

"You're not asleep?"

"No," she said. "And you haven't been, either."

"It's not working," he said.

"I'll call Mills again in the morning, even though it won't do any good."

"That's why it's not working," he said and sat up. "I'm not talking about the sink. I'm talking about you. You're a grown woman and you ain't got enough sense to call somebody else to fix the damn thing? So what if I said call Mills? Son of a bitch won't come out here to fix it and you act like that's my fault. As if he doesn't fix it then nobody can."

"I was just trying to do what you said. I thought that's what you wanted me to do."

"What the hell's that supposed to mean? You act like you don't have a mind of your own. Jesus Christ. I think you want to fight. I think you wait for an opportunity to jump down my throat."

They were trying to keep their voices down. "I don't know who to call—"

"The Yellow Pages are full of plumbers. You know how to use a phone book, don't you? If you want I can go get one right now and show you how to use it. It's real simple because they're all in alphabetical—"

"Go to hell," she said.

Jake flipped on the light and both of them squinted from the brightness. He went to the closet.

"What're you doing?"

"Getting the hell out of here." He grabbed a duffel bag off the top shelf and stuffed it with a pair of jeans and some shirts.

Her eyes adjusted and she said, "Where are you going to go?"

"What do you care?" he said and pulled on his clothes from earlier and started out of the bedroom.

She got up from the bed and followed him down the hall, past the kitchen and into the living room. He put his hand on the front door and turned to her.

"I'm just tired of it," he said. "If work calls, I'll be at the Cardinal." He opened the door and cold wind hit her in the face. She watched him walk across the yard to his truck and get inside. The wind blew over her body and tightened her skin as Jake drove off.

MAGGIE WONDERED IF the fair was as big a deal to the rest of the country as it was around here. She'd seen Reagan's opening-day speech play on the national news but doubted anyone beyond the people in and around Knoxville cared what was happening. Bobby and Pam walked in front of her. They looked around at the exhibits on their left and right. It was a warm day, and she wished now she had worn shorts instead of jeans. A man on stilts was walking through the crowds. He had on an Uncle Sam costume and was twisting balloon animals for children. Pam looked back at her, excited for the first time since they left Fordyce, and Maggie nodded. "Bobby, go with her and hold her hand," she said. "I'm going to stay over in the shade."

They moved toward the man, and Maggie wiped her forehead with a napkin. She bought a lemonade from the vendor and looked at the children through the crowd. Pam was next in line. Maggie smiled at the sight of them, but the worry she had since Jake's leaving was with her. It lived on the edges of her brain. She could not keep it at bay. Even when she was at the store, rearranging the clothes displays or refolding the items on the clearance tables, it worked its way toward her thoughts. *Only two weeks*, she thought. It had to get better. She'd be able to live with this.

The man shaped a yellow balloon into a dog for Pam, and she took it with delight and came running toward Maggie.

"What do you have there?"

"It's a puppy," Pam said and pulled it close to her chest.

"What about you?" Maggie said to Bobby. "Too big for a balloon animal?"

The boy nodded.

They began walking again. The fair's theme was energy of the past, present, and future, and as such, it was, essentially, an energy expo. Most of the exhibits were scientific, and though they looked simple, they still seemed more complicated than Maggie could grasp. They ducked into a large exhibit hall that offered relief with shade and the cool wave of air-conditioning. Bobby, Maggie found, was becoming more and more interested in science, and she let him walk ahead of them and examine each exhibit in the hall for as long as he wanted. A large silver ball was set up in the middle of the room with long blue limbs of static electricity shooting out of it in jagged lines whenever someone touched it. It was called a Van de Graaff generator. Bobby crowded around it along with the other children and parents. The man in the middle of the exhibition wore a white lab coat and glasses.

He was picking out children and letting them come up and touch the sphere while everyone watched the small strikes extend and bend toward each child's hand. Bobby was edging closer to the front, and the man's eyes settled on him. Maggie picked up Pam and put her on her shoulders so she could see her brother step forward and reach out for the swirling charges. Maggie knew nothing could go wrong, but her heart beat faster in her chest. The people around her little boy were closer than she was, and she had a need to reach out for him just as Bobby placed his hand on the ball. She gripped Pam's ankles tighter and tried to slow her breathing. Bobby smiled as he held one tentative finger up to the domed silver, and seeing it would not shock him, he placed his entire hand on the ball and his hair stood up on its ends. Maggie rose on her tiptoes and caught his eyes, and she saw that he fought back a smile.

Even before Jake left, she had thought about how much bigger her baby boy had gotten. She often found herself thinking about his delivery, how he'd come premature and was small enough for her to hold in one hand. When she'd looked at him as a newborn, she never thought there'd be a day when he'd be healthy and strong and able to get along without her and Jake's care. Seeing him in the middle of the crowd, moving away from the man in the lab coat as another child approached, she saw he was still just a little boy, a child. But he was also a boy old enough to recognize what was happening to her and his father. She sensed it that morning when she told the children she was bringing them to the fair instead of Jake—a promise he had made to them before he left.

He had been called into the railroad the night before at three in the morning and was probably still there now. When he phoned Maggie, she had just woken up and the kids were getting ready, waiting on him to show up. "Can you take them?" he said. She pictured him on the other end of the phone with the trains in the rail yard behind him.

"I have work," she said. "You know that."

"It's just one day. The World's Fair doesn't happen every year. Call in sick. I'll call Shelia and tell her for you, if you want."

"No. I'll do it," she said and sat up in bed, his empty spot beside her. They had not spoken as much as she thought they would since he left, and she didn't like the feeling that she was giving in, even if they were talking about something that had to do with their children.

"You'll be okay getting down there by yourself?" Jake asked before they got off the phone.

"Should be," she told him.

"Call me when you get back home," he said. "I want to know y'all are safe."

Now, Maggie lowered Pam down to the ground, and the little girl ran to put her arms around Bobby. To Maggie's relief, he let his sister dote on him and he even bent down to let her pat his head where it seemed the electricity had lived moments before.

"Was that fun?" Maggie asked.

"Yeah," he said, unable to hide the smile on his face.

"Were you scared?" Pam asked.

"No," he replied, but Maggie knew better.

"You guys hungry?" she said.

The children nodded and they went outside to the food pavilion for burgers and fries and sat down at a picnic table.

A big Ferris wheel was above them, and they looked up at the different colored cars moving in a circle. Next to it was a roller coaster, and they heard the occasional screams as it rushed around the rails.

"Can I ride the roller coaster?" Bobby asked.

"Not for a while," she said. "I don't want you to get sick on it."

"I won't get sick. I promise."

"You can't promise to not get sick," she said.

The fair was full of people. The papers said that more than three hundred thousand visited the first week. The lines for the rides stretched out over fifty yards.

"By the time it's my turn," he said, "I'll be fine. Look at the line."

She glanced up to the line and then back to him.

"Please," he said.

"What if your sister wants to ride?"

"She's too short," he said.

A man was measuring children with a long wooden stick, and it was clear he was right; Pam would be too small.

"Okay," she relented. "But you meet us back here as soon as you get off the ride."

He walked to the back of the line, and she kept watch as he moved forward every step of the way. Pam wanted to walk around, but Maggie refused to move. Then the line began to quicken, and Bobby snaked around a corner into the weave of bars that corralled each person to the waiting cars.

She stood up then, taking hold of Pam's hand and moving toward the coaster. Bobby never looked back. He disappeared behind a partition with the fair logo painted on it—a flame-tipped red sun on a white background. She scanned the cars moving out of the bay and didn't see Bobby. And when the ride ended and everyone got off, she didn't see him on the next coaster going up the ramp, either. She suspected she had simply missed him, but when that coaster came back and she still didn't see him coming out the exit area with everyone else, she panicked. She squeezed Pam's hand, feeling the girl's fingers buckle under the pressure and her small hand jerk away in pain.

Maggie lifted Pam on her shoulders once again. "Look for him," Maggie said and heard the pleading in her voice. "Can you see him?" She walked back and forth, the girl bouncing on her shoulders, and moved to the ride's exit and then back to where the line began. Her steps were short and quick, and Pam's feet seemed to kick at her lungs with each movement.

"I don't see your brother. Do you?"

"No," Pam said.

Maggie turned and then turned again, holding Pam's ankles close to her chest. "Hold on, baby," she said. "We have to find your brother."

Maggie swung toward the roller coaster. She saw boys of all kinds. Dark-haired and light-haired. Fat and skinny. Some with ball caps on and others with burr haircuts. She saw sunburned faces and high white socks pulled to the knees, but she didn't see Bobby.

She walked, again, to the exit of the ride and continued to scan the crowd, but everything was a blur of half-faces and torsos. She sought something familiar: Bobby's brown shorts, his red tee shirt, the sound of his laugh or crying. Anything. It was a sea of strangers and strange voices. Then without even knowing she would do it, she began calling out his name.

"Bobby. Bobby Murphy," she said as she walked through and past people. She bumped a man, spilling his drink, and quickly apologized, but there was a terror in her throat and an emptying in her stomach. Her whole body heightened to a sense of numbness as her blood was thinning out. A windstorm of terrible thoughts took her over, and she was held in place by the thought of him being snatched up by some man, led away by his hand into a corner of the fair or some dark-colored sedan in the parking lot. She called his name louder and Pam did too, but still he did not show. A man wearing a blue polo shirt and white visor came up to her.

"Ma'am," he said, trying to get her attention as Maggie stared past him. "Ma'am, are you okay? Ma'am," he said louder.

Maggie looked at him. "My son," she said but offered nothing else.

"What about your son? Is he lost? Where did you see him last?"

Maggie was pulling Pam off her shoulders but holding the girl's forearm, clinging to it almost. "He was just here," she said. "He was just going to ride the coaster," she said and pointed. "I have to find my son."

"Calm down, ma'am. I'm sure he's okay. What does he look like?"

Maggie was still searching. Her eyes had little focus, and she was only vaguely aware of the man's questions and what the right answers to give him were.

"Stay here," the man said. "Don't move. I'm going to find some security."

Maggie wasn't looking at him.

"Ma'am," he said again. "It's important you don't move so I can find you. Don't move." He grabbed her shoulders and looked her in the eyes. Sweat ran down his cheeks. He had a mustache that hung too far over his lip. "Do you understand?"

She nodded and then swung around again. "There!" she screamed. "There." By the picnic tables where they had eaten lunch she saw him, sitting down, his hands in his lap. He appeared scared, his own head turning left and right. She pulled Pam along as she ran toward him, the man following behind. Maggie grabbed Bobby up in her arms and pulled him into her, the boy's arms hanging by his side. She pulled Pam into her as well and held both of her children and kissed the tops of their heads and felt the holes in her throat and stomach closing now, the terror lessening but still running through her veins.

"Thank God," she said. Then, seeing the man, she said, "He's safe. Thank you." The man nodded and walked away.

"You told me to meet you here," Bobby said. "Where were you?" He pulled away from her.

She laughed, arching her neck backward, then pulled him close again. "You're right," she said. "You're right."

MAGGIE WAS EIGHTEEN and a senior in high school when she became pregnant with Bobby. When she told Jake, he never faltered and said almost immediately he would marry her. Twelve years had gone by and on the way to the fair that morning she felt it had simply become too much for either person to pretend the fire and love they held for each other when they were kids was still there, but she had always had a feeling they both felt stripped of something. By the rest of the world's standards, perhaps thirty wasn't that old. In their hometown, though, almost everyone they knew, old and young, had been married with kids by the time they were twenty-five, if not sooner. The hard responsibilities of life seemed to find them before they were even aware, or might have the chance to find out, what waited for them along the corridors of I-75 and beyond.

She had told her mother first about the pregnancy. Then, trying to act as if it were any other day, she had gone to school. All that morning, while in class, she doodled in her notebook and tried to feel the life inside her, to understand how it might grow and become a baby. During lunch, her father showed up, walking right into the cafeteria where all the other teenagers were. His eyes were wild and his rough hands still looked dirty, the nails filled with grease along the cuticles. He had on his gray work shirt, only the front of it untucked from his black pants. She swore she heard his steel-toe boots actually kicking holes into the floor with each step he took toward her. She pushed away her tray and waited with nowhere to hide.

"Get your ass up," he said.

"Daddy?" she said. "What's wrong?"

"You know goddamn well what's wrong."

She rose from her chair, slightly aware of everyone watching them. A few teachers were trying to shuffle down the set of steps from where they watched the students.

"Just a minute," she said.

"I said now," he boomed and slammed his fist down, rattling the silverware and trays. The other kids scooted their chairs away from the two of them, and then Maggie was up, being dragged by the right biceps outside to his car. His breaths were short and heavy, and she'd never believed he was capable of such anger. As soon as they were outside, through gritted teeth, he said, "Who the hell do you think you are?" He still held onto her, and she felt his nails dig deeper into her skin. "You're a goddamn embarrassment is what you are." He let go of her arm, almost flinging it. Rain fell in a drizzle that glazed the sidewalk by the bus drop-off. His truck was parked there. "What do you have to say for yourself?" he said.

"Daddy," she pleaded, rubbing her arm, feeling the beginnings of a sob come on but trying hard to keep it inside her chest.

"Don't," he hissed. "There's no good explanation for it. You get out of my house tonight," he said.

"Daddy," she said again, hearing the weakness and pity of it in her own ears. "Please," she said.

But he had already opened the door to the truck and slammed

it shut. She stood in the light-falling rain, holding her arm. She walked toward him and tapped on the window, but he refused to look at her and put the vehicle in gear. She saw he was crying, his hand still on the shifter, but he would not turn to her. "Daddy," she tried again, and this time the sobs and cries flew out, and when she called for him a last time the word was a broken thing split apart by her emotion.

She had come out of that day hardened and sometimes bitter, she knew, but she had loved Jake and he her. As the first few years in their marriage passed, that was what had allowed her to not be completely stung by her father's words. She and Jake had always known they would be married. The pregnancy only a formality of sorts. Thinking of Jake and the long record of their history together, and the ease with which it seemed to be erased, made her shudder. Jake was a good father, and even with their troubles she didn't think she would have to raise these children alone.

Holding on to Bobby and Pam, she walked with them toward the China exhibit, which everyone was buzzing about. She kept the children close the rest of the day, buying them cotton candy and allowing them to drink too much pop. By day's end, with the sun setting behind the mountains, the children were tired and ready for sleep, but Pam asked to ride the Ferris wheel.

Still reluctant and nervous from earlier, Maggie agreed when the operator allowed the three of them to squeeze into the ride together. They rose above the mountains and the Tennessee River. A faint blue haze hung over the Smokies, and the river was a reflection of swimming lights from the downtown buildings. Up and down they went. The world coming closer and then moving away, and when they were stopped at the top with a chance to look out over the entire fair, Maggie took note of the patterns of people below. The lines for the exhibits and rides like large wooly worms in the shadows, bent and swaying. She saw the neon strings hanging around children's necks and thought of how soon they would fade away to nothing more than colored plastic, all the shine gone.

High in the air the new fears of what she would do with her two children rushed to her, how she could care for them without Jake around every day. She hugged them close as if to make sure they were still beside her. She turned to Bobby. His little-boy looks were as strong as ever, and she touched her stomach, where the fear had been earlier in the day and where she had touched herself when her father pulled away from her thirteen years before. Of course, then she had touched herself because of the life placed inside her and the pain it had caused, and how hard it had been to believe such different feelings could rest in the same spot. After her father had left the school that day, she had gone back inside to finish out the day, refusing to let any of her classmates believe she was different or less than them, pushing as best she could from her mind what the future might bring. That night she packed only the clothes in her room, leaving behind nearly everything else, and went to Jake's.

He held her that night, and for so many after, keeping her close and telling her it would all be okay. She had always believed him, but now, stopped at the very top of the Ferris wheel, she watched the World's Fair. Those thousands of lives blending into one another and the carnival lights, so distant from where they were, and she was faced with knowing she had to make her children believe the same thing.

PASSING SHADOWS

WHEN COLE'S MOTHER died there had been no indication she was ill. She simply went to bed early one evening while he and his father stayed up to watch *Monday Night Football*. In the morning, when he came down for breakfast, Cole saw his father sitting on the couch, holding a cup of coffee in the still-dark living room.

"Dad?" he said.

"Yeah," his father said, soft and staring at the floor.

"You okay?"

But his father didn't move. He kept his head down, and only when Cole walked toward him and stood by his shoulder did he look up to his son.

"Your mother's gone," he said.

Cole searched the room, looking to the windows at the front of the house and into the woods that ran beside the road. "Where? It's so early," he said, scanning the trees he saw taking shape with the first traces of light.

His father rose then, standing so close Cole smelled the coffee mixed with his stale breath. Then his father's hand pressed firmly on his shoulder.

"No, son. I mean, she's *gone*. She passed away last night in her sleep."

Cole's stomach went queasy, his legs trembled beneath him, but he never stopped looking at his father's eyes—his own eyes—as his father's grip on his shoulder tightened.

"I've not called anyone yet. I wanted to wait until you could go in and see her yourself."

Light broke through a cloudy gray sky and began burning off the haze. A wind blew against the house, the beeping of a garbage truck could be heard up the road, and birds pecked at the grass in the yard.

"Go on," his father said, nodding toward the bedroom over Cole's shoulder.

His mother appeared peaceful, as if she were still asleep, and for a moment Cole wanted to believe his father was playing some cruel, cruel joke on him. But when he took her hand in his and felt its cool rigidness, he knew it was true. He knelt beside the bed. Her face seemed softer to him than it had in years, and the crescent-shaped scar under her eye was nearly invisible. He touched it with his finger as he'd done when he was a very small child and remembered all the times she had touched his scrapes with love and care.

He bowed his head, closed his eyes. He thought of how she had made him get up from the couch the night before to give her a hug and kiss good night. In the dark room he breathed in the smell of her perfume, the lotion she used. He took his finger off the scar and rose from the floor, never letting go of her hand. He stood, unsure of what to do, of how he could make some sort of peace.

HE'D RETURNED HOME three months ago after he was downsized from a job he'd never liked anyway. He was unsure of what he wanted to do, of who he even wanted to be, and Boston was a city he could no longer afford. So he packed up everything he could fit in his car and came back home to live with his parents and work for his father's company. The transition had not been an easy one, and in the nights, while he was sleeping, his dreams were still set in Boston. The dark murky water of the Charles flowed through each one, as if leading him out of the light and deeper into an unknown territory. Though he had slept in the room until he was eighteen, he found himself disoriented in the mornings, unfamiliar with his surroundings.

Living with his parents and back in Fordyce had been harder than he expected. He never expected to come back, but leaving had always weighed on him, as if he could never put enough distance between himself and home. It called out to him like some far-off bird's song, rattling in his head, and he'd remember the mountains and the curves of the roads and the smell of dew-heavy air in spring and summer. Before finally coming home he had begun to feel that old pull and thought the move—a reset—was going to be just the thing to get himself back on track. Enjoyable, even.

There had been lots of missteps and starts in his life and at one point—his lowest—he was living in Cambridge where he worked at a bookstore and washed dishes at a diner off Harvard Square. When he woke up in the bone-cold mornings before his shift, he'd look out on the snow-dusted streets, the tiny houses packed so tightly together they appeared to be huddled for warmth, and ask himself if he had missed some sign of what it was he should have done.

His father never asked him what it was he searched for, why he took so many jobs that he was overqualified for. In fact, he had never questioned Cole outright about any of the choices he made, but he always felt he was letting the old man down by not pinning himself to a job and embarking on a career. So when he landed the position at Suffolk in development, coordinating alumni affairs, he was finally doing something he thought his father would find respectable, and it wasn't until then he had the courage to ask his parents to come for a visit. Only his mother came to Cambridge and the small apartment on Bay Street.

"He wanted to come, but you know Dad. He can't stand to miss work," she said to him over coffee.

"He loves work," Cole said. "He helped build that company."

"It's all he knows," she said. "I worry over him. I worry over both of you."

"Don't worry about me, Mom. I'm okay." He saw the wind outside swirling snow off the roofs of cars.

"That's a mother's job. That's what me and your father both do."

"He's not happy about this," he said, raising his eyes around the apartment.

"He thinks you're capable of more."

"I have a good job now. I thought he'd be happy about that."

"He wants you to go back to school."

"For what?"

"For whatever you want. You used to think you wanted to be a biologist."

"When I was eight."

"That's not true. You can do whatever you want. People say that all the time, Cole, but for you it really is true."

He turned from the window when she said this and took in her eyes. She smiled at him, warmly, with encouragement, and then drank her coffee.

USUALLY, THIS WAS the part of the morning where Cole, a week shy of thirty-two but feeling much older, readied for work by standing up from his bed and ironing out the knots in his back that had come with working in the freezer, loading and unloading pallets of food off trucks. The coroner was in the house, and Cole was getting dressed to go back downstairs. His bones cracked when he bent over to pull his socks on. Looking in the mirror at his haggard face, the scrawl of a beard on his cheeks, he wasn't quite sure what he was going to do now, and his eyes seemed lifeless, lamps gone dark.

At the kitchen table, the coroner was filling out a report. He watched the man's pen move across the page in a flurry of checks and hurried notes, and he realized, almost in that instant and in a way that amazed him, what his mother's death meant. There was no one left to work out the silence between him and his father. There was no interpreter left to relay messages. Who would tell both men that they loved each other?

The coroner stood, closing his folder and taking his cup to the sink. "I believe that's everything," he said.

His father was at the dining room table, staring blankly out the window at the woods and road, and it was left to Cole to acknowledge the man. "Thank you," he said. "My father wanted me to ask about a cause of death." This was a lie, but he thought it would sound better if he phrased it that way.

"Can't be sure. An aneurism in all likelihood. Would he like an autopsy performed?"

The words shivered him. Cole ran a hand through his hair, unsure of what to answer and afraid to ask his father who had still not stirred. He'd not said one word after he called 911.

"Tell you what," the coroner said, reaching into the breast pocket of his shirt. His face was fleshy and pockmarked, his jowls shook as he talked. "Have him call later this afternoon, after he's had some time. After you've both had some time."

Cole nodded and took the man's card. "Thank you," he said and stepped outside with the man. Two attendants from the funeral home were lifting his mother's body into the back of a blue-gray hearse.

Cole followed the coroner to his vehicle. "We'll be in touch," he said, shaking the man's hand and feeling how soft and smooth it was. So much so that he had to resist the urge to wipe it against his jeans after they were through.

The coroner drove off, and Cole turned to the funeral home attendants, never taking his eye off the back window where his mother rested inside.

"We'll take good care of her," the older man said. He wore a set of thin gold-rimmed glasses. His son, just a few years older than Cole, was with him, standing by the car. He looked impatient and unpracticed compared to his father. "It's a very tough time for you," the father went on. "We understand that. We want you to know we will do our best to make your family as comfortable as possible."

"Thank you," Cole said, for what seemed like too many times in such a short span. His mother had died, and so far the only thing he'd been able to say about the whole affair was a string of thank-yous to people he'd never met or seen before until today. He'd not even had a chance to talk to his father about it.

The man's eyes saw right into Cole's with such sincere condolence Cole had to turn away, as if he was searching for something he'd lost or forgotten.

Then they too were gone and Cole was alone in the driveway. The beech tree limbs shook in the breeze. He looked to the window, but his father was not there, though the smudge of where his fingers had been was visible under the bright sky.

Inside the house again, Cole ducked into his parents' bedroom from the hallway and heard the water running in the master bath. He called for his father, and the old man stuck his head around the corner, a mouth full of toothpaste, his hair combed and a fresh shirt on.

"Where're you going?" Cole asked, walking into the bathroom.

"The funeral home," his father said, spitting into the sink. He cupped a handful of water up to his mouth.

"Now?"

"Yeah," he said. "Why?"

"You don't want to talk?"

"About what?"

"Mom," he said. "What we're going to do?"

"What can we do?" he said. He put the toothbrush in its holder and flipped the light off, moving past Cole.

"Dad," Cole said.

"Yes," he said, sliding change from the top of the dresser into his hand.

Cole wanted to tell him how empty he felt. He wanted to ask his father if her death felt real to him, if he had already processed what the next step was, and how they went on from here. But looking in the old man's face, with all his stoicism, Cole could only say, "The coroner wants to know if you want an autopsy performed."

"No," he said. "I'm going now."

"Do you want me to go with you?" Cole said.

"If you want. There's probably not much to do, though."

Cole looked at him, unsure what his father meant by saying this to him. "What are *you* going to do?"

"I'm going to sit with her."

Cole stepped closer to the old man, eyeing him, wanting to feel something more than just the loss between them. "Do you want me to call the coroner and tell him?"

"No, I'll do it," his father said. His eyes were already traced with darkened rings. Then he stepped toward Cole and again put his hand on his shoulder, but this time he patted him there and shook him a little. "It'll be okay," he said and walked into the garage, and Cole heard the door opening and the car starting. He watched the

Buick move up the winding road toward town, leaving Cole in the big lonely rooms of the house.

HIS FATHER HAD not made it easy to ask for the job.

"Do you know how many men come to me in any given week looking for work? There aren't six men put together as smart as you working in that freezer."

"I need the work," Cole said.

They were standing outside, beside the grill, and the drippings from the burgers hissed and made the fire rise.

"Your mother and I sent you off to school so you wouldn't need to work a job like that. You've got a degree from one of the best damn schools in America. Doesn't that count for something?" He flipped a burger and looked at Cole.

It did count for something, and though he had spent most of his twenties being shiftless and wandering far more than he sometimes thought he should have, he had finally settled into a life in Boston he'd had to give up.

"Please, Dad," he said at last. "I just need some work for a spell."

"I can't promise anything," his father said and pulled the burgers off the grill. "You better see if your mother needs help," he said, pointing at the kitchen window, where she was cutting vegetables.

Cole walked off, wondering the whole time if his father was standing there and shaking his head in disappointment. He had built a life for Cole that was nothing like his own childhood, and this gave Cole great admiration. He had done that by working an insane number of hours at the office, ninety hours some weeks, and he developed a reputation among his friends' parents for how often he wasn't home or at Cole's ballgames. Work ethic, though, wasn't the only thing that set the old man apart. It was the chances he gave people to work and make a living. When Cole was only nine and ten, he would go to the office with him on the weekends, and on those short rides up the interstate he sometimes told Cole about the country boys he had hired who drove the trucks or who worked in the warehouse. He knew all these details about their lives, the children they had or had lost, the hollers where they had grown up and where their kinfolk still were. He had more in common with these men than he ever did with his fellow executives, and Cole came to understand his father never stopped feeling like a poor country boy himself. He wanted those men to have as many chances as he could give them.

So it never surprised him once they arrived at the office and he had broken free from the rows of cubicles outside his father's door and was roaming the large warehouse, tracing the familiar labels from television commercials—Lay's Potato Chips, Campbell's Soup, Frosted Flakes—all the way up to the ceiling, that every other worker he ran into always said the same thing. "Let me tell you something about your daddy. He's the best man." It didn't matter that Cole's father kept no pictures of him or his mother on his desk; they always knew who he was, and they always wanted him to know just what kind of man he had for a father.

His mother tried to ease his worries as she always had, taking up for his father, explaining in ways the old man couldn't what it was he expected from Cole. "He thinks you're too smart for you own good," she said, then added, "He may be right."

It had been her idea for him to ask for a job. She had smiled when she told him to do it, and before he had the chance to object, she cut him off. "You need your father," she said. "And he needs you too." His whole life she always gave Cole these edicts that seemed so melodramatic and solemn, and he had to laugh them off—and she did too—but he knew deep down how much she meant them.

He pictured her face, the big puffy cheeks, a feature she hated. "I have a moon face, don't I?" she often asked. "No," Cole told her, lying every time. The house was filled with black-and-white pictures she'd taken over the years, and Cole found himself looking at one of him when he was three. He wore a pair of cutoff jeans and held an outstretched paintbrush to his father who was covering a wall. It was always her favorite.

Cole wanted to cry over his mother's death, but he couldn't. No matter how cold and hollow he felt, how broken apart he was, the tears did not come. He wanted her to know just how much he had loved her, and loved her for never giving up on him. He wanted to know what she would say to him about his fear of dealing with his father. What could she tell him when he admitted that he felt he would never measure up to the old man? He compared his own lack of accomplishment next to his father's, and it raced through his heart. It was the thing, in the empty house with rooms full of memories, he saw he had always been doing.

THE SMELL OF flowers and air freshener hung in the air. The carpet was marked with lines from vacuuming. Cole's father was sitting in a high-backed leather chair with brass rivets along the seams. He stayed quiet while Cole paced back and forth, reading the funeral home's brochure, looking over the wallpapering and pictures, again and again. It was restless waiting, especially when his father said and did nothing.

Finally, he asked his father, "Did you talk to Mr. Kirby?"

"Just for a moment. He said he needs a dress for your mother to wear. Can you pick one out?"

"You don't want to?"

"No," he said. "I don't want to leave."

"I can do it if you need me to," he said.

"Thanks. You should go on," he said. "You don't need to be here."

"I'll stay with you," Cole said. "Have you gone down to see her?"

"No," he said. "I will after they've prepared her."

"Are you all right?" Cole tried to read his face, but there was nothing but impassiveness.

"I'm okay. There are some arrangements that'll need to be made. You should call the church and tell them about your mother. Her friends too."

Cole nodded. His father was picking at his cuticles. "Dad," he said after a moment. Cole's father raised his head.

"Do you need anything? Something to eat? Drink?" But these weren't the real questions he wanted to ask. He didn't know how he could simply sit there and do nothing. He wanted to know how the man could spend a life with someone and the moment she was gone not react in some way other than silence.

"No, no. Go on," he said. "I'll be fine. Just do those things for us, okay?"

Cole stood and put his hands in his pockets. "Should I leave now?"

"It's up to you," his father said, standing. "Don't feel like you have to stay with me."

He seemed to be ushering him out the door. Cole nodded and the two men looked at each other, unsure if they should hug or embrace and neither making a move to do so. Finally, Cole patted his father's arm and said he'd come back later to check on him, and then he walked outside into the breeze.

ONLY ONCE DID he ever remember seeing his father angry, and that was after a big fight with his mother. He had come home from baseball practice, hearing the shouts through the windows of the house as he walked up the driveway. He opened the door to see his mother crying, two glistening streaks of tears running down her face, but her chin was pointed straight at his father, who was leaning back against the stove.

"Go to your room," he said when he saw Cole.

The shouting continued once Cole was in his room, and the last thing Cole heard was the slamming of the door and his father's car moving away from the house. He lay in bed all that night waiting to hear him pull the car into the garage below his bedroom. Three days passed, and still Cole never heard from him. Not even a phone call. On the fourth night, Cole heard the car outside his window but not the garage door opening. Then his father's footsteps were downstairs, his Florsheim shoes clicking against the hardwood floors. The shower turned on in the spare bedroom, and moments later, as he stayed still in the darkness, tracing the edges of the ceiling fan with his eyes, his father's car started up and the sound of the engine moved farther away from their home. In the morning, on the kitchen counter, four new one-hundred-dollar bills. Below them was a note that only said, *For groceries.*

Even then as a twelve-year-old boy it said something to him about how he should act if he ever found himself in a similar sort of conflict. It reached out to him almost as strong as any hug he had ever received from his father, assuring him that he would take care of them no matter what happened.

Their reconciliation was quick, and no one, not even his mother who loved to talk to Cole about all the details of her life, ever said anything about it. His father had simply shown up one day at Cole's practice, the white sleeves of his shirt rolled to the elbows and his tie loosened at the neck. "Ready to go home?" he asked as Cole walked up. Cole's throat clenched when the old man spoke the words, and he'd only been able to nod, and then his father's arm was over his shoulder, patting his back and guiding him toward the car.

It was hard for Cole to look at his father and not remember how he looked that day. Still young, still strong. Some part of him always believed it was his father who made everything better, despite his quiet ways and unwillingness to talk. As he got older, he knew he could never know the entire story, the words that are exchanged between a husband and wife and the promises they make to themselves and for their children. He never let go of the idea it was his father who went to his mother. It was the money on the counter, perhaps, the sight of it, that fueled his belief.

COLE WENT BACK to the funeral home at eight in the evening, bringing a dress for his mother and letting his father know the obituary would be in tomorrow's paper. The old man nodded in affirmation at the last piece of knowledge and ate just half of the sandwich Cole had brought him. They sat together in the room where the visitation was going to be held, staring at the space where the casket would sit. It was lit with two soft overhead lights, and already the front of the room was filled with peace lilies, bereavement wreaths, and the petals of countless flowers.

"I can't believe this," Cole said, only to break their silence.

His father didn't respond. He looked at the old man's jaw, then his hair, grayed on the edges and thinning on top. The wrinkles around his eyes weren't visible, though. He appeared younger in this light. Cole thought about his father's leaving so many years ago and how he had never come to Cole's room and said something to him. Why didn't he wake his only child in the middle of the night to tell him it would be okay? It had taken everything for Cole not to race out of his room and into the kitchen to grab him. As a boy, he thought that had been bravery on his part, how his father would handle the situation, but here, in the dim light of the funeral home, in the company of his father, he knew it was only cowardice. Because what would he have done if he'd gone out to him only to have his father squat down and tell him he was never coming back?

The next three days were going to be filled with cards and warm wishes. Serious handshakes, somber hugs. He'd been to a dozen visitations in his life, but couldn't once remember ever actually attending a burial. He thought of the pair he and his father would make, both dressed in black suits, each showing the other in their features—the past and the future. Beneath them his mother lay on a cold table somewhere, while in the back of the funeral home the director and his wife were probably just clearing the dishes from supper, settling in to watch a movie before a long night of peaceful sleep.

"I'm going home," Cole said.

"Good," his father said. "You should. Get yourself some rest. Thanks for coming by."

"Thanks?" he said. "She's my mother. I loved her too."

"I didn't mean it that way. I'm glad you came by. You didn't have to."

Cole didn't know what else to say other than that he was welcome. Then, "Are you coming home soon?"

His father half-grunted and shook his head.

"You need some rest too," Cole said, but his father didn't turn to him again.

Cole put his hand on his father's shoulder, remembering all the strength once held there when he was a boy, and then he left.

THERE HAD BEEN a woman in Boston. They had been drifting apart for a while by the time he lost his job, and if he had honestly thought he could salvage their relationship, he would have stayed. But she wasn't ready. That's what she told him. She didn't know about marriage, she didn't *know* about him the way he said he knew about her. They had friends visiting from out of town, and they had taken them to the North End for pizza and sightseeing. She told him all this inside a bakery while their friends toured the Old North Church. His face had gone flush with anger and embarrassment, and a pit below his chest opened up with a burning, melting pain. It was the first and only time he ever felt the physical ache of heartbreak. The breakup had made going home easier, but he had moved enough in his life that he knew he couldn't outrun his problems. She was still with him in his thoughts far more than he wanted. He had thought to call her and tell her about his mother, but when he picked up the phone all he could do was trace his finger over her name on the cell phone's screen. She was the only person he wanted to talk to and yet he couldn't call her. They had parted on good terms, made promises to keep in touch after some time had passed, but he didn't know what he would say to her. *Comfort me*, he thought. *Come back into my life and comfort me*, he wanted to say, but her decision had been that she didn't want to be a part of his life anymore.

Clutching the phone, he walked through the house and turned on lights. He went to every single room, flipping every switch, and when he looked out the windows, it was so bright he couldn't see the night in front of him. Then he went outside to the road, each window glowing in front of him. Had it been just a week before and he had come home to this sight, his mother could have been in any one of those rooms. Had it been just months before he would have still been in Boston, in the arms of the woman he thought was going to make him happy for the rest of his life.

He sat down in the middle of the road and pulled his knees into his chest. The sky above him was cloudless, and it was an endless field of stars. He took in one big deep breath and exhaled. Finally, he thought, the tears would come. But as he continued to watch the windows, hoping for the passing of a shadow, some sign of movement, his eyes only welled.

IN THE MORNING there was no sign his father had come home. Cole had fallen asleep on the couch with all the lights still on. He called the funeral home, and they said his father was there. Cole dressed and drove to meet him. When he arrived, his father was where he had left him, sitting in the same chair, in the same pose, and Cole wondered if he had moved at all from the spot or gone outside, at least, into the air and paced. The next two days it was the same thing. He refused to leave the funeral home, and every time Cole came by to check on him, his father always seemed surprised by his presence. Mr. Kirby told Cole he'd seen similar grieving before, but nothing quite like this.

"He sits all day," he said. "He doesn't speak. He must have loved your mother very much." Cole knew he said this in a tone meant to let him know his father's grief was, in some way, honorable.

Cole handled most of the details of the visitation and the funeral, his father agreeing to everything he put in front of him and signing all the forms. On Friday night Cole greeted the people who came to the funeral home, standing up for each person to shake his hand or give him a hug after they had viewed his mother and accepting their soft-spoken words. His father, clean-shaven and showered, stayed seated. What Mr. Kirby didn't know was that while his father mourned, Cole had been shuffling through old pictures of himself and her and of their family. He too had spent restless nights, but his were spent in a house that hadn't been home in a long time and that now took on an even more distant feeling with his mother's death.

His father had hidden, and by the last night of the visitation, Cole was unable to even look at the old man. He cut a small figure. His handshakes were limp, his eyes lost to some other place. And of all the things Cole had ever felt guilty about in his life, none of them compared to the contempt he held for his father in the dim funeral home. Though Cole had not seen him shed one tear, he looked at his father's grieving as a weakness. He was the one who should have handled the details. Instead, he had forced Cole to be as stoic and reserved as he was, and as they drove out to the cemetery inside the funeral home's Cadillac, Cole knew this was what he resented most.

The familiar shapes of the mountains that set the boundaries of Fordyce rose up before the windshield in the distance, and the land's pattern seemed to wrap around him like some warm quilt. Side by side they sat in the car, each man looking out his own window, and side by side they stood at the graveside service while a small crowd of friends and family gathered.

The preacher read the Psalm and gave a meditation on death, mentioning a few personal aspects and stories about Cole's mother. Cole didn't listen. Around him he watched the people nodding, praying with the preacher, clutching purses and tissues in their hands. There had been moments in the last few evenings when all Cole wanted to do was shake his father, to pull him out of the chair and drag him outside and ask him what went on inside of him. *I've known you all my life, but I don't know who you are or what you want.* He had come back to Fordyce with so much shame, and for the first time in his life his father wasn't the strongest person in the room.

Then the preacher quieted, and Cole felt the finality of his mother's death being laid upon his shoulders. His father was stone-faced, and Cole noticed in his expression, in a way he knew shouldn't have surprised him, how wrong he'd been. For three nights he had lain in bed once again, waiting to hear the old man come in the door, the jangle of his keys being laid on the counter, his footsteps on the stairs toward his room. He had stayed in bed with his hands behind his head, staring at the dark, listening so hard, so intently, his head hurt, but not once did he rise from his spot and run to his father. Just as he had when he was a boy, he waited on him to make everything better. His father in just three days' time had withered away under the soft lights of the Kirby Funeral Home while Cole had been unable to say the simplest words to him. They had both failed each other. And in the clear day, with the sun growing brighter by the minute, as if he could see it pulsing in the blue-dream of sky, Cole began to feel his mother everywhere in his thoughts. She bound the two men, pleading from the other side, it seemed, for them to move toward each other.

Then his father's hand was at his elbow, the grip pinching into his skin, and Cole led them both to the casket. Sweat beaded at his temples. His father leaned into him, and as he bent over with his free hand to scoop up a small patch of dirt, the grip on Cole's elbow tightened. The old man held out the dirt, his hand shook over the casket, and his whole body was buckling, pulling down on Cole's arm, but Cole stood firm, widened his stance by a half step. He watched his father open his palm and, like smoke, the tiny granules spread into the air, and the two men stood at the gravesite while everyone in attendance drifted away, leaving them alone.

THE BEGINNINGS OF A STORM

A FTER WORK, JAMES rushes home to scrub off the specks of asphalt and grime of exhaust from a ten-hour workday. His jeans lie in a wad on the motel room floor, and in the front pocket is eight hundred dollars, all in twenties—an entire week's pay. Most of that will be gone by Monday when he'll arrive back at the airport to get behind the wheel of a bulldozer or front loader, hungover and cotton-mouthed. But now, in the cool stream of water, the money represents nothing but possibility and access, two complete days of not hearing the loud whine of diesel engines or jet planes rising from the earth. He takes a long drink from one of the beers he's brought into the shower. He has denied himself this specific pleasure all week, trying to practice some measure of restraint and discipline until Friday afternoons, when often he gives in to his impulses. On the drive home today he stopped at the corner store on Lamar and bought a sixer and two tallboys and set them on the passenger seat, waiting until exactly 5:00 p.m. before he cracked the first one. Until then the cans seemed to stare, to bubble with life just a foot from his reach. When the digital clock on the truck's stereo tumbled to the magic numbers, he was in a winding line of cars by the university. He grabbed the first can from the bag and popped its top all in one motion, just as a couple of blonde, long-legged sorority girls crossed in front of his truck. He raised the can to them and called out "Cheers!" as they walked right on past, turning their heads just enough so that their hair became filled with sunlight.

He turns the water off and finishes his beer, crushes the can, and steps onto the cold tiles. He checks his hair in the mirror and wraps himself in a towel. He's been living in this motor lodge for six months, ever since he and Lisa split their marriage up. The walls are thin, marked by stains that appear to be from an electrical fire, but the carpet in his room is less dank than in the first three rooms the owner showed him. He pays the man $125 a week in rent. The TV and air conditioner work and that's all he's really paying for. He bought his own sheets and bedspread at Walmart, and those are the only luxury items he's afforded himself. Everything else he has is a ragtag collection of his old life. If Lisa saw him now she'd see what he can't: that he's given up.

A young black woman on the television says the temperature was over 100 today, the heat index 115. The room is hotter than normal. He walks to the air conditioner and feels nothing but warm air blowing out of the vent. He reaches down into the cooler and pulls out a fresh can of beer and places it against the back of his neck. Bright light streams through the cream-colored curtains. Through their sheerness he sees his pickup truck and remembers when it was shiny and new. Lisa had come home with it. A gift to get him started, she said. He was doing landscaping then and had assembled a crew of six. He had dreams of growing the business, telling Lisa his back wouldn't last forever. She'd gone to her father and gotten the money for the truck. That started a big fight between them.

"I'll never live it down," he told her.

"He wants to help. He believes in you."

"You believe in me. He loves you. Never wants to disappoint you. Your problem is you're spoiled. You don't want to work."

"You need a good truck to haul your equipment. Besides, we're going to pay him back. I promised." She was calm and refused to take his bait.

"We?"

"That's right," she said. "Us."

He relented then, and that night they drove the pickup downtown to Gus's Fried Chicken, and afterward they walked over to Beale Street and drank beer in plastic cups and watched the tourists around them go in and out of the neon-lit bars while they milled about, listening to the covers coming out of B. B. King's club. He bought her a carnation, and afterward, on their walk back to the truck, she stopped underneath the refurbished Orpheum Theater, the marquee and awning a sky of bright white bulbs, and he snapped her picture with his cell phone camera. He still has it, transfers it from one phone to the next even though it's been six years since he took it and the truck is now dented along the fenders and back bumper, with rust settling into the crevices of those scars.

He shakes his head as if he can expel the memory and brings the can to his lips and takes a deep drink until everything in it is gone. And then, in a move he saw his father's friend do once when he was a boy, he licks the rim to get every last drop of alcohol.

He grabs his watch from the dresser. Jenna's not due to arrive for another few hours. He dives his hand back into the cooler and this time comes out with a fifth of Very Old Barton. It is the bourbon his father used to drink, and he doesn't even bother with the paper cups on the bathroom sink. The bourbon is cool and sweet. He sits on the edge of the bed, intent on working himself into another state of being, but then his phone buzzes. "Jimmy!" Keith calls to him. "You going to see that hot little piece of ass tonight?"

James rolls his eyes and sighs. He's been working with Keith for two months on the construction job out by the Memphis Airport. A new office complex. Keith's the closest thing James has to a friend these days. Sometimes he thinks Keith tries to pretend Jenna isn't what she is, that her encounters with him are exclusive, dates.

"Don't be that way, Jimmy," he says. "I hear you getting all huffy. I'm just asking. I bet she's a toe-curler, ain't she?"

"What do you want, Keith?"

"You're a real gentleman, aren't you? Won't give up nothing."

"What do you want me to say?"

"I want you to tell me you're going to fuck her six ways to Sunday. I want you to say you'll fuck her so hard she'll scream *my* name."

James has to smile at that one. He says, "Never heard that one before. Your name, huh?"

"If you can manage it."

James gives a soft laugh.

Emboldened, Keith continues. "One time I got this hot little thing to blow me in the pew at church. Man, what I wouldn't give to be seventeen again."

"Congratulations," James says, an edge returning to his voice.

"I'm just making conversation."

"Is that what you call it?"

"What are you so damn prickly about?"

"Nothing," James says. "It's hot in this damn room." He takes a quick drink from the bottle.

"It's hot in this whole damn city. I should move to Canada. This shit is Africa-hot."

"You'd freeze your ass off in winter."

"I like cold. I like bundling up and facing the elements."

"It's more than elements up there."

"What's that mean?" Keith says.

James shrugs to the empty room, tells Keith he doesn't really know. He has done this more and more of late. Saying things that really have no meaning, just because they sound good to his ear.

He doesn't feel like talking to Keith. He just wants to get through this night and then the next. He wants, somehow, to both face and forget the life he now owns.

"After you're done with that little piece, why don't you call me later?" Keith says. "I got an idea for us."

"I might," he says, and before Keith can acknowledge his reply James hangs up.

He considers supper and stands and feels the beginnings of a buzz—a warming in his ears. It's not unpleasant, but he needs to get out of the room into some AC. He is searching for his keys when a knock comes at the door. It's Jenna.

"You're early," he says.

"It's a slow night. I saw your truck."

The sky has changed color, and gray swirls of clouds give off the hint of a breeze. He studies them.

"You going to let me in?" She tries to push past him, but he doesn't step aside. "What gives?"

"Nothing," he says, still focused on the sky. "Come on." He retreats and she locks the door behind her.

"You need to open a window in this place."

"There's beer and brown liquor in the cooler," he tells her.

"I didn't come here to drink," she says. She is already pulling her shirt off and stepping out of her jean shorts. She walks over to the bed and slides under the covers, waiting on him.

Despite not being ready for her, he feels his erection against his jeans. He unsnaps the buttons on his Levi's and rolls on a condom. In minutes her small legs are wrapped tightly around his back. Right before she comes she will ball her hands up into little fists. He loves this moment. He keeps his eyes open when he's with her working for it. He sweats through every pore in his body, every aching limb and muscle in him throbbing as he rocks atop her. He slips his arm underneath the small of her back to pull her light frame off the bed so that he is cradling her in one arm. He looks into her face, a little pockmarked and weatherworn but soft in the eyes and mouth, and he sees who she was and might have been if not for this or that, and he grinds through his own feelings until those fingers of hers clench the air between them and then he bears down harder, rocking the two of them faster, grabbing the top of the mattress to brace himself. Jenna lets out a full-throated cry at climax, but James won't allow himself so much as a sigh. He seems to have gone somewhere else in his mind with these final few movements, reminding himself of where he is and who he's with, eliminating almost all pleasure from the act. He gently lays her back down on the bed, her body covered in his sweat and he smelling of her sex, and pulls the sheet over her curled legs and goes to the bathroom. He never takes up the space beside her, preferring to get in the shower while she rests and let cold water sting him, as if desensitizing himself from what's just occurred. She has told him before it's different with him, but he doesn't want to hear it, though he feels it might be true, with the way she carries on.

As he steps into the shower he feels her hands on his shoulders. He turns with a fright. "Get out," he says. "Get the hell out." She holds her hands up but doesn't seem afraid. She doesn't speak and turns from him and he lets her go. He showers quickly, and when he comes back out, wrapped in a fresh towel, she is still there, watching television like it never happened at all. He figures that's how it is when you pay for it. They don't fight you or want anything from you. There's no complication of emotion.

"I'm sorry about earlier," he says. "I didn't mean to shout."

"You don't have to worry about me," she says. "I just wanted to rinse off. Didn't think you'd mind."

She gets up and goes past him, and he knows the reason he

minded has something to do with a boundary of intimacy he didn't want to cross. He puts his clothes back on and waits for Jenna to come out, and when she does, he flips off three twenties from his roll of money and puts it on the dresser and tells her he's leaving.

"Where are you going?"

"I don't know."

"Want me to come with you?"

The question is an odd one, as if she's pressing him. He feels himself tilting his head to examine her. "I'll be all right," he says.

"You call me anytime," she says, wringing her wet hair.

"Close the door when you leave," he tells her. He can't get out of the room fast enough, and when he's inside his truck, he pauses to collect his breath. The sky is darker, the clouds thicker and the night moving in. He drives to a filling station, and in its convenience store he fixes himself up with two hot dogs and buys another sixer. He heads east on Poplar, passing Overton Park where a yellow flag on the golf course is ruffled by the wind of moving cars.

He rides with the radio low and a beer between his legs, careful not to take any sips whenever the truck is lit up by oncoming cars. He's headed to his old house, another bad habit he can't seem to break. It began months ago when he drove by on a Friday because he simply missed Lisa, their old life she no longer wanted. He thought he might walk up to the front door, coax her into a dinner, but when he pulled up there was an unfamiliar car in the driveway. A Saab. He didn't believe she could have found somebody that quickly, so he parked down the street and watched the house. Watched it so long he fell asleep behind the wheel and woke at dawn to see the Saab covered in dew. An hour later a man walked out. Someone a little bit younger than him with big shoulders and a tan face. A square-jawed, bushy-eyebrowed fucker is how he's described him to Keith. He considered following him, but he stopped himself. What he did do, though, was come back the next night and every night after, and when that piece of preppy Swedish shit was in the driveway, he parked right behind it while Lisa had her date inside the house where he once took his morning coffee. Behind the wheel of the truck—*their* truck, he thought—he failed at trying not to imagine what she must be doing with this new man in her life.

He stopped only after she called to say she had put his stuff in boxes and he needed to come over and pick it up. That night she told him about Hal, who was nowhere to be found. Then she told James, "You look gaunt." That was her word.

After putting the boxes in the bed of the truck, he checked his face in the rearview mirror and noticed how sunken his cheeks were. Haunted would have been the better word, he thought. She never mentioned him sitting in the driveway.

He slows the truck down and sees Hal's car. It's a mistake to be here, he thinks, but he doesn't turn around. He studies the house and can't believe how unfamiliar everything looks even though not one thing has changed since the last night he spent there. The wisteria hangs from the arbor, the crepe myrtles have blossomed. The lights are on and the curtains pulled back, and he sees Lisa and Hal moving through the rooms. It appears they've just eaten supper. Her black hair is up in a ponytail, and she moves briskly at the sink, scrubbing the dishes. Hal kisses her neck, his arms wrap around her from behind, and she laughs at something he says, falling into his embrace. James's face and stomach burn. Then Hal moves away and goes to the living room and turns on the TV and falls onto the couch. James finishes a second tallboy and plucks a fresh beer from its ring. Then Lisa is done at the sink and her back turns, and he sees her in the dining room, turning out the lights. He waits for her to appear in the living room beside Hal, but she doesn't show up in the picture window behind the couch. He keeps waiting, watching. Hal's head turns, snaps to the driveway. James eyes the kitchen window through the twilight and makes out her shadow and then her face against the glass. The front door is thrown open and Hal stomps toward him. Before James jumps out, he tries to find Lisa once more but sees only darkness filling the window frame. He moves quickly toward Hal, leaving the truck door open, and the cab's light spills onto the concrete. The two men meet in the yard.

"This has got to stop," Hal says.

"That's my house."

"It was your house."

"Look here, you son of a bitch—"

Hal nods toward the house. "She's the only thing that's kept me from grabbing my pistol, you know that?"

"You think you're the only motherfucker in Tennessee that owns a gun?"

The two men edge closer to each other. James's head stirs from alcohol and adrenaline. Then Lisa is there with them and James turns to her, ready to reason, to show her how crazy she is to be with this asshole, but before he can say any of this the flats of her palms are on his chest, soft and warm, and she guides him backward. She looks directly at him, as if Hal isn't even there, and tells James *he's* acting crazy. He can't come by anymore. Doesn't he have any pride? Things aren't going back to the way they were, and the sooner he accepts that, the sooner he can get on with his life. And when she says this he understands what he's just witnessed between her and Hal.

She has gotten on with her life. This drops him quicker than any punch. Hal steps away from the two of them. The winner, James thinks. He tells Lisa he's sorry. He won't bother them anymore, but he speaks to the ground. He extends his hand out to Hal because he feels it's all he can do, this one small act of grace. They shake. James gets into the truck and drives away.

"YOU DID WHAT?"

"I wasn't thinking."

"Wrong," Keith says. "You were thinking too damn much and that's why you did it. Damn, Jimmy." It's loud where Keith is. James hears music and voices. "Hold on," Keith says. After a moment it's quiet. "Where are you now?"

"On my way home."

"Fuck that. You need a drink. Come out to Wild Bill's."

"Only college kids and tourists go out there anymore."

"The band's good. I got a table."

"I think I should head home," he says.

"That damn room ain't no kind of home I ever been in. You come out here or I'll drive over and get you."

He reluctantly agrees. The air is thick with humidity, and he wonders when those damn clouds are going to burst. He makes his way to Wild Bill's. On the curb he pulls a plastic flask from the glove box, unscrews it, and takes a swig. He swirls it around and tries to eyeball how much is left, but for the first time in a long time, his heart isn't in it and he throws it back in its place.

The sidewalk vibrates from the bass inside the juke joint, and he shoves his way inside to find Keith in a corner table near the band. It's at least ten degrees hotter in the bar than it is outside, and the women dance with their hair matted to their necks and foreheads. Their bodies curl and contort next to one another, and he navigates past a pair of hips to make it to Keith.

"Took you long enough," Keith shouts over the noise. He pushes a chair toward James.

James sits without speaking. He taps the table, but not in beat with the music, and eyes the quart of beer on the table.

"Want some?" Keith begins pouring into a plastic cup. "It's warm but it drinks the same as cold."

James sips slowly. His mind keeps going back to his house, to Lisa's palms on his chest. Polaroids fill up the walls of the joint, and he searches as if he will find their smiling faces in the throng of people having a good time.

The band takes a break and Keith leans over. "Tell me what happened."

James takes a drink.

"Can't tell anybody else, you might as well tell me," he says.

James starts at the beginning with Jenna, how she tried to enter the shower and how it set him off. He leaves out the part about spending all that time in Lisa's driveway. Tells him how Hal threatened him with a pistol and how he threatened him back.

"He said that?" Keith says.

"Yeah. Crazy fucker."

"You even own a gun?"

"No, but I can get one. Anybody can get a gun."

"True enough. You should have strung that little shit up by the nuts. Wouldn't have done any good, but you'd have felt better for about fifteen minutes. Maybe twenty."

Keith's a few years older than James. Ex-navy. He has scarred knuckles, and where his hairline begins, a scar as long as a finger points downward, almost bisecting his forehead. He's probably the last guy in the world James would ever mess with and the only one he thinks he can't outdrink. Keith turns around and surveys the crowd, as if he's leaving James alone, though they share the same space.

James watches everyone dancing and drinking, the smiles that stretch their faces, and wonders what they see when their eyes pass over him. If they can even see him.

"Forget it," Keith says, turning back.

"Forget what?"

"She made her choice. You couldn't have done anything different."

"I could have been better."

"Shit. Tell me something I don't know. We all could be better, but you were who you were and that's who she fell in love with. Then she moved on. I'm going to get more beer."

He twists through the crowd, grabbing a woman around the waist and dancing with her a moment before letting her go and sidling up to the bar. He catches James's eye, nods toward the woman, and winks. She has on an electric-blue dress, dark brown hair falling to her shoulders in small waves. She walks toward James and asks, "Do you want to dance?"

He shakes his head. "I like sitting. But that fella right there is going to dance with you all night."

Keith heads over with two more beers, and James gets up and offers her his chair. "Go ahead," he says. "His name is Keith."

"You're leaving?" Keith says.

"She was looking for you. She's always been looking for you."

"What?"

"Go with it. Thanks."

"For what?" He puts the beers down, quickly asks the woman to hold on a second. "Where you going?"

"Motel."

"Good. Monday?"

"See you then," James says. "Good luck."

The temperature has dropped when he gets back. Leaves and trash fly by him and the tail of his unbuttoned shirt billows. It's very late. The wind suddenly stops and the world becomes still and silent. Abandoned. In the sky the clouds are milky white and gray and on the horizon are bright swatches of orange and yellow as if they are morphing into nebula—the one term he remembers from an astronomy class at the community college ten years ago—the beginnings of a storm.

Jenna stands outside his door. She looks almost the same as earlier, and he tries not to think about where she's been since then. She moves to the truck, and when he gets out, she says she's been waiting on him.

"What for?"

"I missed you." She thumbs the buttons on his shirt and slips a finger in between the fabric, and her nail is cool against his chest.

The straps on her top fall off her tanned, freckled shoulders. He notices she's highlighted her hair, a detail he missed earlier, and he runs the backs of his fingers across it.

"You didn't notice earlier," she says.

"I had things on my mind."

"And do you have things on your mind now?" Her whole hand is inside his shirt now, rubbing his breastbone.

He thinks of how she bucks under him at his touch, the way she bit his bottom lip earlier, and the shower he took afterward when all he wanted was for her to be gone when he came back to the room but was so grateful when she was still there.

"You going to let me in?"

He unlocks the door and they walk in together, and before he can snap on the light she moves against him, strokes him outside of his denim, but he pushes her away, gently, and turns on the light. He wants to take his time.

He steps back to admire her. She's knock-kneed. A petite woman, her hair almost brittle in its new blondness. He asks her to undress and waits until she is naked before he undoes his belt and pulls off his boots. He won't let her onto the bed until he's naked too. He refuses her help with his clothes so she stands not knowing what to do with her hands. But once they're both unclothed, he turns her so he can sit on the bed and kiss her abdomen and run his fingers along her rib bones.

"It tickles," she says.

He smiles. He glances at the nightstand, where condoms lay beside the alarm clock, and he leaves them there.

He pulls her onto him so that she straddles him, and he hardens. Her small breasts are pert and firm. Her nipples bloom at the touch of his lips and she moans and begins to work her hips. He allows himself to close his eyes and listen to her breathing speed up, to feel the hotness of her breath against his neck as she reaches down and takes hold of him.

This is not how it has ever gone between the two of them, but he is falling away. He lies back flat underneath her, his arms splayed above. He fights against the warmth and sensation he feels. He watches the motion of their sex, thinks of the skin against skin. He closes his eyes again, and gone from his mind are the room they share, the broken air conditioner that hums loudly in the corner, the incessant noise of one motor after another that fills his head all day. He can't even picture Jenna's face. He can't see Lisa or the first night she led him to her bedroom and undressed him in the dark and when they were finished how she pressed herself close, all of her softness against him, and he put his arm around her and made a silent promise to never let go. He can't envision anything except that in the morning this woman he doesn't love, that he'll never love, will be beside him and that outside the red door of this space they now share is a world kept at bay by a lock that costs three dollars at the True Value.

Jenna quickens her pace. She brings her hands down to James's chest. She digs her nails into his skin and it peels back from her scratches. He winces, but she doesn't stop. She's calling his name. Over and over she says it. James. James. James. He rests his hands on top of hers and he feels his heart beating. There is the sound of their flesh coming together in fast, hard successive beats, and Jenna lets out a wild scream. With that James opens his eyes and lifts himself up and flips Jenna onto her back and grabs her as he always has. Without knowing how to phrase it, what he wants from her— to see in her—is tenderness, but she is languid. So he grabs hold of her hair near the scalp and tightens his grip so that her eyes spring alertly wide. He no longer fights. He slows down and then he pushes deep into her. Her mouth makes an inaudible O. Then he's working, steadily increasing his pace. His legs and back cramp, but he continues, trying to move as deep and as fast as he can with each motion, looking right into Jenna's eyes. She is right there with him, her face ablaze, clutching at him with her legs and arms. At the height, as everything in him pours forth, he nuzzles into her neck and falls beside her.

His head's awash in endorphins, and now it's Jenna who rises from the bed and goes to the bathroom. The shower turns on. The sheets beneath him are soaked with sweat, but he doesn't move. He can't. He rubs his eyes with his palms and listens to the water falling against the tile. He rolls over and puts on his boxers. He reaches for a beer from the cooler and rests the cold can on his chest. It sends a shiver through him.

One night, early in their marriage, Lisa went outside to watch the sky just before a hard rain. She sat on the trunk of her Camry with her eyes fixed in wonder on the swirls of light in the sky. "Come back inside," James said. "It's dangerous out there." He was in the doorway that led out to the carport of the little house they rented on Jefferson Avenue. "You ought to come here," she said. "You worry too much." The air sirens sounded right then, and James noticed how empty the streets were. "Will you come in now?" he said. Reluctantly, she came inside, where the television showed reporters downtown by the river, standing in rain slickers, the sky behind them bursting every few seconds like a firecracker. Lightning slammed the ground, and the power went out and the streets were pitch black. Rain fell like tiny hammers against the roof and windows. The wind blew hard, and they heard limbs breaking from trees. A loud, piercing whine of splitting wood rushed over the house, and they knew a tree was going to fall, so they huddled together in the middle of the living room. Lisa clung to him, and he covered her head with his hands in the dark room until a tree crashed through the back of the house into their bedroom. Lisa screamed, and he held onto her, rocking her. Tears were in her eyes and he asked if she was okay, but she didn't say anything, so he guided her head to his shoulder, ran his fingers through her hair, kissed her temple. "I'm here," he told her. "I'm always right here."

The water shuts off, and James turns his head to see Jenna standing in the bathroom doorway toweling off. "I should go," she says.

"You sure?" he says. "Might be nice if you stayed."

"I don't think so."

"Want a drink before you leave?" He holds the unopened can up to her.

"No. I have a long night ahead of me."

"I see," he says. He sits up and picks his jeans off the floor and fishes out the wad of bills, flipping off double what he paid her earlier.

She comes to him, cinching the towel around her chest, and grabs his hand. "Keep it."

"No," he says, pushing the money toward her.

"This one was on me," she says. "I wanted it."

"I did too," he says, his neck bent upward to look her in the eye. He wants to hold her cold, clean body, but she turns away, lets the towel drop. She shimmies into her shorts and pulls on her top.

When she faces him again she gently traces the marks she's left on his chest, as if she's a painter admiring her work. "I was a real wildcat tonight, wasn't I?"

"You were something else," he says, rising off the bed.

They stand close. She kisses one set of marks then the other, and the water from her hair runs in beads down the length of his torso. "I wasn't the only one," Jenna says.

He knows life turning on a dime is cliché, but that's what happened to Lisa and him. It's as if he merely blinked and she was through with him and the world shifted in ways he never thought it might. A big wind howls against the motel room, and Jenna is making her move to go, unlatching the chain. "Wait," he calls and pulls on his jeans. She stops. They can go anywhere his cash will take them, which he knows isn't very far, but will she go with him? Jenna is silent at this, and in that silence he knows he won't ever outrun the ghost of his marriage, that he gave the last of what he considers his real self to this woman before him who is a prostitute and who is ready to walk out into the night and away from him forever.

"I can't do that, James," Jenna says. "I've got to leave."

She opens the door, and with perfect timing, the storm roars in, crowding out all other sounds. Jenna runs for it and, barefooted, James steps onto the breezeway and watches her run through the rain, her small steps splashing in the parking lot. He calls for her, but she can't hear him over the hard sound of water pelting the earth.

SOLID GROUND

JUST SAW HER get swallowed whole. She might have been twenty yards away, and then the earth was opening up and she was gone. I was on my front porch gathering the mail when that pretty young woman came past in her car, bobbing her head to some song on the radio, and then the worst sound I've ever heard came tearing up from the ground. The concrete crackled and screeched and her car vanished. She screamed the whole way down. I couldn't hear that, but I saw her mouth open and the tendons in her neck straining. I didn't know whether to go to her or stay where I was. One by one the doors on our street opened to take inventory of the noise, and then once we saw the damage, we made our way to the hole, searching into its blackness and then lifting our heads back to one another. We couldn't see anything except for the broken chunks of asphalt and dirt. It was like the earth had been hollowed out and there was no trace of that car, only slivering earthworms burrowing back into the exposed soil. The pit was so deep I thought of it going all the way to China like we believed when we were kids, but then I just thought of that hole going on forever—through the earth and into space. I imagined that poor woman falling without end.

I gave myself chills with such thinking, and I backed away and went right to the porch and sat down. The police and fire departments showed up and started clearing people out. Seemed like half the crowd moved onto my front lawn and all of them snapping

pictures with their phones. I hollered to one of the officers, Icie
Harp's boy Randy, and told him I didn't want them on my lawn.
It wasn't that I was worried about the grass or my flower beds like
I told him, but that I needed space. I needed to be able to go into
my house and try and forget that dark emptiness. Before long I
knew the television crews would show up and start interviewing
every hick we have in town, making us all look like a bunch of
fools—that's what makes for good news these days—when what
really happened was that a woman was disappeared.

The officers and firemen pushed the crowd toward the sidewalks
to make way for search teams and vehicles, but as those men went
to work, rigging themselves up in climbing equipment and surveying the hole, they kept glancing back over their shoulders. Like the
rest of us, they couldn't turn away.

"They'll stay off the lawn, Mrs. Anderson. I'll make sure of it."

"What about that woman?" I said.

"They'll do what they can to find her."

"She's gone," I said. Men were now lowering themselves down
into the hole.

He didn't even react. "We don't know that. You should go inside
and rest. I'll come get you for a statement in a little while."

"What sort of statement?"

"You were the last person to see her," he said. "You were the first
person to see this." He turned to the hole.

"I don't want to talk about it."

"We'll need your statement to file a report," he said.

"There's nothing to say."

"We just want you to tell us what you saw."

"What I saw is what you see there." I pointed to the assembled
crowd. I stood up and started into the house, and Randy stepped
toward me, or at least I thought he did, and I held my hands out for

him to stop, which confused him. I didn't want to be bothered by him or by anyone for that matter. I went inside and locked my door.

"Mrs. Anderson," he called through the glass. "I didn't mean to scare you, but I'll need to come back later."

I remained quiet. His dark figure came through the curtains, head cocked to the side, listening. Finally, he stepped away and I did too. I went to the sofa and sat down with the lights off. I kept remembering the earth ripping apart and seeing that woman's honey-colored hair, her throat fully exposed to the light.

THE NEXT MORNING, yellow tape surrounded the scene. There were some gawkers, but mostly it was just neighbors who'd walked down the street for coffee. The dog walkers cinched their leashes around their hands when their dogs began to circle the hole, sniffing and prodding with their muzzles, tails pointed toward the sky. Icie's boy was down the street, parking his cruiser and setting up traffic cones.

For most of the night I had stayed by the window, watching as the rescue teams moved in shifts. Three went down and three came back up. Bright floodlights tried to show them a path and lit up the street and the front rooms of the house. From the minute she fell, something inside of me sensed I would never see the woman again, that none of us would, and yet I still wanted very much to walk out there and peer down once more.

When my husband Everett was alive he used to get mad at me about the way my imagination could run. He said I dreamt too much and wasn't practical, but I used to tell him being practical doesn't allow for any joy and what good is a life without joy.

"But you always go dark," he said. "You never think about the good that can come from something."

He may have had a point. I am prone to melancholy, so when

I walked off my porch and into the yard, I tried to imagine that woman landing someplace safe and gentle. I tried to think of where that might be and what came to mind were those gilded images of heaven in the Bible I gave up on long before I was an adult. They're just too perfect and too out of sync with what's actually beautiful on this earth and in this life, so I pictured her falling into a field of blue wildflowers and clover or tall grass near a hillside shaded by oaks and sycamores with a picnic blanket spread beneath their leaves and the sun overhead and a cooling breeze. A blue sky dotted with puffy clouds. Then I had to shake the image from my head because it was too damn foolish given how she had left, given the ugliness and violence of how she was taken.

"Ready for that statement, Mrs. Anderson?"

It was Randy. He's nearly the same age as my son, and I can never think of him as an officer of the law but rather as a boy who is playing dress up. I see him as a child, riding his bike across my lawn and jumping the sidewalk. I keep expecting him to tell me he has a Halloween party to attend, but he is a man now with a wife and child at home.

"How's your mother?" I said.

"She's fine. Says to tell you hello. She saw your house on the news and asked after you. I told her you were feisty as ever."

"Don't go spreading rumors, Randy."

"No rumors, ma'am. Just the truth." He smiled big and wide, and I thought to myself he must be a good son.

"What do you need to know?"

"Just what you saw."

"Who was she?" I said.

"Excuse me?"

"The woman. Do you know who she was?"

"We haven't a clue. No one has reported a missing person. As far as we can tell you're the only witness. Everyone else was inside when the sinkhole opened up."

"Only me."

He nodded.

"She was driving down the street without a care." I stopped. I didn't know how to tell him what I saw. I had convinced myself overnight the young woman looked me in the eye as she fell below the world, that I was the last person she saw before darkness overtook her.

"Mrs. Anderson? Can you go on?"

"She didn't see it coming. She was singing, mouthing along with the words. Then there was the sinkhole opening up and it was over. It was so fast and so loud."

"Anything else? Did you see a license plate? Do you remember the make of the car?"

"The car was light blue. Japanese. That's all I can recall. The things that must have run through her head once it started," I said.

He penned something in his notepad and told me he would type it up and bring it back for me to read over if I wanted. I was about to say no, that I'd said all I needed, but something told me I should tell him I wanted to look at it one more time. Just then the radio on his shoulder crackled.

"Go ahead," Randy said.

A clear voice came back. "We've got another sinkhole."

He turned to me. "I've got to go, Mrs. Anderson. I'll stop by later."

Then he was running toward his cruiser and hopping in. The roof flared blue and the siren rang through the neighborhood trees. I had the urge to get in the car and follow, but I didn't want to be in the way. When I turned the news on an hour later, there was Randy in front of Mills Hardware, saying nobody was hurt and answering questions. The phone rang and I checked the caller ID.

"Hi, Sam."

"Mom, are you okay?" His voice was urgent.

"I'm fine. How are you?"

"I saw the news. Right in front of the house?"

"It's nothing to worry about, though another one just opened up across from the hardware store."

"Is there any damage to the house? Where were you when it happened?"

"I hope Mills is okay," I said. "He's getting so old I can't imagine how he keeps a store these days." I walked to the front of the house. I couldn't stop looking at the spot.

"But what about you? Should I come home?"

"You should always come visit your mother. You and your sister both should come home more often, but you don't need to come home on account of this. It's just strangeness. Untelling what's caused it."

"Fracking," Sam said. "All that damn fracking. Those fuckers just keep tunneling through the earth like a bunch of overgrown ants. They'll suck the earth dry until we're all on fire."

"You don't know that. And stop cursing."

"We don't *not* know it. Remember the earthquake last year? And those others up in Ohio? That's all because of fracking."

"Well, son, you're not the one that has to live with it, are you?"

The line went silent. I shouldn't say such things to him because I know he is concerned—and probably right—but I'm the one that lives here. Not him. He left when he went off to college, and he's never come back and he's not going to. Before he could say anything more I saved both of us and said, "I'll be fine. Have you talked to Heather?"

He gave me a reluctant sigh but answered. "I talked to her yesterday. She seemed to be doing good."

"And when are you two going to come home?"

"We think at the end of summer."

"Well, I'll be here. I'm not going anywhere. At least I don't plan on it." It was hard for me to say more, to tell him I miss them, and that the days get lonelier with each year. They are in the middle of their lives and I remember what that was like for Everett and me, but our only aim was to have them, to raise them right—to be true and good people. They want more than that, it seems, and we encouraged them to leave, to experience a world past Fordyce. They listened to us and they have gone. My loneliness, in this way, is my own doing.

"I'll call again tomorrow," Sam said.

THE NEWSWOMAN FROM Lexington, thankfully, wasn't some young child fresh out of college. She appeared to be in her early forties, though her hair was stiff enough it could have stopped a brick. When she came to my door, I politely declined, though she tried to insist I was "integral to the story." I told her if she wanted to do some good, she should find out who that woman was and locate her people. That's what was most important. She left the porch with a short cameraman trailing behind her, and they set up camp on the sidewalk.

I went up to the second floor and watched her from behind a parted curtain. Nobody was lining up to talk to her, but nobody walked away when she approached either. Past her, the firemen were still at it, still going down in threes, but their attitude was a lot different than on that first day. They laughed aboveground and sipped on coffee. They might as well have been standing around a fire in someone's backyard. No one cared about that girl anymore. No one, it seemed, except me.

That night, after I watched our little town on the news, I went outside. They had already given up night searches. Police barricades and heavy equipment surrounded the hole, but nobody was there. I squeezed past a barricade and ducked under some police tape. The neighborhood slept, and I shined a flashlight into the opening. I saw what I expected, but then I sat down and let my legs dangle above the dirt. The asphalt still held the day's heat, and I ran my hands along the road's broken edge and felt the soft crumbling of it at my fingertips. The sky was full of stars, and I turned off the flashlight so that I was in the dark. I pictured that poor woman once more. Where was she headed? Who was expecting her? What kind of life had been taken? The crickets' whine was high in the air. I have more days behind me than in front of me, which is something I've thought about more and more in the last five years since Everett's passing, but I don't know how to make them last or count. And that girl was gone before life even began for her. Without thinking much, I found my foot searching for a place to step, my body lowering itself into that hole. There was a makeshift ladder constructed for the rescue workers that was only four rungs tall, like one you find in a swimming pool, but it was on the opposite side of me. The flashlight I had was small enough to be held in my mouth, so I turned it back on and placed it there and then bent my neck downward to see where my feet might land if I pushed off with my arms. There seemed to be a ledge of dirt that would hold me, so I took a careful step forward and felt its solidness. Then another.

My eyes were level with the road, and below me it was as if a path opened up into nothing. Nothingness, I corrected myself. I wanted to sit down in that space and let the earth cover me, but why I wanted to escaped me. I didn't want to die; I wasn't ready to leave this life, but maybe I wanted to know what it might feel like to be below rather than above. I made a motion to sit with a slight shuffle step to my left and slid, the dirt giving way underneath me, and I let out a scream that made the flashlight fall from my mouth and tumble quickly toward the darkness. I flailed my arms toward the edge and grabbed the jagged asphalt and managed to keep myself from falling. I kicked like a cartoon character trying to find a foothold until finally my toe struck something solid. I was sure I was going to fall, and confronted with the danger, my heart beat faster, my fear churned, and I pressed my body as close to the edge as I could. Soft dirt touched my cheek, and then, despite myself, I felt wet tears at the edges of my clenched eyes. I opened them wide to see only the night, and then, inch by inch, I made my way to the ladder where I pulled myself up to the road and then lay flat on my back, collecting my breath but unable to stop the tears.

THREE WEEKS LATER the sinkhole was filled. They did bring in geologists from the university and some structural engineers to study the hole, but they said there was too much earth to move and too much to risk by peeling the road back to search any longer. So they showed up one day and dumped load after load of concrete and sand into the pit, and then they poured new asphalt and tamped it down with a road roller. I watched all this over the course of four days, and when they were done a black flat rectangle covered the street, and somewhere underneath it all she was still there. I thought of her beating against the roof of her car and somehow making her way out, crawling through all that sediment and dirt only to find one more layer of darkness she could not claw through. It kept me up, and I found myself going out there nearly every night, standing right in the middle of the newly repaved surface—beside where I had lain.

Cars rolled right over top of it, and with each one I waited, expecting the earth to open up again, but it never did. I thought of the one time Everett and I went to New York. We had been planning that trip for months, and two days before we left I took ill with a terrible cold and fever. We shouldn't have gone, and as we walked up and down Fifth Avenue I shook with chills. Every step of the way Everett said we could go back to the hotel room, but I wanted to keep going, to keep looking in those big store windows at clothes that were more expensive than our mortgage. I wanted everything. At Bergdorf Goodman there was a scarf in the window that stopped me in the middle of the sidewalk. A marvelous golden cashmere with specks of marled blue and fringed ends. Everett didn't even have to ask what I was looking at. "Let's see how much it is."

"We can't afford it," I said.

"We can if you want it."

"It's not practical," I said, using his own argument against him.

"You can't always be practical. You've got to enjoy yourself." He winked and tugged at me, but I didn't budge. I don't know if I had ever wanted anything more, and yet I couldn't take one step toward the store.

He walked in without me. And though I put on a show of being angry and upset, of talking about the expense, when we got to our room that night I pulled it from its box and tissue paper, and the first thing I did was brush the soft fabric across my cheek.

We went out that night and I put the scarf on, and I loved it so much I didn't want to take it off when we sat down to dinner. For a few hours my fever and chills left me, and on our way back to our hotel, every time we passed a window or mirror, I stopped to notice the scarf, not believing it was mine. I clutched at the fabric as if it might fly away. On the sidewalk those metal grates from the subway whooshed hot air past my knees. I hated walking over top of them, fearful they might give away.

"Let me on the solid ground," I told Everett, and he traded places with me, smiling like I was a silly child.

At Mills Hardware I walked up to the resurfaced road, noticing its blackness already fading.

"Hell of a big hole," Amos Mills said, coming out from the store.

"I've seen bigger," I said.

"Yes you have," he said. "I still can't understand how a car disappeared. I can't believe nobody has come to search for that woman."

"Maybe she got turned around and was lost. Just passing through town on her way to someplace else."

"Must have been. I feel for her family. They're going to come calling one day. They'll figure it out and they'll show up and you'll see them, Alice. They'll be standing right outside your house looking at a discolored patch of road, and maybe everybody else will believe them to be crazy but you'll know who they are and why they are there."

"I never thought of that," I said, "but you're right."

"I don't envy you that one." Then, changing the subject, "How are the kids?"

"They're fine. Planning to visit soon."

"You don't think they'll ever grow up when they're babies and you're up all night after them, but then they leave and you don't know if they'll ever come back, do you?"

"That sounds about right," I said. "And yours?"

"They're fine. They'll come back for Labor Day. You think it's finished?" he said, pointing to the hole.

"What do you mean?"

"Are they done opening up?"

"My son doesn't think so," I said.

"I hope he's wrong."

"Me too," I said.

Later that night, I called Sam and Heather. I needed to hear their voices even if it was for just five minutes. They told me they would come at the end of the summer to visit. They promised. They asked how I had been, and Sam, trying to take on Everett's role, asked how the house was, if it needed anything. In some ways, it's quite sweet how they try to take on our old roles and in others I can't stand it, but I was lonely and I needed my family. Heather told us about a new patient, a child actor she said we would know if she could tell us her name, who had been coming to her for a month for counseling. We listened to the more interesting details and tried to guess at who it was, but she wouldn't give a name. Then, feigning sleepiness, I told the children I had to go. Hearing their voices had made me lonelier, and when I got off the phone, I thought I would just go right up to bed. I began flipping off lamps and light switches when the moon came out from behind a cloud and its white light fell on the road, on the patch. I opened the door.

The wind was in the leaves and I smelled rain coming, but the light was on the road. I walked behind the house to the shed and pulled out an old pickaxe of Everett's and carried it out to the road. The wood on the handle was worn smooth. I took a mighty swing and jabbed into the patched surface. The axe bounced right back, not even nicking the asphalt and nearly toppling me, but I steadied myself and I took another swing. Then another. I tried to hit the same mark to soften the spot. The wind blew hard and the moonlight left and I struck the road again and again, trying to keep up a rhythm, but I couldn't. Breathless, I dropped the axe and sat down on the curb. Blisters had already formed on my hands, and I rubbed them. The asphalt had what looked like only a scratch on its surface. I was never going to break it.

THE END OF summer arrived and with it Sam and Heather. I spent a week getting the house all straight for them and going to the grocery for their favorite foods. It took my mind off the awful events of the spring, the image of that poor woman. The two of them home were something like a storm, and the house, for a few days, was alive like it used to be with their energy and talk, meals around the dining room table, and the steady hum of a television or stereo in the background. Heather and I cleaned out the attic, and Sam took care of my landscaping, asking how the pickaxe had become so bent and nicked, and when we went to church everyone told them how happy I must be to have them home.

I was happy to see them. We sat down in a pew in the balcony, and I took note of the cracks in the eggshell-colored plaster. It is a good old church, comforting, and I felt safe between my children, the first time I had ever had such a feeling—that of the protected rather than the protector. The preacher gave his sermon about how Jesus said He would never leave us, that He would never desert us, and I thought about how Everett and I shouldn't have waited so long to have them because the truth of life is I *will* desert them. Everett already has. Life is an odd miracle to me. It is so simple and true—the movement of breath into a body and its exhalation—and then, like those breaths, it is fleeting, but with such hard parting.

I'd been looking out the window every day for a couple that might have resembled Everett and me to show up and stare at the road, but no one came. It was as if that woman, that girl, had no people. The preacher read from the book of John, quoting Jesus, and I took up Sam's and Heather's hands and gave each one a good squeeze, which they returned. They were leaving in the morning, and I would count down the days until their next visit. I thought I might cry if I focused on it too much, so I picked up a hymnal and thumbed through its pages.

After lunch, I went up to the office and turned on the computer, and I started looking up sinkholes on the internet. There was our town. There was the news article from the paper and one on CNN.

An "unknown motorist" each one labeled the woman. She couldn't have always been unknown I thought. Not someone who screamed for the life inside her all the way to the end.

The children were in their rooms, readying suitcases for an early morning drive to the airport. They refused to let me follow behind in the car and watch them off, and it was as if I had already begun to allow the knot of loss and leaving to form below my sternum. I wanted them both to stay, and yet I knew I could never ask them such a thing—a life here is not what we ever wished for them. Just then Heather's voice called to me and I rose.

She was standing in the hall, holding my golden scarf.

"Mom, this is gorgeous."

"Your father bought it for me when we went to New York."

"Why didn't you ever wear it?"

"I did there. It never seemed to fit in here, and I could never find the right occasion for it."

"It's lovely," she said, thumbing the fabric.

"What is it?" Sam said.

"A scarf," she said, holding it out to him. "She's never worn it."

"I did once," I interrupted.

"You've kept it in the attic all these years?" Sam said.

I nodded. "Take it," I said to Heather. "Your dad would be happy you have it, and I will be too."

"I can't," she said.

"You're going to get it one day," I said. "You're both are going to get everything that's left, so you might as well take it now while I can see you enjoy it."

"Mom, that's so morbid." She turned to her brother who turned back to me, but I only shrugged my shoulders.

"But it's true. Take it. I want you to. Here." I took the garment in my hands and placed it around her neck and knotted it for her. "You look beautiful. Doesn't she?" Sam nodded. I stood behind her and faced her toward the mirror, and then there was Sam looking too. The three of us alone in the hallway. Heather turned and kissed my cheek, and the fabric brushed my neck.

"Mom?" Sam said. "Do you know those people?"

Through the transom window above the front door we saw a man and woman standing in the road.

"They've been out there for fifteen minutes," he said. They haven't said a word to each other."

I put my hand up to my heart. There was a genuine ache and pain, and I stood between Sam and Heather and I knew.

"I'll be right back," I said.

"Who is it?" Heather said.

"The parents," I said. "They've come to see her." I noticed a bouquet of wilting flowers in the man's hand. They had on church clothes.

"You want us to go out there with you?" Sam asked.

"No, you two just get your things together. I'll be back in a minute." I opened the door and the rush of a breeze entered. The couple lifted their heads, and I walked down the steps to the sidewalk. The man put his arm over the woman's shoulder and she clasped it.

I was aware of Sam and Heather standing in the doorway, so I turned to them and waved for them to close the door, and they obliged. Then I stepped off the sidewalk and called to the couple.

SILER, KENTUCKY, 1970

N O ONE WAS surprised when news spread that Cheeks Mahan killed Riley Lawson. After all, people knew the story. Riley had married the Mahan girl, Della, when she was nineteen and almost immediately began pounding on her. When she came home to visit her family for Sunday dinners after church, she wore the bruises of her young love under her eyes and on the slim part of her wrists. When she was a girl, no one had ever seen a child with such life in her, never understood where she got that energy and bounce to her walk, the shine in her hair. When they looked at her parents—Cheeks who was an old man before he turned forty, his back gimped up from working in the mines in his twenties, his hearing gone from running dozers in his thirties, and her mother, Marlene, with a frame as fragile as a bird's but a mouth that cut wounds deeper than the valley they lived in—it was hard for anyone to see much hope or happiness that might lie in between the walls of their home.

But legend and rumor can only explain so much, and what happened, of course, changed them all, and maybe none more than the boy, Duke, who handed his father the 12-gauge shotgun that pumped the slugs in Riley's body and who still, sometimes in the night, hears the shot.

The marks of Della's beatings had bothered them all, but not as much as they did Cheeks. He had always believed the girl's spirit was like a thing of defiance that could burn like a strong fire even after a bucket of water has been poured over the flames' tips. It was what, he thought, gave her her beauty. And though Marlene saw it too, she had envied and resented it, and in some small place inside her had been happy when Della decided on that son of a bitch Riley Lawson three years before.

All that changed when Della finally moved home, leaving Riley for good they thought, near the end of June, just when the wet heat of summer was really starting to build in the valleys and hang in the treetops of the mountains. But every week on Friday, after Riley had been paid and run out to his cousin Pete's place, the bootlegger, for a half case, he came calling on Della, and she would meet him halfway, talking in the yard.

Cheeks had warned Riley not to come around and told Della she needed to leave him be, but neither listened, and on one muggy night, with the last remnants of firecrackers and Roman candles shooting off somewhere in the distance, Riley drove into their yard, the tires of his beat-up Dart skidding brown streaks into the grass. This was not the night Cheeks took the boy's life, but they all thought it would be, and when Della got up from the couch and ran to the door, Cheeks pushed her aside and told her to stay still. Riley cut the headlights off and stomped his boots into the earth, hollering her name, asking her to come outside.

She watched from the window, and Duke stood behind her, looking over her shoulder at the dark figure in the yard. Riley's steps were unsure, and Duke watched his father turn the doorknob and step out onto the porch with his shotgun down by his side. "Don't move," he said to them both as he crossed the doorway.

The heat entered through the open door and hit their faces like a wet towel. Riley stopped his shouting when he saw Cheeks. He took on a calm look and narrowed his eyes toward the shotgun. He called out for him to shoot. "I don't want to live without her. Shoot me, old man. Right here," he said, pointing at his heart. "Blow me away."

At that, both men stepped forward, Cheeks from out of the doorway, the lights of the living room glowing behind him, and Riley stumbling, tripping on a rock and falling to his knees.

Cheeks put the shotgun back down to his side then, and Riley lowered his head, letting his chin bob against his sternum.

"I love her," he said. "I don't want to die."

Della broke for the porch. She stood in the damp night, locked in place, her eyes shifting back and forth to the two men she loved more than any others in the world.

"Go on," Cheeks said. "Put him in his car and get back in the house."

She ran into the yard where Riley was kneeling and pulled him up, supporting nearly every ounce of his body on her shoulders, and dragged him to the car.

"Baby," he said to her when he was sitting upright. His blue eyes were swimming in the moonlight, and his black bangs were stamped to his forehead with sweat. "Come home," he said. "Come back to me." Even with the alcohol in him, he meant it. He knew there was no other woman he wanted in his life.

Della wanted him then too. She wanted to frame his face with her hands the way she had on their wedding night when they'd driven down to Eagle Falls and sat on the rocks watching the water crash, the mist swirling in her hair. She could feel her back lean forward, the muscles in her jaw tense as she readied to kiss him when Duke came from behind her and said, "Daddy says to get back inside. Let him sleep it off."

The moment was lost. She pulled back and followed her little brother into the house.

"You ought to know better," Cheeks said when they came inside. Marlene was sitting at the kitchen table, drinking coffee.

"Please, Daddy. Not now," Della said.

"After all you've been through with him," he said. "You'd think—" but he didn't finish the sentence. He put his hands on his hips and looked down at her, the scruff of his beard shadowy on his face.

"You can't go back to him, Della," their mother said, breaking the silence in the room.

These warnings didn't matter. Three days after Cheeks raised his rifle at Riley for the first time Della snuck off in the middle of the day to see him. Duke was in the mountains, scouting deer for the fall, and saw the blue Mustang—a present from Riley to Della on the night he proposed—cutting swatches through the thicket of trees.

He was halfway up the hillside and knew there was nowhere else for Della to go that day. He watched the car hug the curved yellow lines in the road and listened to the deep grumble of the 351 engine rise through the air. He pictured Della behind the wheel, her hair flying all around her face, the dark brown of it contrasted against the white upholstery.

Duke thought he was starting to understand what it meant to be a man and felt as if he was coming into his own manhood more and more with his new growth-spurted and filled-out frame. And because of this, though she was ten years older than him, Duke saw how easy it was for a man to love his sister and her beauty, to want to follow her. He'd been too young when Della first met Riley Lawson to remember much, just eight, but he'd always been wary of him. Everyone knew the stories about the Lawsons. There was Butch, the oldest, who'd been kicked out of the navy (after earning two Purple Hearts) when he'd hit his commanding officer and hung him over the edge of the ship by his ankles, screaming at him until a half-dozen seamen grabbed hold of both men. Loyal, the middle boy, stole hubcaps and sold dope over in Fordyce, and once when he'd been at the Trademart Shopping Center, two boys came out and jumped him with a baseball bat, only to have Loyal somehow take the bat away from them and beat them both black and blue, busting their car windows and then slitting their tires.

By those standards, perhaps, Riley Lawson wasn't as tough as his brothers, nobody could say for sure. The legend of their stories had outgrown the substance of each man long before Della had met and married Riley. She had ignored those stories, passed them off as mere gossip, and fell in love. The night Riley proposed to Della he'd won the Mustang in a poker game over in Rockholds. Right after he picked the keys off the table, the story went, the man he'd won it from had come at Riley, chips flying off the table in a rain shower of red, blue, and white plastic discs.

Some said the man should've known better. Riley wasn't just thick-chested. He was quick; his fists could fly like hummingbird wings. He beat the man's face in until it looked like somebody took a mallet to a steak. The whole left side of the man's body seemed to drag the ground, and when Riley was done, they said, he pulled a pistol from under his denim coat, held it over top of the man, and pressed it into his broken and crooked nose, bending it straight.

"You're lucky I didn't use this," he said and spat.

But Della didn't know this. She'd only known half the truth; that he'd won it at a card game. She was too sick with love and happiness, with that incredible energy of hers packed with good- will to believe such things really happened—even in this sort of rough country and life. She accepted the car with glee and drove Riley and herself all the way over to Middlesboro that night, wind- ing through the mountains so fast on some of the turns that Riley thought for sure they'd head right into the bank, and they found a spot near the Cumberland Gap, inside the national park, and made love under the stars with the lights of the car cut off but the radio playing Joplin, the Dead, and then the Lovin' Spoonful over their naked bodies.

Della couldn't see a time when her love for Riley would fade. And after they were married, she never thought for a moment that her love would not calm him on those nights he came home from playing cards or running through the hills with his friends and he'd get that angry, sick look in his eyes like a lost dog that's been attacked. Nobody knew it, but Della believed in her own spirit as much as everyone who saw it. She felt she could will herself through the worst moments with an intensity of focus that had been the trait of her people, that was carried in both her mother and father and passed on to Duke as well. She was singular in her ability to love Riley through to the end.

As Duke saw the Mustang blow through the turns, the old fear he carried as a younger boy brewed in his belly. He felt the acids there churn his throat raw. He wondered if this might be the time when Riley, the man whose family history had been littered with rumors, would reveal himself in some awful way and finally break his sister's spirit.

THE ENTIRE FAMILY carried the same fear as Duke, and when she returned home that night, it was as if each of them felt a chip of themselves had been taken through the countryside to Riley's during the day. They sat at the dinner table, and Marlene leered at her daughter with a look so disgusted and filled with loathing that Duke looked down at the floor and Cheeks finally said, "She's a grown woman, Marlene. She can do what she likes."

Marlene slammed down a bowl of mashed potatoes on the table.

Cheeks held up his hand before she could speak and said, "There's nothing left to say."

More than the others, Marlene took Della's running off as an act of personal rejection. It was a commentary and a punishment, she felt, for all the terrible thoughts she had of her daughter over the years. She'd always known the girl was ageless. Her skin was smooth like soapstone and she wouldn't begin to wrinkle until well into her fifties. But the envy she'd always carried for Della had relented the first time the girl came home with bruises under her eyes and a cut in her lip. She'd undressed her that night, just like when she was a baby, pulling back the covers on the bed in Della's old room and helping her in. She wet a rag and brought cotton balls dipped in alcohol and cleaned Della's face and iced her bruises. And when she came home the last time, her eye swollen shut, red patches of Riley's skin under her nails, Marlene stayed by her daughter until the sun cracked through the curtains, and she realized she had fallen asleep in the slat-back chair with her head resting on Della's stomach, the slow movements of the girl's breathing having lulled her.

It wasn't just that Della had gone back to Riley, sneaking off while Marlene was at the clothesline and her father was at work. It was more than that. It was the color in her cheeks, full and bright with the rouge of love as anytime she, Cheeks, or Duke could ever remember. The prance of a young girl in love washed over Della, lifting her spirit back to its rightful place. Marlene thought, whether Della knew it or not, she was going to fall harder than she ever had before. It was just a matter of time.

Della made three more trips to Riley's, and though she knew her family knew, she never admitted to it. She let the truth go unsaid and came into the house doing her best to hold back her smile when she thought of the way Riley smelled pressed next to her. The feel of her skin next to his, the sweat they created forming a bond of recognition and familiarity she craved and missed and that she acknowledged in soft, clenched cries of pleasure at his touch.

Before leaving on her fourth trip, though, she announced her intentions to her family, making them aware she and Riley were getting back together and that she was moving back in with him the following week.

Marlene left the room at this, slamming her bedroom door. The noise had such loudness and finality it shook Della and Cheeks. Cheeks, always given to wishing the best for his daughter, never sure how to approach her about much other than to tell her she was a good girl, shrugged his shoulders and stayed quiet.

"I guess you've made up your mind," he said at last.

"I have," she said. "I love him."

"And what about before?"

"He's changed."

"That's what he's told you, but has he? Can you see the change in him?"

Duke watched Della move forward and grab their father's thick arm and pull near him, resting her head against his shoulder. "He's changed, Daddy. He won't treat me that way again."

AT BUFFALO CREEK, where their house was, Riley had been drinking since two in the afternoon. He'd taken his rod and reel down to the pond and intended only to drink a couple while he fished. But the sun seemed to penetrate his skin after the first beer, mixing with the alcohol to give him a tingle. It was a feeling more pleasant than he had expected, and when he finished the four cans he had brought, he went back to the house for more. He was celebrating, he told himself. Della was coming to see him tonight, and then next week she'd move back in for good. He'd won her over again, and this pleased him more than the smell of her perfume that lingered on his fingers for the last two weeks long after she had left. Ever since that night when Cheeks had raised his shotgun at him, he'd known that there was nothing he wanted more than her, nothing he wouldn't do from now on to get her back. He'd been wrong to hit her those times, but it was the drink that made him unsure of his own thoughts, much less his actions. When Della left him, he began to change, to see what he needed to do to be with her and become a new man.

By six that night he was in a daze. He sat in front of the television watching the game of the week—Braves vs. Cubs. The picture and sound kept fading in and out and he knew he needed to get on the roof to turn the antenna, but he was too drunk to climb a ladder. So he sat there with the static-covered images of the television and drank his beer, waiting on Della to arrive.

On the other end of the countryside, Duke was outside in the car, sitting behind the wheel and tuning the radio when Della came out on the porch ready to leave. She was running late after Marlene refused to come out to fix dinner, so Della had put on a pot of soup beans and baked some cornbread. Duke smelled the beans simmering in the house, mixing with the milkweed at the edge of the front yard by the gravel road. Della wore a pale yellow dress with a blue floral print, and her hair was pulled up in a ponytail, the wisps of her auburn strands brushing her neck.

Duke grabbed the steering wheel and imagined he was driving. He leaned his body into turns but did not make shifting noises with his mouth the way he did when he was a smaller boy. He thought of Steve McQueen in *Bullitt*, and pictured himself driving the Mustang down 92, racing on the straightaways. He wanted to know what the wind in his hair felt like at eighty miles an hour.

"Going somewhere, little man?" Della said to him. Her little brother was the true mixture of their parents, she thought. He had the crook in his nose of their father and the soft, round cheeks of their mother.

"Just imagining," he said without looking at her.

"Imagining? Not playing, but imagining?"

"That's what I said."

"No need to get rude with me. I'm just asking," she said, bending down to the window and crossing her arms on the sill. "You want to drive me over to Riley's?"

Duke looked at her. Della smiled at him, her face clean and fresh, too pretty for such a rough man.

"Well?" she said. "I'll let you."

"I'm not old enough. Besides, Daddy wouldn't let me no how."

"He doesn't have to know everything."

He knew she was serious now. The sun came out of a cloud cover and shined down on the hood of the car and the blue paint sparkled, forcing him to squint his eyes.

"I'm only going for a little bit," she said. "Let your big sister teach you something. It's not that far, and if you get bored we'll just come on back home."

Duke sat still, looking at her, grinding his fingers around the steering wheel.

"Okay," he said.

"All right," she said and stood up, tapping the roof with her fist. "Let me back it out of here and get us on the road, and then once we're out of range from the house, we'll trade spots. Run in and tell Daddy you're going with me."

Duke ran inside. Della had never seen her brother move that fast, and she laughed at him as he ran so hard he tripped on the first step and caught himself before he fell flat. She put the car in reverse, holding it with the brake and waiting for him to come back out. The boy practically jumped into the seat and slammed the door. Della laughed and then began backing down the driveway. She hung her arm and head out the window to see where she was headed. Beside her Duke took notice of how she did this and of where her hand was on the steering wheel and of what the gauges all read. He'd never paid such close attention to the way a person drove a car, and when Della had the car straightened out, she put it in park and they traded places.

He sat down before she did and felt the way he had when he saw his first deer last fall and raised his rifle toward it, bringing its heart into the sight of his barrels.

"Now," Della said. "Just put it in drive there, but don't give it any gas. Let the car move forward on its own."

Duke felt the car lurch forward, the tires digging into the gravel. Every so often Della steadied the wheel for him, but he got the feel for it right away and gunned the gas just to feel the tires spin in the loose rock. Della screamed when he did this and then broke out into a laugh and slapped her brother on the arm, and Duke smiled for the first time since they got in the car.

She stayed close to him as he drove to Riley's, but Duke had a knack for knowing when to brake and how much pressure to apply on the curves. Her little brother wasn't so little anymore, and she watched with delight the way he was holding onto the steering wheel with white knuckles and his tongue slipping out of the corner of his mouth. She promised Riley she'd only come over for a bit. She told him her parents had not taken the news well, and having Duke along would give her the excuse she needed to leave early and come back home to try and make it right with them.

Riley heard the car in the driveway and got up from the couch, taking the last long pull on his beer and throwing the can in the trash. He grabbed another from the fridge and went outside to meet Della.

"What do we got here?" he said when he saw Duke step out from the driver's side.

"I let him drive all the way over," she said. "He did a good job. He's a natural."

Riley popped open the beer and took a drink. "That's an awfully nice car to let him learn on, ain't it?"

"It's fine, Riley. I was just letting him have some fun."

He ignored her. "You like driving that car, boy? You feel like a big man now?"

Duke stopped walking, felt the sun starting to dip behind the mountains and knew that dew was going to settle soon.

"Answer me, boy."

"Riley, my God. What's your problem? Leave him alone."

"Stay out of it," he said to her and took another drink.

"You know how I got that car, boy?"

"Jesus Christ, Riley. You're drunk and you're acting like an ass. We're leaving."

"The way I'm acting," he said. "I'm not the one letting some little shit ride around the countryside in a goddamn Mustang. My goddamn Mustang at that."

"Your Mustang? I thought you gave it to me."

Riley walked toward Duke, the rage building in him from some place, he didn't know how or why, that had something to do only with him being a Lawson and this was who he was. Duke stood still and tried to get a bead on Riley's eyes and what they were saying. He remembered the deer from the fall and how he'd let his sights wander from its heart to its face. It stood in the clearing nearly a hundred yards away from him, but Duke swore he saw the gloss of those big black eyes like onyx and that was what made him pull his shotgun down.

"I asked you a question, boy. You know how I got that car?"

"Riley," Della said coming behind him, pulling at his arm. She'd seen this look before. "Of course he knows. I told him you won it in a card game."

Duke looked at his sister, and though he didn't know it, his eyes betrayed her. Riley saw this and pressed further.

"What about it, little Duke? You don't believe I won it playing cards, do you?"

Duke looked at Della then Riley. "I've heard stories."

"Like what?" Riley said. He drank the last of his beer, finishing it by Duke's count in three long pulls.

"What've you heard, Duke? Tell your brother Riley what it is you've heard." Riley crushed the can and threw it at Duke's feet.

"That's enough, Riley. Let him alone." Della grabbed Riley by the shoulder and tried to turn his body toward her, but he shrugged her off and pushed her to the ground.

"Don't lay your hands on me again, woman." He raised his hand to her and Della cringed.

"Duke, are you a storyteller? Tell me your story. Tell me what you heard."

Duke looked inside the car where the keys dangled from the ignition.

"You think you're going somewhere, Duke? You've got a story to tell me," Riley said.

Della came in between them. "Get in the car, Duke," she said.

Duke made a move for the door, but Riley reached around Della and grabbed him by his hair.

"Not until he tells me a story," he said and jerked the boy

backwards. Duke fell to his knees in front of Riley and looked up at him and saw his blue eyes brimming with cold and frost. Della beat at Riley's chest.

"Let him go," she cried. "You're hurting him. Let him go. Goddamn you, Riley Lawson."

Duke screamed and tried to raise his body, but Riley gripped his hair tighter and powered him down to the ground.

Duke's face was pressed to the earth, and all he could see were the tops of Riley's worn-out black boots, the laces undone and frayed. Then he felt Riley lean down near him, Della beating at his back, but he kept ignoring her.

"What story did you hear, Duke? What was it? Was it the one where I beat a man within an inch of his life? Was it the one where I pulled my pistol out and straightened that crooked nose of his? Which one was it, little boy?"

Duke smelled the beer on his breath in hot waves. Turning, he saw the stubble on Riley's face and his yellow teeth.

"I don't know anything," Duke said and tried to look at Della.

Then Della reached around Riley and dug her nails into his neck and ripped them up along his cheek, and Duke felt the grip on his hair release in an instant. His nose fell into the grass and he pushed himself up.

"Get in the car, Duke," Della said, backing away from Riley.

Riley was touching his face and looking at the dabs of blood on his fingers, and he walked in a slow and assured stride toward Della.

"Start the car," she said.

"Goddamn you, Della," Riley said and lunged at her, but she ducked away from him and scratched his face again and ran for the car. She made it to the door as Duke turned the engine and got in.

"Go," she said. "Go."

Riley was doubled over and wobbly from the beer. He looked at the two of them and tried to get his wind, but the beer was too deep in his system. He had to squint in order to see, and it was getting dark now. Lightning bugs floated in front of him, and tree frog croaks filled his ears.

Riley fell to his own knees now, vomiting as they backed down the driveway. Della reached over and pulled the lights on for Duke, and they saw Riley stand in the yard and head toward his own car.

"Hurry, Duke," she said. "Get us home."

Duke pushed the accelerator to the floor and felt the car respond with the urgency he had inside himself. He took the curves wide, wavering over into the other lane before centering the car while Della kept screaming for him to be careful.

He pulled off 92 and onto the gravel road that led to their house. He fishtailed past the other small homes, their windows now boxes of light. The Mustang roared into the driveway, and Della reached across him again and laid on the horn in one long continuous motion until Cheeks came on the porch.

"Daddy," she said, running from the car when she saw him. "Riley's coming after us. He'll be here any minute now."

Cheeks ran down from the porch in his socks. "Marlene," he yelled. He met Della in the yard, but she was hysterical and he couldn't understand what she was saying. All he could make out was something about Duke and how angry Riley looked, how she'd never seen him that way. He passed her off to Marlene and put all his attention to Duke then.

"Where is he?" he asked, looking Duke in the face.

They were in the house now, and Duke watched Marlene sit with Della on the couch and saw Della bury her head in between their mother's shoulder and neck, her own small shoulders bouncing up and down. He was looking so closely at Della that he didn't hear his father.

"What happened?" Cheeks said. He was frantic and scared. Duke wasn't looking at him, and he slapped the boy across the face without heat but quickly. "Damn it, son, I asked you a question."

But Duke couldn't see anything that resembled love or feeling in his father's eyes. All he saw was the same flame of fury he'd seen in Riley Lawson, and he moved away from his father, unsure of what to do, whether or not he should run for the door, all the while looking back to Della.

That's when he felt his father's hands on his shoulders. "Get my rifle," he said and shook Duke by the arms. "Hurry."

Cheeks put his shoes on, though he knew it wasn't going to go that far, that he'd never step outside.

"Daddy," he heard Della say.

"Quiet," he said to her sharply. "I hear his car coming down the road."

Duke brought the shotgun in and Cheeks checked the chamber.

The night was on them now. A crescent moon seemed to be held up in the sky by the cedar trees on the mountains in front of them. Two streams of light from Riley's car ran across the yard, and he stood in their wake.

"Where is she, Cheeks?"

"She's safe from you," he said.

"We've done this before, old man. You can't keep her from me. She loves me and I love her."

Cheeks stayed quiet, watching Riley's slow steps to the house.

"She'll just keep coming back to me," Riley said.

"Until you kill her," Cheeks said and pumped the shotgun. The sweat in his palms started to build.

"I love her, old man. I ain't going to kill the woman I love."

"You don't know what it is you love."

"How would you know, old man?"

"I know your kind."

"You ain't seen half the Lawson in me. You're lucky for that."

"Maybe so," Cheeks said.

Duke watched all this from behind his father. He saw Riley's big chest heaving up and down with his breaths, each one he thought might be the next to rip the black tee shirt he had on right down the middle. He took a step forward, and like before, his father warned Riley. For a moment, Duke thought it would be the same. He thought Riley would cuss his father and crawl back in his car, and then his mother would take Della to the bedroom and stay by her again through the night. Only this time, he thought, maybe Della wouldn't go back to Riley, that this would be the time when she learned he would never change. And these thoughts calmed Duke. They made him feel safe and secure, and the things he had feared in the last hour fled his body and he could almost see himself making plans for tomorrow, for the new spots in the forest where he might be able to put a deer blind.

But then his father said, "This ends tonight." And it happened.

Riley Lawson ran toward the porch in long, pounding strides. Cheeks Mahan backed up into the living room of his home, and when Riley Lawson hit the last step and was no more than four feet from crossing the threshold of their home, Cheeks Mahan pulled the trigger and Duke, Marlene, and Della saw a spark fly out from the barrels and a cloud of smoke and the gaping mouth of Riley Lawson when the slugs tore through his shirt and chest and ran out through his spine. Blood splattered on the walls and his big body fell forward to the floor and, for a second or two, he seemed to crawl like a worm, but they didn't know toward what. Some would say later it was toward the woman he loved until he died, and others said it was toward the life he didn't want to lose.

THIS MUCH IS true. Cheeks Mahan shot Riley Lawson and watched him die in the same living room where his children, Della and Duke, learned to walk. When the sheriff and coroner came out to claim the body, they did not ask any questions of Cheeks other than what they could already see. "Did he try to get in your home?" Cheeks nodded yes, and the sheriff told him he had a right to protect his own. He did not go to jail. He did not get questioned. He did worry that once word got out there would be retribution, but if Butch or Loyal or any other Lawson wanted to honor the memory of their kin, then so be it. He would be ready.

In time, Della moved to Williamsburg where she got a job as a secretary for the county school system and married a boy named Hamlin from Goldbug. Marlene was a more agreeable grandmother than she ever was a mother and found in babysitting her grandbabies all the joy of parenting she'd never felt with her own children. The day Duke Mahan turned sixteen Della drove up to the house with her husband and handed him the keys to the bright blue Mustang he'd driven just four years before. She'd kept it up all this time just to give to her baby brother, and the engine still hummed like it was new.

Duke took the keys from her and thumbed them in his hand. He could still see red blood spreading out from under Riley Lawson's body, pooling at his elbows, and the look in his father's eyes when he stood over the dead body, calm and matter-of-fact. He remembered the sheriff's hand on his father's shoulder, not comforting him, but approving him. There were Della's cries that night. Nothing but whimpers and the small fight of her and Marlene as their mother tried to keep her from looking at the body and blood that was left behind. But what he remembered most was the car moving under him, his shoulder slamming into the door when he turned onto 92. It was in that moment—when he felt his ears pricking up in the night, his sight honing in like a hawk—that he understood the time and place of his youth, of nearly everything that would follow, and the undeniable feeling that he could run from nothing.

WASHED AWAY

I F I THOUGHT anything about the rain that afternoon we left our new house, it was that it might turn to snow by nighttime. Robert drove me through Fordyce and showed it was a little town. The high school football field sat right in the middle of everything, only a block away from Main Street, which was lined with a few stores and banks, a restaurant or two. We drove through downtown and back toward the highway, past the drive-in theater and the trailer park sitting beside it. I wondered what it was like to sit on your porch and see all those actors so large on the screen, almost looking down on you, but not to be able to hear what they were saying. Fordyce, like the valley where his parents lived, wasn't what I had dreamed of when I married and came to America with Robert, but at least it was a town, and I thought that it would be enough, for a little while anyway.

We got back to his parents' home and the rain was heavier, but mostly it was just steady. All through the night it came down, and in the morning the creek behind the house had risen level with the bank. The temperature hadn't dropped below freezing, but the water fell in cold, stinging drops and soaked the earth. The road was filled with puddles, and the gravel from the roads had washed out into some of the yards. The sky was a solid sheet of gray clouds. I don't think it stopped raining for almost eighteen hours, and the radio was calling for flash floods all over the county. We lived with Robert's parents, Owen and Evelyn, and they didn't seem worried about the weather, and because of that, I didn't think much of it either. Robert and I had been having problems, and I believed moving to Fordyce, getting out from under the roof of that tiny house, was going to be the break we both needed to begin our lives together.

WHEN OWEN WENT out to the porch the next afternoon, he asked me to come sit and talk with him. That was one of the good things about living in the house. Owen always wanted to talk to me. He liked to listen to the radio, and every time Loretta Lynn came on, he'd look at me and say, "She's a Kentucky girl, you know. Just like you," and he'd laugh out loud and slap his knees. Even in old age he stayed young-looking. He didn't give way to shrinking like my own parents had. He'd grown a beard over the winter, thick and red mixed with gray. He ran his fingers through it, scratching his neck, and I saw his fingers bowed and crooked from arthritis. The rain was a drizzle by then, and it fell sideways in a cold mist that brushed against my cheeks.

"It's too cold out," I said.

"Ah," he said and grunted. He kept his wood for whittling in an old Coca-Cola crate, and he pulled it in front of him and handed me a piece of wood and a knife. "You need to have something to do when you sit out here with me," he said. "That'll keep you warm." He had always liked carving things for me while we talked, a canoe or a gun, but some days he just stripped the bark and the pine, and the soft yellow wood fell in curls like candle wax on the porch floor.

He'd hold out that smooth little rod he'd made and ask me questions about home. He was always curious about the mountains near Masan, and he picked up another piece of wood and pulled another knife out of the front pocket of his jeans. "Tell me about those mountains again. How high do they rise above the ocean?"

"It's not how high, Owen. It's the view. It's walking to the top and being out of breath and looking down on the earth like a bird. The ocean stretches out and meets the sky, and you can only tell the difference between the two where the sun splits them in the distance. And then you can see the people riding bikes, walking, driving cars, in, out of the maze of streets, and imagine where they are going. The Lord looks down on us this way," I told him. "He picks us up and points us in different directions."

It always made me sadder to talk about Masan, to think of Korea, but I liked remembering, and I thought it was important to picture those scenes and images in my mind. I never wanted to forget my home.

"To hear you talk, you sound like an old country boy," Owen said. He had started cleaning the bark on his piece of wood. I was sitting on the edge of the porch with my back against one of the beams, looking at him and then up to Gatliff Mountain.

"What's that mean?" I asked.

"Your voice," he said. "My boys—even Robert with all that schooling, all that college—none of them can stand the thought of leaving this place. They'll never leave these hills. No, sir. They'll always be country boys. I don't know how you left home the way you did."

A pack of dogs came down the road then, their fur in wet clumps, and they chased one another's tails, barking and yelping. Mud covered their legs as they ran off and up the mountain. I watched them and caught sight of the dozers and dump trucks moving at the very top. It was such an ugly scene with those mangy dogs and the yellow machines on the hill covered with black soot. The noise from their engines and the barking of the dogs swirled around me. I never understood, from the first day we arrived, what drew Robert back home. How could what I saw before me pull at him and make him miss that place? But I also knew that what Robert had longed for were the very things I was beginning to miss about my own home. That valley shaped him and made him. Even though I wanted to escape Korea, I understood that Masan was what defined me.

"You don't think he'll ever leave?" I asked Owen. "Never?"

He took a long strip of bark off the wood. "I don't reckon," he said. "He went all over the world in the army, and the first place he came back to was here."

I held my own piece of wood in my lap. My hands glistened from the drizzle, and I scooted back onto the porch a little closer to Owen. He instructed me on how to strip the bark and told me that the knife he'd given me was "sharp enough to cut frog hair," but I wasn't really paying attention to him. I was wondering if he was right and that Robert would never leave the hills, and if that was true it meant I would never leave the hills. I thought moving to Fordyce was only going to be a beginning for us. I thought that the future was spread out before both of us, letting us walk in any direction we wanted, but the truth was the future was where Robert pointed us, and we were never going to leave Kentucky.

I held the knife out before me, and then the wood. I thought about how sharp that blade was, how easily it cut, how simple it was to shave the bark. Simple movements shaped everything. I pushed the blade away from me, down the length of the broken limb. The resistance was smooth, and the strip curled backward, tickling my knuckles.

"Good, just keep that up," Owen said.

I continued just to try to take my mind off everything, but it was hard to concentrate. I wanted to leave the house again and go into the forest, as I usually did when I felt overcome, but I couldn't do that. I'd done that too much, and a part of me wanted to take what Owen said and deal with it. That seemed like the adult thing to do.

I watched Owen carve the pine into the shape of a man. And then he took up another and started carving a woman. He began telling me a story I didn't listen to. He had set me on the path of my life without knowing it, forecasting the landscape that would dominate my life, and there was nothing but ugliness in it. Mud and trees and loud machines. When I was a girl and we were without food for days, I would become so hungry I pinched myself just to feel something other than the hunger. I saw the tip of that knife, and I wanted to prick my finger to see the blood come out of it in a little trickle and have that small burning and pulse in its tip.

Owen leaned forward and spit his chew of tobacco into the yard. He had finished telling me a story. It had been about Robert, but that was all I knew, though I heard him clearly say, "Yes, Robert's always had a one-track mind about things. I never could figure him." He looked down at me and at the wood I had whittled. "That's good," he said, taking it from my lap and holding it up to his eyes. "You're a natural. You're going to do just fine."

THE RAIN STOPPED for a few hours, but the clouds lingered over the house and the mountain. Evelyn had begun working in the garden early that winter, cleaning out the weeds and turning the soil over. Robert said his mother was always anxious during the winter and that each year she seemed to start on her garden earlier. I had been helping her, but with the rain falling there was nothing to do but watch the puddles fill and sit with Owen on the porch, listening to the radio. I wanted to tell Robert about what Owen had said and ask if he thought it was true, but we'd already had so many talks with both of us trying to control our frustrations, and I knew when he came home that night I wouldn't say a thing. I didn't know where to start, anyway, and once I started I didn't want to feel the exhaustion those fights brought on and the questions they made me ask about him and about my life.

It was already past suppertime when Robert finally walked in the door from the bank. He was always staying late. His tie was undone, and his eyes had no glimmer. Evelyn had put a plate of food for him in the oven, and I got it out and fixed him a glass of ice water and sat with him at the table.

He ate the food, and we made small talk. Robert knew something was bothering me, but he didn't ask what it was. He told me on the weekend we would go to Lexington and shop for some new things for the house. When I nodded my head, not looking up at him, he finally asked what was wrong. I tried to pretend I was sick, that I was tired, but he knew better.

I tried to keep what I was feeling inside, but I didn't know how to hide anything from him. He put down his fork and pushed his plate away. He took a deep breath and ran his hands through his hair. It had grown out since the fall from his army haircut and hung in small curls over his ears. I saw the traces of stubble on his cheeks; he'd rushed out without shaving that morning. "Nothing makes you happy," he said. He stared at me, and I thought of the first time I saw him in the restaurant in Korea, looking starched and fit in his uniform, and how that one chance moment had led us both to the kitchen table of his parents' home, my life completely altered and given over to him. "It's true," he said. "Nothing I do is good enough for you."

"Don't say that."

"Why the hell not?"

"Because it *isn't* true."

"It sure as hell feels that way. You're not happy here. You're not happy with me. You're not happy with what you're doing. You're not happy with living in this house. I make these changes for us, and it's not good enough. You were happy yesterday morning in town, and now I come home tonight and it's the same old shit."

I hated when he talked like that; as if he thought he could shut the whole conversation down.

"You don't think I have a right to feel unhappy?"

"A right? You've got a right to feel whatever the hell you want, but I've got a right to not feel like every bad thing in your life is my fault."

Owen and Evelyn were in the other room, and I heard the television. This was the first time we'd ever argued out in the open. I wanted to keep my voice down, but Robert was beyond that. He got up from the table, taking his plate to the sink and setting it down with a crash. "What else can I do, Shin? What else have I done wrong?"

"I didn't even say anything," I told him.

"You don't have to. That look says enough. It questions and judges me more than anything you ever say."

"That's not fair."

"What's not fair is not trying," he said.

"What does that mean?"

"If you can't give this place a chance, you can't give us a chance." He was at the sink, his hands holding the counter behind him, and glaring at me. I refused to back down when he did that, so we stared hard at each other, both of us searching for an answer to our troubles. That small kitchen held us like an eggshell—tight, leaving us unable to twist away from each other, and just as fragile. "I can't do this tonight. I can't go through it," he said.

"Run away," I said. "That's what you do when it gets tough." Our voices were clear by then. There were no sounds in the house but our words in the air. "Go run to your brother's and leave me here alone like always. Go run wherever it is you run to."

"You don't know what the hell you're talking about," he said. He came toward me, and we stood face-to-face. I thought about my mother and my father and those times when I knew she pushed him with her words so hard that he would strike her, when she kept going to the edge of his anger—and hers—so she could feel her bones rattle. I'd always wondered why she did this, had never understood what made her want to feel that kind of pain, but with Robert in front of me I knew then—with his eyes both angry and distant—that it was a kind of pain you can deal with. You can pack ice on a bruise and nurse yourself through the throb. The ache in your heart can be made physical, and all that you are dealing with below the surface, that you never let anybody see, is brought out to the light. But Robert was too good a man ever to hit me. He knew I had tested him, and I saw his eyes change in that moment. I had hurt him, I saw. He didn't cry, but what was in him looked worse than a man fighting back tears. It was defeat. And confusion. It was everything he had wanted and dreamed of evaporating.

I saw it and I said nothing. I was too cold then and too young to know how to handle what we were in. All I had for models were my own parents, who I'd seen love each other all my life, but who I had also seen hate and push each other. Maybe I thought that's what a marriage should look like, what it is made up of, but I don't know for sure. He brushed past me and went to the car, and the headlights lit up the rain like crystal. It was falling heavy again, and for the first time all night I heard the drops on the roof. Slow and steady they fell, thumping time with the seconds.

ROBERT WAS STILL gone the next morning at breakfast. I sat with Owen and Evelyn, and while I expected them to be angry with me, to say something about our fight, they didn't. I was sure they blamed me for his leaving, and I should have stayed in bed all morning and not come out of the room until they were both off and doing their own business or chores, but I hadn't. When I woke that morning it was to the sound of more rain. On the radio they were talking about floods in Bell County and that we weren't far behind. After breakfast Owen had me go out on the porch with him, and I thought he was going to ask me about what happened the night before, but he just took up his whittling and asked me to turn the radio up louder.

"Too much rain," was all he said as he sat down in the chair. "Nothing good can come from this much rain."

I was thumbing through a magazine, only looking at the pictures, and my mind was on Robert and if he was going to come back that night, if he was ever going to come back. I'd split something in him and in us. And if he never came back, how was I ever going to get out of that valley? I didn't think Owen and Evelyn were going to help the woman who ran their son off from his own home. Most of all, though, I just wanted to make it right between us. We were moving soon. We were going to have our chance, and that was what I wanted to focus on. *People change*, I told myself. Owen could be wrong, I thought. Our lives were up to us and not anything else. I should have never let what Owen said affect me so much.

"You're a lot quieter this morning than you were last night," Owen said. *Finally*, I thought. *Here it comes*. Before I could say anything, he looked up at me. "Couples fight," he said.

"We have been a lot lately."

He nodded and went back to his wood and didn't say anything else. He knew there wasn't anything he could tell me.

We sat on the porch an hour, maybe more, and the rain slowly stopped. Poplar Creek began overflowing its banks, and the water was brown and muddy.

Then we heard it.

A rumble up on the mountain, louder than anything I'd ever heard up there before. It wouldn't have surprised me as much had it not been such a slow morning. The bulldozers and dump trucks hadn't been circling on the carved-out chunks of mud and earth like usual, and it was one of the few times when the valley had been peaceful.

Owen stood up and pulled his cap off his head. "That's a loud sound," he said.

I walked out to the edge of the porch but couldn't see anything. "I can't tell what's going on. Can you?" I asked.

Owen went into the yard, still carrying the stripped wood in one hand and his knife in the other. "They supposed to be done stripping that side of the mountain there," he said, pointing with the knife.

Above us two men jumped into their bulldozers and another four or five men ran and hopped in their pickup trucks.

"Something's scared them awfully bad," I said and realized how much I was beginning to talk like Robert's family.

"They running like scalded dogs on top of that hill."

"What for?"

"I don't know, but I'm going to walk up there and see." Owen folded his knife and put it in his pocket. He started down the road and I followed.

"They're not going to let you up there," I said.

"I've lived here thirty years. I ain't never seen men move like that unless somebody's trapped in a mine, and they're just stripping these hills. There ain't a mine shaft for anyone to be trapped in. Something's bad wrong on that hill."

"How can you be sure?"

He stopped in his path and turned around. I saw Robert in Owen's cheeks and eyes. His eyebrows were gray at the edges, still with hints of red in them. "I just know," he said and moved up the hill.

He stepped on briars and held them down with his foot for me to cross. They grabbed and clung to my jeans, scratched little cuts along the backs of my hands. Owen didn't want to use the main access road. He wanted to make his own path. I wiped sweat from my face and looked to the top. We were halfway there, but it was a steep mountain. Mud stuck to our shoes, and it made the trail we were walking slippery.

"Come on now, Miss Shin. We're almost there."

He held out his hand for me to grab and pulled me up to a level place.

"This shouldn't be so hard," I said. I was trying to catch my breath and bent over my knees.

"You just not used to these mountains the way I am. Come on," he said. "Let's find out what's happening."

Owen took big steps up the slope like he was twenty years younger. He pushed away tree limbs as we got higher and then used them to pull himself up. He didn't slip once, even though his shoes and the bottoms of his jeans were caked in mud. I followed him up the mountain, doing my best to mimic his movements.

The closer we got, the clearer the men's voices became. They were frantic. "Hurry up, Cole!"

"Goddamnit, Artemus, I need you over here now."

"Where in the hell is Lonnie with that dozer?"

"What is it?" I said to Owen. "What are they yelling about?"

"It's the impoundment," Owen said. "Something's wrong with it."

"What's that mean? What's an impoundment?"

"It's a big pond they keep all the waste in from the mining

process. They dam off the waste and filter the water through it. See there," he said and pointed.

I stood on my toes and looked, but I couldn't see anything except the bare mountains to the right of us that stood even higher than Gatliff Mountain.

"On the other side of all that is the waste. All the watery sludge and slate they don't use they put in there. Like one big toilet." He walked toward the men but was stopped short when another man spotted us and came over.

"Sir," he said. "You can't be here right now. You're on private property."

Owen looked at the man and tilted his head. "Lowell Deaton?"

"Yes, sir."

"You're Charley's boy, aren't you?"

"Yes, sir."

"What's happened here, son?"

Lowell snuck a glance over his shoulder and took in the other men running to the impoundment. They had pulled off their coveralls to move faster. There was so much shouting and so many engines coming to life that all sense of a plan seemed to have vanished. I peered down the mountain, seeing how far away the house was from us.

"I can't tell you that, sir."

Owen stepped closer to the man, who now looked like a boy. Maybe twenty, my age, at the oldest. "Lowell," he said. "I live three hundred yards down this mountain. That's my house right there," he said and nodded over his shoulder. "If something's wrong, I got as much goddamn right to know as anybody."

The boy fidgeted, unsure of what to say to Owen. Owen stepped even closer, removing all daylight between him and the boy, and Lowell Deaton buckled. He leaned to Owen's ear, as if someone might hear him if he was too loud, and said, "The impoundment's busted. All this rain has put pressure on the walls, and now the slurry is seeping out and cracking through the dirt."

"Are you going to be able to fix it?"

He shook his head. "It don't look good. Now, you've got to get before they see you and me," he said.

Owen squeezed the boy's arm, and Lowell moved away, toward the crowd of workers. The dozers and backhoes were pulling out clumps of earth in big raking motions and pushing the mounds of earth toward the waste site. I wasn't sure what was about to happen, but I got scared when I saw that. Something about the faces of the men running the dozers showed they knew what they were doing wasn't going to be fast enough.

"We better get down the hill," Owen said and grabbed my hand. "Go down the access road. It don't make a damn who sees us now."

I made my way toward the road, all the time looking back to see what kind of progress those men were making, who were covered from the waist down in nothing but that thick slurry, like wet, black concrete. They began to backpedal away from the spill as the sludge pooled around their feet, filling the tracks of the trucks and dozers.

Owen never turned, though. He kept going down the hill toward the house. I didn't know a man his age could move so fast. The last time I turned, I saw just how massive that impoundment was, and I couldn't imagine how much it held and what would happen if all of it ran down the mountain. The men were now jumping in trucks, piling into the back of the beds. Their shovels submerged. We made it to the bottom, and any minute I knew they'd pass right by us.

At the house, Owen ran in, tracking mud everywhere. Evelyn jumped up from the couch and looked at him and then me, too alarmed to say anything to either of us. Owen grabbed the phone in the kitchen. "Robert, you need to get home right away, son. We've got to get out of here. The impoundment on Gatliff is giving out. It won't be long before it's completely gone. I don't know how much time we have."

Evelyn's face fell at that. She knew exactly what that meant, and that was when I became very afraid. She moved past me to see for herself what we had just run from, and then she came back to Owen. He had not yet hung up. He held the phone tight in his hand and nodded. "Okay, get here as soon as you can."

When he was off, we both looked at him, expectantly.

"It'll be at least thirty minutes for him to get out here. Evelyn, go in the kitchen and put some food up for us. Shin, go get some clothes for us and put them in a suitcase, and make sure we have flashlights, batteries, and matches."

"What are you going to do?" Evelyn asked him.

"I'm going to go tell these other people in the valley we ain't got much time."

But outside the window, already, the trucks came racing off the mountain and driving down the road. Their tires spit dirt and gravel, and they honked their horns as they went, some stopping at houses along the way. I saw the men telling the families to leave, to get out of the valley. Other men jumped out of the trucks, and their wives came running to them with babies in their arms, their other children following behind. Then they were lifting the kids into the back of the pickups, and the wives were holding the children close to their chests, and the trucks were off again.

Now cars and trucks were screaming down the access road, but they weren't stopping. These were the men who didn't live in the valley. Even when they rounded the corners, there were no brake lights flashing. I couldn't move my hands to put anything in a suitcase, and then it was too late for us to do anything but run.

The sludge and water didn't come on us all at once, but it came quickly. It broke through the impoundment and carried a chunk of dirt as big as a car down the mountain into the road. I screamed when I saw it, and Owen called from the porch for us to just get out of the house. "We don't have enough time," he said.

He carried a flashlight and grabbed Evelyn's hand. "We've got to get to higher ground," he said. We went to the backyard, its field of tall grass pulling at my knees as we made our way to the base of the mountain behind the house. Our feet sank in the mud with each step, and it was so hard not to check and see if the dirt and sludge was right on our tails. I saw the sludge slip over the sides of the mountain, pouring through the trail Owen and I had just made, crashing onto the little road, filling the ditch, and trembling over. It was less than fifty yards from the house, and I kept hoping the water wouldn't make it that far, but we all knew it would. Stunned, we stopped for a moment and watched.

The slurry built up and crossed the road—now mailboxes were floating—and with one big surge it ran into the yard. It moved the way lava does, and I heard the earth rumbling above us. A pickup truck washed down the mountain and crashed to the ground and then was picked up by the current of waste, moving away from the house. The porch was covered now; one more minute and the house would be ruined. Evelyn covered her mouth and reached out as if she could stop it by will. Owen grabbed her and pulled her close. "We've got to get up this mountain," he said. "There's no time."

We crossed Poplar Creek, stepping into the cold water. We were soaked up to our hips. The sludge was in the field now, all the way up to the windows of the house. It kept coming at us, and we waded through the creek, the water rising past our waists and the muddy bottom filling our shoes. We scrambled on our hands and knees out of the water and just kept climbing. It didn't seem like we could get high enough on the mountain; we just kept moving as fast as we could. Mud covered our clothes and lodged underneath my nails. I felt little nicks from the bushes on my hands and face. Evelyn's hip was hurting her, but Owen held her and pulled her up with him. We climbed so high we were even with the top of Gatliff and saw across the field to the busted dam.

"It looks like someone stuck a ton of dynamite in there and blasted a hole," Owen said.

Sludge kept washing out of the hole, filling the valley like a bathtub. Trailers and homes were swept under its weight and floated in the sludge. I saw fish on top of the water. Along the mountainside other people were scrambling up, and then we all saw it. It was a man. He was shirtless, trying to wade through the sludge but being swept up in the power of its current. His head bobbed up and down, under, and then reappeared, his face and hair covered so that all we saw was the opening of his mouth as he gasped for air.

"Lord, God," Evelyn said. She stood up, we all did. But there was nothing we could do. He was trying to reach us, but it was useless. The sludge, somehow, came even faster, ripping through everything. He grabbed hold of a telephone pole, and the force was so strong his body was laid out flat. We couldn't hear his screams for the sound of the sludge flooding the valley, and then we saw it pull his clothes from his body, and he lay in the sludge naked, his white skin stained black, his arms still clinging to the pole. He kicked his legs like a fish fighting the current, but we saw one arm slip and then the other, and soon his body was moving away from us, turning and twisting in the mess. I covered my eyes, not wanting to see if he was swallowed under.

We sat down then, unable to speak or look at each other. The other families on the mountain were sitting now too, and mothers held their children close to their chests. Some of the miners who had run down the mountain were pacing near the creek bank, watching the blackness rise closer to all of us.

"How long will it keep coming out of there?" I asked.

"It's untelling," Owen said and sat. He pulled his chewing tobacco out of his back pocket. "All the waste goes into that impoundment. Hell, there could be ten years, maybe more, of buildup in that damn thing. It's only going to get worse."

Babies were crying, and men were cussing. Screams and shouts all around. The walls of houses caved in, broke into pieces, and were carried away by the sludge. It kept pumping out of the hill like a broken spigot.

"My God," Evelyn said, and that was the only sound from any of us for a long time.

I've never felt so helpless as I did that day. All around me the world turned black, the valley one big spilled bucket of paint that none of us could use but that would color our lives forever.

The rain started again, a big cloudburst, and this seemed to push more sludge out. There wasn't a blade of grass or garden patch in sight. Trees shot up from the black water as if we lived in a swamp now instead of a valley. Owen held Evelyn close to him and rocked her into his side. I still don't know how she didn't cry at seeing the tiny house, the only one they'd ever lived in once they married, fill with all that waste.

All we could do was wait on Robert and his brother, Johnny, to show up and come get us. We didn't know how long that would take or if he'd even be able to reach us from the road. In the distance the sludge had mixed with the creeks. Two ingredients not meant to make anything.

The valley was gone. All that was left was that murky water, and I saw how far it spread up the base of Gatliff and all the way down the road out to the main highway. From where we were it looked almost as large as a lake and the mountains around us like islands waiting to be devoured and covered. For hours we sat on the hill, shivering in our wet clothes and not knowing what to do or how we were going to get someplace safe. I had my head down when I heard the motor on the little johnboat and looked up to see Robert and Johnny waving at us. Robert's shirt and face were covered in grime, his brown jacket soaked like a wet paper bag. Owen helped Evelyn, and we walked down the mountain. The sludge had come over the creek, twenty yards up the hillside.

"All the houses are gone, Dad," Robert said. "Nothing's left."

"Only the foundations, I guess," Owen said. "We'll build ours back, though. Take us a little bit, but we'll put it back together," he said and squeezed Evelyn.

"Maw, you okay?"

"I'm fine. My hip's hurting, but that's all."

Robert stepped out of the boat and came to me. He didn't know if he should hug me or not, so he rubbed his fingers across the back of my hand.

"How bad is it?" I asked. "We couldn't see where it ended."

"It's not stopped," he said. "It's spread nearly all the way out to the Cumberland River. Dead fish are everywhere, some even in trees. It's pretty bad. I don't know how y'all survived."

We watched the water fill the valley, churning the earth into a paste of mud and mixed branches. The paltry little houses in the valley, some no bigger than two rooms, with their slanted roofs, the shingles worn thin and flapping in the wind, were crushed. It didn't take much for the water to wash away those homes, those lives. And really, that's what it did. It took away the one thing most of them had free and clear in the world.

I looked at Owen and Evelyn. I saw their lives, already drawn, already lived. Gone. Erased. The shavings brushed away with the hand of God and being cleaned with His tainted water. A shiver ran down my back, and I shook myself. What had we been doing for the last half year? What were we planning? Owen kissed Evelyn on the neck. It was something he never did, and that's when I knew they both saw the finality of their lives, and I thought of my own parents.

It takes us all a long time to see our parents as just human. I knew that despite my father's faults, he did love my mother. When she sang in the courtyard he went outside and sat beside her and chewed on a piece of dried squid and listened to her voice. She had this way of hitting every note with just the right amount of emotion, and if she sang something sad, I could see her eyes well up and get glossy, but no tears fell down her face. She wouldn't let them. She just held those notes a little longer, her bottom lip quivering. When she was done my father would take her hand and rub it, setting it in his lap, then pull her body into him, and she would sing again.

"It'll be okay," Owen said to Evelyn. "We'll be all right. Haven't I always figured something out?"

She just nodded to him then and smiled.

Owen led her to the water's edge. Night was closing in. The water on the mountain was so thick it looked like we could walk across it. The boat was too small for all of us to fit in, so Robert told Johnny to take their parents out and then come back for the two of us.

I watched him help Evelyn into the boat. He held her arm until she was sitting all the way down, and then he stepped away. Above all, I knew I had married a good man. He came to me, and we watched them back away from us, the three of them waving. Johnny called out to say he would be back soon, and the three of them waved.

Robert put his arm around me, and for the first time in a long while, I leaned into him, almost putting all my weight on him. All I wanted to do was fall down, to lie with him and not think so much anymore.

"It's going to take a long time before things get back to normal," he said. "I can't believe what's happened. Look at it, Shin. Nothing's the same."

He smelled like the rain and cold. I pushed closer into him. "I'm sorry," I said. "I don't know how to make myself happy. I just wanted us to be on our own and to feel like you and I were starting a life together. Nothing's worked out like I thought it would."

He pulled away and looked down. I bit my lip and looked out over the water, as if some answer was floating in that disaster.

"What are you saying?" he asked.

"I thought my life would be different. I thought when we came here life was going to get easier, better than it was, but it's only gotten harder."

"It's been a tough day, and we had a fight. Things *are* going to get better."

"No, they're not. It's all going to get harder now. I was so happy that you and I were going to have our own place, but then your father said you would never leave Kentucky. And that's what I was upset about last night. I didn't dream of this, *Yobo*. I didn't dream of leaving my family to come to this place, but I came here because I love you. And now, just when you and I were going to have our chance, that's going to be changed again, too. Owen and Evelyn will need to stay with us, and until you and I are alone, I don't know how we're ever going to have a chance to be with each other, to learn to love each other in the way we need to."

Robert picked some dead leaves off a tree and crumbled them in his hands. I watched the pieces fly out onto the sludge as he shook them free.

"What do you want me to say, Shin?"

"I don't want you to say anything. I want you to do something. What do you think I do down here all day? Who do you think I talk to? I mean, really talk to."

"I know it's hard now—"

"You don't know, Robert. You don't."

"Let me finish," he said.

I sat down and closed my eyes. Rainwater seeped through my pants, cool and slow. I didn't want to be angry with him, not after a day like this, but it was all I could feel for him then. I opened my eyes and saw him kneeling beside me but looking away toward the impoundment.

"How fast did it happen?"

"Fast," I said. "It felt like it would never stop. We ran away from the house and watched it rise."

"They've lost everything," he said. "Everything they worked for. All of them, not just Mom and Dad. I don't see how something like that can happen. What's the reason?"

"There aren't reasons for everything, you know that. Some things just are. Some things just happen. It's what you do afterward that counts most."

Robert turned to me then, and I curled my knees close under my chin.

"You can't fix everything. You can't get back what's lost," he said.

"You can try, though."

"And then what?" he said.

"And then," I said and pulled him down next to me, "you see what's left of what you had and look for where there is still work to be done."

Across the water we saw Johnny's light, its beam twinkling like a star as it cut in and out through the trees and bushes in front of us. The little motor puttered a soft whine.

"I'm glad we've got a way to get back," I said.

"It'll be good to warm up."

Robert put his arm around me. Somehow, even then, I knew the hardest days of our lives might still be ahead of us, but I also felt with him beside me, with us moving to Fordyce, that the flood, no matter how ugly and devastating, was going to be a salvation of sorts. Maybe I just wanted to believe that, to find some way to make my own sense of what had just occurred. But we were going to leave the valley, and even if his parents came with us, it would still be something of a new start. Johnny's light grew stronger as he made his way. I couldn't see as much of the valley the closer he came. All I could see was the long beam of light growing smaller, pushing into the center of its source, where it grew brighter, until it was in our eyes and his voice called out for us.

SATELLITES

ALICE IS NEARLY finished with her father. They have spent this morning with only the crisp sounds of grooming—spritzes of water, the snip of scissors—hardly speaking a word to each other. She had planned on telling him she was moving out of the house, that it was time for him to come back home and take over the farm again, but he had arrived late, eyes puffy and bloodshot, smelling of Nicorette gum and too much aftershave, and when she hugged him, he felt thinner and smaller than the last time she saw him, and she was stifled. She went about cutting his hair, thinking the entire time how to broach the subject. Then, just as she readies herself, Angie Johnson comes ambling through the door of the salon. She's a chatterbox and the sight of her, though usually unwelcome, brings a grateful reprieve.

"Well, look here," the woman says. "Amon Hampton. How are you doing this morning?"

Alice feels her father's shoulders tighten underneath his smock.

"I'm fine, Angie. Yourself?"

The woman sits down and grabs a magazine off the coffee table and says she's fine too and peeks over top of her magazine.

"It's so good to see you two together. Especially after the year you two have had. It's good of Alice to take care of you."

Her father's shoulders wrench higher. She readies to speak when he beats her to it. "We're getting along," he says. "We're doing okay these days, aren't we?" He lifts his eyebrows to her in the mirror.

"Almost back to normal," Alice lies. She makes a few more cuts, levels up his sideburns, and then plugs in the hair dryer to blow the cut hair off his clothes and neck. The whir of the machine drowns out the television Mrs. Johnson has now turned on, and her father fidgets in the chair, ready to go. He is already rising before she has dusted off his neck. He pulls out his wallet.

"Let me give you something this time," he says.

"You can pay for mine," Mrs. Johnson says. "When you get our age, it's up to the children to take care of us. But, Lord, don't I hate it." She smiles.

He holds some folded money out to Alice, but she shoos it off. They hug again and he says he'll call, more for Mrs. Johnson's ears than hers, and walks out. She thinks to follow him and that what she needs to say shouldn't wait all day, until she closes the shop. This is the worst he's been since her mother's sudden passing, since both of their worlds were flipped and rearranged, but before she can even make a step, Mrs. Johnson is heaving her big body into the chair and starting in about her "grandbabies."

Alice nods and listens, but she is elsewhere. She trims the woman up, places the foil patches in her hair and brushes dye along each swatch. After she's done, she puts her under the dryer and tends to the other tasks of running the salon—taking phone calls, marking new appointments, sweeping up scattered and fallen hair. She wants to call her father and check on him, set up a time for them to talk, but she is too busy to call. One customer after another keeps popping in the doorway, and when she finally has a free minute toward the end of the day, the boy from the AutoZone next door comes in and says Terry Thompson has just released all the animals out at his place.

"When?" Alice asks.

"I just heard it on the radio. Must have been an hour ago," the boy says, pushing his baseball cap back on his head. He's so casual about it. He often comes in the salon on his breaks and reads the magazines or watches the television. And he always has a story. A bigger gossip than any of the women that come in here, Alice has sometimes thought. He has no idea she has animals of her own at home or that Thompson's house is close enough to the farm that she fears they are in danger.

Alice says nothing, but her eyes go to the traffic out front, and she doesn't expect it to be moving along steady and unalarmed.

She shuts up the salon, leaving in a fright with all the lights turned on. She speeds home through the business district and every few seconds expects something to leap out from behind a building, but all she sees are people running errands. Grocery. Doctor's office. Hardware store. By the community college, students cross the street with their hands cinched around their backpacks' straps, worry-free, even though the radio has confirmed the boy's story and message boards have been rolled onto the shoulder of I-70 with alerts that read WARNING: WILD EXOTIC ANIMALS LOOSE. The announcer tells everyone to get inside and stay there.

She makes it to Kopchak Road, to a turn she's made a thousand times in her life without any problems, and then her stomach lurches. Instead of stepping on the gas, as she normally would, she puts the car in park. Terry Thompson's place rests on a soft hill of grass to her left, and if not for the police cruiser's lights swirling in the misty, late afternoon at the top of his driveway, nothing would seem out of place.

Tigers and lions. Leopards. Grizzlies. Monkeys, too. Nobody knew for sure how many animals in number or species Thompson kept up there, but Alice remembers him building the compound, the cages shipped in on flatbed trucks. Word got around that Jack Hanna came in from Columbus to check on the animals at one point, but that wasn't verified. There wasn't much she'd ever been able to verify about Thompson. Not that she'd tried much. Rumor said he was a mobster from New Jersey on the lam or in protection after testifying against his mob bosses. The one time she saw him up close—at the Kroger with two grocery carts filled with only steaks and whole chickens—he looked like any other person in any other grocery store in any other town. She was surprised by how normal he appeared. Khaki pants, white collared golf shirt. No sweat suit or gold chains. He smiled, soft and sheepish, and asked how she was while he pushed those overflowing carts ahead of him. No one wanted those animals up there, and people who had been invited to see them said they lived in filth and Thompson had no business keeping them.

A truck comes toward her now and in the back are two sheriff's deputies in plainclothes holding big black assault weapons in their hands. A chill spreads through her. The truck slows and the two men stare. They are only boys, she thinks. Not much older than twenty-five and doing their best to appear grim and tough. The driver, who has on his uniform, rolls down his window.

"You need to get on, Miss. We got an emergency."

"I know," she says but makes no move to put the car in gear. She is focused on the boys, the muzzles of their rifles pointed skyward. She chances a question. "How bad is it?"

"I can't say for sure, ma'am." She shifts her attention back to the driver, knowing he sees her as older now than he did at first. He looks to be her age. His hair is close cut and gray at the temples, and his eyes are the palest blue she has ever seen, like they have the faintest dab of paint in their irises. He might be someone she went to high school with, but she cannot place his face.

"Have you seen any of them?" She puts her hand on the gearshift. He shakes his head. The boys in the back of the truck fidget with their rifles; they no longer eye her. The driver must be their commander.

"What will you do to them?"

"We'll take care of 'em," he says.

"Meaning what?"

He nods to the back of the truck, presumably to the younger officers and their rifles.

"Just like that?" she says. "Not a single thought about it?"

"It's them or us," he says. "Not much choice, is there?" But it's not a question. "You have to go," he says. "It's not safe here."

She looks at the hillsides, the grass and trees, the sway of the land, her father always called it. She grew up five minutes from here and has always felt nothing but calm on this road and drive to home. She rolls her window up without saying goodbye and guns the engine of her car, causing the tires to squall.

As she approaches the farm she sees the two horses and herd of goats huddled at the far edge of the field to the left of the house, at least a hundred yards away from the barn. She skids to a stop in the driveway, and the house blocks the view of the animals. The barn doors sit open thirty yards away directly in front of her. Phone in hand, she presses it to her forehead, knowing she must run for it. She closes her eyes and works up her courage. Then she is out of the car and moving through the gate and yard. She ducks inside, momentarily collecting her breath, then grabs two lengths of rope by the stalls for the pair of horses and comes out, facing the field. She makes out their pawing and stomping in the grass. If they were people they'd be cowering. The adrenaline in her veins causes her to shake. She imagines torn animal fur and gnashing teeth, and before she can let herself think much more, she sprints for them, forgetting that inside her house on the hall closet's top shelf rests the shotgun and its slug-filled shells.

She counts to three and takes off. The soles of her ballet flats slide off her heels and slip and slap against the wet grass, and in two forceful strides she kicks them off. Her toes grab at the damp earth and her lungs seize with strain. She is careful not to come up on the pair of chestnut beauties right away and reaches slowly for their haunches, clucking and cooing between breaths, until they feel her hands. She runs her palms down the length of their bodies, talking the whole time in a soft voice. Their big muscles twitch with unease and they snort, jerking their heads. At any minute they could run all out, away from her. Once she is in front of both horses, the goats bay louder. She senses trouble near but can't bring herself to search the woods.

She pulls the ropes from her shoulder and loops each around the horses and her gloveless hands tug at their fighting necks to guide them back across the expanse of field. She tries to be quick but not hurry, that little nugget of John Wooden's that her high school basketball coach said time and again. She clucks and coos some more, but the horses step gingerly, as if testing each patch of turf for firmness and solidity. The ropes serve more as conduits for the electrical current of their fear than leads. Thompson's house is a mile and a half north. with nothing between it and Alice but treeless slopes. She steals a glance in its direction, feeling that ever since he brought those animals to Zanesville they have been lying in wait.

Step by small step she keeps the horses moving and then, halfway to the barn, her cell phone rings. Startled, both horses rear up on their hind legs and their stomachs stretch ten feet above her. "Easy, boys. Easy." She pulls down on them as gently yet as forcefully as she can, but the phone cycles into its ring once more and the horses rise back up, lifting her arms with them. Her shoulder sockets pop. The rope fibers dig in and split her palms. She straightens, gives each rope a good snap, and settles the horses, and they seem to calm and focus, like scolded children.

Once she has marched them into the barn, she shuts them up in their stalls and nearly collapses from the effort. She sits on the ground and cold air burrows into the open wounds on her hands and sweeps over her wet and muddy feet. She curls her toes against the barn floor's dust and makes her hands into fists, feeling the sting of the burns. The goats are still alone, and she forces herself back to the entryway. They have moved even closer to one another in their corner of the field. For over a year she has been there in the early mornings to find every one of the newly born kids, sometimes coming as twins and triplets, sucking from their mother's teats. She has cuddled them close to her, savoring the soft fur and the kissing of her knuckles. And, in a small way, with each arrival they have reminded her of the children she will never have, of how quickly that part of life sped right past her. There's no way to get them all moving in the same direction toward the barn and she doesn't think they'd all fit anyway. Then there is still the matter of Thompson's animals, of how many might be near, and the fact she is without her rifle. She can't save them.

Behind the barn, the mountain that borders the field is covered in spindly beeches and poplars that sway between cedars. Everything is quiet, too quiet, and though she can't see anything, she is sure a pair of large, spark-filled eyes gaze down on her. Spooked, she retreats inside, slams the barn doors closed, and climbs to the loft where a glassless window looks over the field and gives her a clear line of sight to the goats. She pokes her head out the opening and turns her head to the motionless woods. She reaches in her pocket for her phone and calls her father back. He answers on the first ring, and something in his voice tells her he is panicked but trying to remain calm.

"The sheriff and his deputies are out now," he says. "They're going to kill 'em."

"I know. I saw them earlier. Where are you?"

"In the truck headed back. I was in Granville when I heard."

"What were you doing over there?"

"We can talk about it later."

"What if there isn't a later?" she says.

He tells her not to be dramatic, to sit tight, and then asks what the news is saying.

"I'm not watching," she says. "I'm in the barn." She tells him about the boy coming in the shop, the horses, and how she is readying to go in the house for the shotgun once she has the nerve. She settles against the wall and pushes her feet out in front of her. Tips of hay prick through her jeans. Then a loud rifle shot echoes out. She leans forward and twists to her knees so she can see out the window. Her mind returns to the pickup truck from earlier.

"Don't go anywhere. It's too dangerous to run for it," he tells her.

Her head is outside, searching and listening in the dimming light. "I can make it to the house," she says.

"You can't outrun a damn lion. You stay right where you are. I'm on my way to you."

The goats clamor louder. They have huddled so close to the corner of the fence she is certain they are trying to push it down and break free.

"Is there anything on the radio? Do they have a count?" she asks.

"They're not sure." She can tell by the faint sound of his voice he's dropped the receiver below his mouth. "Maybe five lions and fifteen tigers."

"I should try to save them," she says under her breath, to herself, in a way that acknowledges, with finality, that the tight-packed mass out in the field is helpless.

"No," he shouts, and it startles her. "I'm twenty minutes out. I've got my rifle. We'll walk into the house together."

Another shot explodes in the air. Then another. Boom. Boom.

Boom. She's never heard such loud and rapid gunfire in her life. The blasts seem so close it's as if the compressed air of each one pushes against the barn. The goats run in small circles and criss-cross one another. They seek escape, and yet they cannot stand the thought of not being near the others. Then she sees it in the woods. She pulls her head back in and drops the phone in the hay. Obscured by the trees and more than forty yards away, a lion prowls through the woods. A female. Lean and lithe. The animal's coat stretches taut over its muscles. Alice has never seen such power. It walks unhurried, surveying, and the animal's slow swaying tail only adds to its sense of indifference. The goats spot it and scramble. Their chatter rises and Alice waits for it to attack, but it walks along the fence, eyeing the goats as if curious.

The horses go crazy in their stalls, and the hair on Alice's neck rises. She hears her father's voice pleading to tell him what's happening, asking where she's gone, and she kicks the phone away from her, burying it in the hay. Suddenly she hates this barn more than she ever has before. She sees his dark figure—his suit coat flapping in the wind—as he trudged across the field with his head bent forward and sought refuge here after the funeral. She was left alone to deal with everyone in their house, to take their hushed condolences, their hugs that lasted a moment too long, while he hid, probably shoveling out the stalls and keeping himself busy so he wouldn't have to deal with any of it. It had always been where he ran when her parents got into a fight, and though they were loving parents, she sometimes found herself, especially these last few years, playing traffic cop to them both, trying to ease and explain their angers. After her mother died her father could no longer stand the thought of living in the house and asked her to take it, to take care of everything. She hadn't expected it to hit him that hard and rather than draw them closer, the grief—the new responsibilities he foisted on her—has driven them to their own corners.

The goats frantically search for shelter as the lioness creeps along the fence line. Then it jumps over and lands in a sprint. It is so assured and strong that there is grace and gentleness to the movement. Before Alice can register just how fast it is, the lion has plucked a goat from the ground with its jaw and blood sprays from the felled animal's neck across the lion's snout. It pushes the goat into the ground with its forepaws, and Alice lets out a loud shriek. She can't bear to watch the rest, but the animal cries of the goats and the roar of the beast cut through the night and haunt her as she hugs herself and covers her ears. She refuses to look out the window again even after her father pulls up and lays on the truck's horn in one long continuous note. When her phone rings she must dig through the hay to find its illuminated screen.

"Are you still in the loft?"

"Yes." Her chest heaves. "Can you see it?"

She does not know that the lion stands before him, its mouth covered in blood. "Yes," he says softly.

"Where?" she pleads. "Is it in the field?"

"Stay where you are."

She calls to him, and he says nothing in return. Alice scrambles down from the loft, skipping the last three rungs of the ladder and falling to the ground and skinning her knee. Night is falling, and the truck's headlights fill the slits in the doors' cracks and frame. She throws them open to see the lion between her and the truck. Amon steps out of the vehicle, and the animal doesn't flinch. It merely turns its head to them both.

He brings a rifle to his shoulder. His fingers fumble with the safety and his arm shakes. The lion roars, and its bloody mouth and whiskers are gruesome in the stark lighting.

"Get back inside!" he screams. "Close the goddamn doors!"

She doesn't move. She sends up a prayer for the lion to simply move on, thinks now she should have lied and told him she was safe in the house. He is on the verge of getting mauled and killed, and it will be her fault. She almost yells, "Be careful!" but realizes how pitiful and ridiculous that will sound and knows he won't listen anyway. He'll do what he has to save her, and there is a rising guilt for her earlier thoughts about him up in the loft, about the last year of their lives. The animal steps toward him, and having seen it move, Alice knows it can close the gap to him in a second. She raises her hand, as if reaching for him, and her father keeps his eyes steady. In a blink, and with great relief, the lion darts right and sprints off, toward Thompson's, and as soon as it is gone her father hurries toward her. His artificial hip makes running out of the question, but he does a sort of skip and hop until he is beside her. She clutches at his arm and pulls him inside. He puts the rifle down, and they can feel each other's hearts beating hard and fast.

"Daddy." Her voice is helpless.

"I'm right here," he says.

He locks the doors. She knows it is now safe, but that doesn't make it any easier. Then she feels his arms wrap around her with the force of someone drowning. She is so stunned by the strength of his embrace she nearly steps back to take in his face, but then he is shaking with the short spasms that indicate crying, and she presses her cheek against his rumbling chest. She whispers, "I know."

He finally releases her and turns to wipe his eyes. Over his shoulder he asks if she is ready. He puts a hand on the doors. She says yes. He grabs the rifle and unbolts the doors and peeks out before opening it all the way. He gives her a flashlight from his coat pocket and instructs her to stay close behind him, and they step into the night.

Wind rattles tree branches. She aims the flashlight's beam in front of their feet and keeps her attention there too. Her father's head swivels, taking in everything around them as they make their way to the back porch where she unlocks the door. Even after they have shut the door and turned on the kitchen lights, her chest is still clenched and knotted.

He sets the rifle on the table. They go to the living room to watch the news, but her father falls in a slump on the couch, as if everything, at last, has spilled out of him. They watch the reports on the animals and without speaking they are both looking for a glimpse of their lion on the screen, but all the footage shows are the killed animals laid out side by side, mouths agape, like drying timber on Thompson's property. It's been a long while since she's heard a rifle shot, and she finds herself at the window wanting to hear their sonic echoes once more and know it's all finished.

Behind her Amon has closed his eyes, and she calls to him in a whisper, afraid to wake him if he's sleeping. He doesn't stir, and as she looks on him her heart breaks for him. Their love and their loss have gone unacknowledged for so long they have become like two satellites that circle the same empty space. She thought there would come a time when they could get back to normal, and she's tried not to resent neither his asking nor her agreeing to live on the old farm, but she misses the rhythms of what she must now call her old life. She sees in his weakened figure the only way to convince him to come back to this house is by telling him that she's not going anywhere.

She takes an afghan from the back of the couch and places it on him and goes into her parents' bedroom to make up the bed. She has avoided it and not once slept in here, instead sleeping in her old room with its twin bed. She works fast, pulling the musty sheets off and replacing them with fresh, clean ones. Her shoulders ache from stress, and she sits on the bed after tucking all the corners and closes her eyes, rolling her head in circles to loosen the tension.

She hears a door close and opens her eyes. She comes out the bedroom and down the hallway. The afghan is folded and the television turned off. She calls for Amon, but the house has no answer. In the kitchen the rifle is missing. She picks up her phone.

"Where did you go?"

"I'm at the foot of the driveway," he says.

She opens the front door and a breeze shivers her. Exhaust clouds the truck's brake lights.

"Come back inside. There's nothing more to be done."

"I'll keep watch and check around the house after a while. I want to make sure you're safe."

"But *you're* not safe out there."

"Better me than you."

"That's not true. You were just sleeping."

"I feel fine now."

She doesn't want to fight him but must keep him talking. "People say he loved those animals." She grabs a coat from the hook and puts it over her shoulders and stands in the open doorway. "None of this makes sense."

"You can't make sense of it. You know better than that," he tells her.

She lifts her chin to pull the coat tight at her collar. Stars fill the sky, and she is about to tell him it's a beautiful night, something he has pointed out to her all his life on nights like this, when he speaks first.

"They're saying he killed himself."

"Who?"

"Thompson," he says. "That crazy bastard." He tells her how the man unlocked the cages then took a pistol and shot himself in the head.

She doesn't know what to say in response but stares into the black distance toward Thompson's and imagines the man outside in the light of day, going about the business setting free the animals with a ring of keys in one hand and a pistol in the other. The simple movement of turning a key has wrought so much chaos on their lives. Then, remembering, she says, "Why were you in Granville?"

"I should pay attention here," he says. There is heavy sighing and the rustling of him adjusting his posture in the seat. She tries to picture him down there in the cab.

"Why were you there?"

Another deep breath. "I was looking at some land," he says. "Just outside of town."

"What for?"

"I'm thinking of buying it and moving there."

"When were you going to tell me?"

"Soon," he says.

"You'd just leave?" she asks. "You've never lived anywhere else."

"There isn't anything here anymore," he says. "Just you. And you've got your own life. I know you've put it on hold because of this year."

He stops short of saying he is sorry, and Alice is glad. She doesn't know if she could stand to hear it. As she looks down on the truck, thinking about the heat in the cab, the radio stations that are nothing but static at this hour, how he's all alone, surrounded by the night, she knows he will walk away, that they will continue to drift even farther from each other. And she wants to say to him it doesn't have to be this way and they can talk about her mother and what he misses, what life has been like, but she knows she can do nothing for him but go on being his daughter.

Resigned, she is ready to tell him good night and to come inside when he gets tired when she hears a sound. "Did you hear that?"

"No," he says. "Let me cut the engine."

The parking lights and brakes shut off, and only the slight metal tint of the truck glows in the darkness.

"It sounded like the lion," she says.

"Your mind's running wild."

"How can you be sure?" she asks.

"I can't."

"Daddy."

"It's late, honey. I'll come up to the house in a little while. You go rest. Sleep."

"You promise to come back?"

"I do," he says.

She thinks about the lives that have come to pass for both of them and how each has been littered with the unexpected, and it's not lost on her that this is the definition of life. She never thought she'd be a spinster, living in Zanesville, traveling roads she grew up on. He thought he'd be a grandfather and still living on this farm he built. They both thought it was only a routine surgery. Where life once seemed about possibilities it has now become about making peace with what has transpired.

She ends the phone call, and as she does the truck comes to life. Taking her time, she goes to the closet and pulls on her tennis shoes and a sweatshirt and steps out the front door. She glances left and right like she's about to cross a busy street, and then takes off down the hill, keeping her focus on the burning red of the taillights. The heavy footfalls jar her. When she arrives at the truck she beats on the door and pulls at the locked door handle. She's startled Amon and in the confusion he hits the gas and the engine revs loud and high before he reaches across the seat and opens the door.

"You scared the life out of me," he says, breathing heavy.

"I didn't want to be alone," she says.

"You should have gone to bed," he says flatly then hands her the shotgun.

She rests the stock on the floorboard between her feet and keeps the barrel toward the windshield. He stares at her, no longer startled, or even seeming to be afraid. "Like you did," she says and looks at him crossly, and he shrugs his shoulders. "How can I sleep when it's still out there?"

"You don't know that it is."

"Then why are you here?"

"Because it might be and you're my daughter and I'm supposed to take care of you."

"I'm a grown woman. I've been taking care of myself for a long time now."

"I know you have." Then after a beat of silence, he says, "When you were a baby and couldn't sleep your mother and I drove you around town. She always made me drive, and she'd sit in the back of the car with you," he says and eases the truck onto the road.

"Think it'll work tonight?"

"No, but it won't do us no good to just sit here." They have a small laugh, a leavening of their anxiety.

He drives slow enough that she hears the tread on the pavement. She doesn't ask where he is headed, and when he steers toward Thompson's, she keeps quiet still. At the head of Kopchak Road traffic cones have been placed to block the way to the compound. He pulls past them, taking the truck onto the shoulder.

"Don't," she says.

"I want to know what happened to that damn lion."

Up ahead, blue cruiser lights turn round and round, spreading over them in intervals. A deputy throws open the car door and comes out waving his hands and a big Maglite. They've made it far enough down the road to see the animals on the ground, lit by emergency floodlights. They stare past those ghosts and up into the shadows on the hill, imagining what once lived there and what that man set free to be destroyed.

The deputy bangs the fender with his hand and Amon rolls down the window. "You see that roadblock back there?" He is a young man and he is jittery with wide eyes and a small crack in his voice.

Her father ignores the question. "Have you gotten all of 'em?"

"I asked you a question," the deputy says.

"And I asked you one." He adjusts his hands on the steering wheel.

"Daddy," Alice whispers.

"You need to turn this truck around and go home."

"Did you kill all those damn lions?"

The deputy ducks his head and pushes back the brim of his hat to eye the shotgun. "I won't tell you again. Go home and put that rifle in a safe place."

"It's safe where it is," her father says.

The deputy stands and reaches for the radio receiver on his shoulder.

Alice quickly leans across Amon and tells the officer thank you, that they'll be on their way.

"That's a good idea," the deputy says and points the flashlight on Amon's face and keeps it there as Amon rolls up his window and throws the truck in reverse, spinning the tires.

He drives them back faster than when they left and stifles a yawn. His face is lit from the dials on the dash, and he looks even older than she remembers, worse than this morning.

"I'm going to sell my house," she says, deciding it right then. "I'll stay on at the farm, and I want you to come back." She can't even begin to picture a life in which she never drives to the farm again and sees the house and its black shutters from a hundred yards off, the gray and weathered barn tucked against the mountainside. "We're getting older, Daddy—"

"Speak for yourself," he says, cutting her off. He grins, though. He sits up higher in his seat. "I'm not coming back. I won't be a burden to you," he says. "I don't know if I can be in that house anymore." His voice has gone soft and it's the only time he's ever said anything about the grief that drove him away from the farm. She knows his memories of the life he once lived on the farm pull at him every day because they pull at her too. She misses her mother as much as he does.

"We don't have anyone but each other," she says. And the truth of it, spoken for the first time, fills the space between and around them.

They turn down the road for home, and the lion stands in the driveway. It faces the truck and lets out a loud roar. They stop. The truck's radio hisses static. Alice thinks about the remaining goats in the field, the never-ending rawness of this day, and grips the barrel of the shotgun. The lion moves toward the truck and roars again. From the corner of her eye Alice is vaguely aware of Amon reaching for his cell phone in the cup holder, hears him explain the situation. She is focused on the animal, its eyes and movements.

"We can go get one," she hears him say. "We just talked to one not five minutes ago."

Alice spins in the seat. "No," she says. "We can't lose her. We have to keep her in our sights." And with that she jumps out of the truck with the rifle raised to her shoulder.

"Alice! No!" He is out too, shouting from across the hood.

The lion is twenty yards away, directly in the halogen beams. Amon waves his arms and hollers at the animal, trying to distract it. He slaps the hood, hollering, "Hey, hey, hey." Alice is so stunned she can't tell him to stop or ask what he's doing, but the lion takes the bait and charges. It springs into the air, disappearing from the lights briefly, and Alice aims down the sights and fires into the darkness. An awful, anguished cry pierces the night.

The shotgun's recoil sends her backward and she nearly topples. She regains her footing and fires the second barrel and as she steps forward, the fallen animal is in front of the truck, wounded, on its side. Blood spills from its rib cage and its breaths are fast and deep.

Amon, in his retreat, has fallen behind the truck. She sees him on the ground, rubbing his hip, and she comes to him and crouches down. They both see the animal's mouth open, as if it wants to ask for help. The barrels of the gun throw heat onto her cheeks. She grips her father's arm and helps him up, and then they stand over the lion, awash in brightness. Neither of them can speak. Alice's hands and body vibrate. Her ears ring in deafness, and together they watch the animal's final moments—its fight for oxygen and inability to lift its head from the grayed asphalt. Before they place the call to the police and then walk inside to talk about their own future, Alice thinks of an African prairie and dry heat. How far this animal is from where it should be, how it can never go back there, how cold and alone it must feel on the ground in this strange land with the last swell of its lungs drifting past the two figures before it, who appear suspended in the light.

ACKNOWLEDGMENTS

These stories have appeared, sometimes in different form, in *Narrative, Blackbird, Ocean State Review, Still: The Journal, The Pinch, Catamaran, Catapult* and *Kenyon Review Online.*

I DIDN'T ALWAYS want to be a writer. I wanted to be an astronaut first. My dad would take me to the small chain bookstore in our hometown, and I would pick up all the books I could on space, the moon landing, the space shuttle, NASA. At home, Dad and I read them together. Later, I'd attend Space Camp after winning an essay contest to attend sponsored by a local civic organization. Maybe that was the first parting of ways with the original dream, of writing being something that interested me nearly as much. Well, that and my experience at Space Camp proving not to be all that interesting or fun. But when I think about being a boy and wanting to be an astronaut, I'm struck by two things. The first is that it wasn't a fad or notion of being a boy but something very real for me. I grieved when the Challenger exploded and became more determined to become an astronaut. The second is that both my parents encouraged me. It wasn't just the trips to the bookstore and the library to research space, it was the way both of my parents actively helped and researched with me. Whatever my dreams were, they were both right there. They never steered me away from what I aspired to. As long as I put in the work and time, they would put in just as much to make sure my life was the one I wanted. That's why this book is as much a product of them as it is of me. I'm not sure how you thank someone for giving you the courage and the opportunity to pursue your dreams, but Mom and Dad, you made mine possible and you never made them seem impossible, which, as a parent now, I understand is the greatest gift you gave me. Thanks to my brother Tim, who put up with a cranky and sullen unemployed early-twenty-something for two years, paying the lion's share of our rent and grocery bill while I worked part-time jobs and wrote stories. All he said to me was, "If you want to be a writer, go write. I'll take care of everything else." And he did. He always has from the time we were boys until I was an adult, and when hard times came again for me later, he was there to help me through once more, pick me up when I was down, and show me that I could withstand and bear more than I thought. This book is also a product of his faith and support in me.

After my family, there are so many people to thank that I feel like I could go on saying thank you forever, for longer than the thirteen stories in this collection. My teacher Mary Ellen Miller at Western Kentucky University changed my life. She noticed my writing and encouraged it, mentored me, read every page I wrote as an undergrad with interest and care and a deft hand. She did not live to see this book's publication, which is one of the few regrets I have in this life—that it took me so long to get a book out in the world for her to see—but I would not be the person or writer I am without her. I'm thankful each day that she was the professor who walked through the door of my Intro to Literature class freshman year. Otherwise, I'd be practicing law and wondering what might have been. Dan Myers, Charley Pride, Patti Minter, and Cassandra Pinnick were also professors and mentors who went beyond the call for me, who still influence how I teach and mentor my own students now. Thanks for giving up so much of your precious time to me. Ned and Elizabeth Stuckey-French were my North Stars in graduate school. Great writers who became great friends. They kept me between the ditches and made me better at every step.

Ned, breaded tenderloin awaits us. Mark Winegardner pushed me harder than any teacher I've had and showed me the kind of work I needed to do in order to be the writer I wanted to be. David Kirby and Barbara Hamby kept me sated and sane and were a model of graciousness—as well as devastating good looks!—and kindness I'll never forget.

Thanks to the editors who believed in my work and published these stories, particularly, Tom Jenks and Carol Edgarian at *Narrative*, Mary Flinn at *Blackbird*, Nicole Chung at *Catapult*, and David Lynn at the *Kenyon Review*. And thanks to Mike Curtis as well, whose kindnesses kept me afloat when I wanted to drown. Thanks as well to the National Endowment for the Arts, the Ohio Arts Council, and the Kentucky Arts Council. All provided much-needed financial support and encouragement at critical stages in my development.

I am fortunate to have more mentors than any one man should, and I want to make sure Steve Yarbrough, Townsend Luddington, Hal Crowther, Tom Rankin, and Jill McCorkle all know how much I appreciate them—on and off the page. As a young man, I was always observing you as a way of being in this life. To Lee Smith, I would have never made it this far without you. I am a failure at being the kind of warm and generous mentor and person you are, but I do try to follow your example. I hope this book is worthy of all the time you have given to me over the years. And to Richard Bausch, where to begin? I thieve from you every time I set foot in a classroom, using your words, your careful consideration of this writing life, as instruction for my own students. After all, nothing I've come up with on my own seems better than how you put it to me when I was your student. Thanks for the laughs, the drinks, and teaching me the life. Every day as your student and friend has been an education and more than I could have hoped for when we first met.

Mark Carothers, Kyle McGown, and Ben Nunery, thanks for being there at the beginning and all the days since. Bill Eville, Ali Salerno, Quentin James, Zach Martin, and Jason Nemec—a Hall of Fame caliber graduate school cohort—thanks for keeping the lonely days at bay and the writing on the level year in and year out. Zack Adcock and Wendy Sumner-Winter helped me through Memphis. Dave Lucas is my favorite poet, in part because he has fed me the most. To him and Amy Keating, thanks for making Cleveland feel like home, for being the best of friends. Phil Metres taught me how to be a professor when I was a kid walking into my first job, and his steady hand has kept guiding me ever since. My colleagues at Denison University, Margot Singer, Peter Granbois, David Baker, Ann Townsend, Jack Shuler, and James Weaver, have never wavered in their support for my writing and teaching—cheerleaders all. I'm fortunate to have found myself in your good company and at a university that values our work in and out of the classroom. Josh Finnell, never forget lunch is from 11:30–1:30 at Huffman. Pizza for dessert. Chris and Kelly Molloy thanks for being on the journey with me. And to Silas House, the first writer I ever knew. You're my other brother in this life. I always have your back.

To Lynn York and Robin Miura, thanks for bringing this book into your fold and careful hands. I couldn't have landed at a better place with better people. It's a great gift to work with a press that is doing so much to support writers and great writing.

When I got engaged, a student of mine asked me how I knew Mary was the one. It was an easy answer. She taught me what real love is. Mary, I hope you can count on me the way I have come to count on you. You helped give me a life I thought I might never have, that had passed me by. I am rich in gratitude to many people, but you're the only one I share all my joy with. I love you.